Under the Paris Moon

A WHIRLWIND ROMANCE

BOOK ONE

REBECCA HEFLIN

UNDER THE PARIS MOON

REBECCA HEFLIN

Cover Design by The Killion Group, Inc.

Published in the United States of America by:

Rebecca Heflin Books, LLC

ISBN: 9781736660027

www.RebeccaHeflin.com

Acknowledgments

To Susan. You fought the battle and won.

When I began writing *Under the Paris Moon*, little did I know a few months later my oldest and dearest friend would learn she had breast cancer. What's more, little did I know, a month later, I would be going through the same stressful situation, only in the end, my biopsy was (thankfully) benign.

My heroine, Ellie, my best friend, and I all learned of our breast cancer/suspected breast cancer through an annual screening mammogram. Ellie's and Susan's outcomes were excellent because the cancer was caught early. The importance of breast self-exams and screening mammograms cannot be overstated. If you're a woman age 40 and above, please get your screenings. It could save your life.

Quote

You're my serendipity. I wasn't looking for you. I wasn't expecting you. But I'm lucky I met you. ~ Park Jimin

Prologue

"*Excusez-moi—c'est mon taxi*," the woman says, as I move toward the taxi pulling up at the curb. Although her French is quite good, she has enough of an American accent for me to realize she is not from France.

"I beg your pardon." I step aside. Who am I to stand between a beautiful woman and her taxi? And this woman *is* beautiful. Striking really. Tall and regal with hair the color of polished silver, shot through with pewter and charcoal. Broad sunglasses obscure her eyes, but her wide mouth and full lips beg to be kissed. She carries herself and the small pink bag from one of the local vintage shops like she means business. *What's her story?*

Then a thought occurs to me. I flash my most charming smile, the one that used to make women around the world swoon, then wait for recognition to dawn on her gorgeous face. Nothing. *Huh.*

Maybe my sunglasses and baseball cap are a better disguise than I realized. Or maybe her sunglasses hide her reaction. Okay, then. "Where are you going? Perhaps we could share the taxi." I flash another trademark thousand-watt grin.

"You're American, then?" she asks in surprise.

It is easier to just agree than to explain. "Oui," I say with a wink.

She frowns and shakes her head. "I'm not sharing a taxi with a stranger."

So she really doesn't know who I am. Suppressing the gut punch to my ego that follows, I try again, pouring on the charm that won over even the most recalcitrant co-star. "We could introduce ourselves, and then we wouldn't be strangers."

She scoffs. "No, thank you," and tries to move around me to open the door.

I reach for the door handle at the same time, brushing my hand across hers, and the zing at the contact shoots down to the soles of my feet. She must have felt it too, because she jerks her hand away as if she's just touched a hot iron.

"Please, allow me." Those lush lips thin in annoyance as I reach for the door again, and she gives me a suspicious look, as if I might climb into the cab behind her. Or jump in before her.

I can't resist. "It's April in Paris!" I sing the line from the classic song and lift my free hand to encompass the City of Lights dressed in her best spring fashions. "What more do you need?"

Nothing. Wow. Tough crowd. Resigned, I open the door to the driver berating us in French about whether we are getting in or not.

"*Oui, juste moi*," she said, emphasizing there is no "we."

She slides onto the seat, and I catch the flash of a smooth thigh when a breeze lifts the hem of her fuchsia sundress. Before I close the door, I prod once more. "When was the last time you smiled?"

She reaches for the door handle and says with a straight face, "June 5, 1989," then she slams the door shut.

I bark out a laugh and shake my head. Damn, she is intriguing. But I have no time to pursue this woman. I have to get back to my hotel for a social media campaign my agent and I predict will resuscitate my dying career.

Chapter One

DAY ONE

Eleanor

Why I let my best friend, Maddie Gallagher, talk me into this, I'll never know. I collapse onto the bed with a sigh, not caring if I rumple the new deep violet silk Dior cocktail dress.

Yes, I do know, and Maddie is right, as much as I hate to admit it. I need a break. Before I left, Maddie reminded me it's only one night. I can hear her too-cheerful voice, "Then you have nine whole days in Paris! The art museums, the food, the shopping! Get away from the legal, personal, and professional drama in your life right now. What have you got to lose? Go. Find your happy."

I snort. My "happy" isn't going to be with some overpaid pretty boy . . . though a little shopping in Paris—and a free stay at the Four Seasons, no less—wouldn't be amiss. Now I'm in a suite in Paris with a view of the Eiffel Tower, because Maddie entered me into a contest without my knowledge—or permission. And believe it or not, I won, so here I am. Well, at least the four years of French in college and the decades of continued practice won't go to waste after all.

So, after my obligation tonight, I'll take Maddie's advice and take full advantage of the remaining nine days in the City of Lights. Then I'll return home to face the mess I left behind and do my damnedest to get my life—my new *single* life—back on track.

By the way, I'm Eleanor Marshall, or Ellie to those who know me. And I'm a fifty-something divorcee.

I know what you're thinking, and you'd be right. I am a cliché and, damn, I hate it. The devoted wife of nearly thirty years thrown over for a younger woman. And not just *any* woman, but my soon-to-be former business partner.

My suite, the aptly named Eiffel Tower Suite, is all crisp whites, cool beiges, and understated elegance. The vases of cream and pale pink roses lend a heady fragrance to the space, which is absurdly large for one person, with a dining room, living room, and office, in addition to the private bedroom and luxurious bathrooms. Yes, that's plural. The suite has a guest bath too.

But the best part? The expansive terrace that wraps around the suite on three sides, offering panoramic views of the Eiffel Tower (of course!) and Paris's main sites. My gaze sweeps the bedroom. This suite for ten nights must be setting Geoffrey Harrison back a good sum of money. I don't know what his game is, but I hope whatever it is, it's worth it. Speaking of . . .

Sighing, I rise and slip my feet into a pair of classic black Louboutin pumps. Eyeing the colossal basket of fruit, chocolates, and bottle of champagne that greeted me upon arrival yesterday morning, I select a chocolate and pop it into my mouth, letting the rich dark flavor melt on my tongue. The attached card reads:

Welcome to Paris. Please enjoy. I look forward to

meeting you tomorrow night.
XOXO Geoffrey

Once again, I roll my eyes over the message. *Oh, please.* Like he actually selected the fruit and champagne instead of his publicist or another flunky.

I pick up the Judith Leiber evening bag I'd discovered in a vintage shop this morning, and with one last glance in the mirror, mutter, "Let's do this."

Stepping out of the elevator into the impressive Four Seasons lobby, I pause, drawing in a deep breath to quell the nerves at the thought of meeting a man I wouldn't recognize if he came up and kissed me. My fault, really, since I could have easily Googled him. I scan the lobby for a likely suspect: a man in a suit who appears to be looking for a woman he has never met.

The lobby exudes luxury and sophistication in a harmonious blend of classic and contemporary styles, creating a rich, timeless atmosphere. An enormous chandelier dripping with crystal teardrops hangs from the high ceiling, casting a warm glow on the inlaid marble floor below it. Towering arrangements of white roses, orchids, and hydrangeas set against the black lacquer display tables warm the otherwise cool space.

I turn my attention to the seating areas that have been carefully arranged to offer comfort and privacy. Plush sofas and armchairs upholstered in rich fabrics, inviting guests to relax and unwind. Like my suite, the color palette is neutral, featuring soft tones of beige, cream, and gold, creating a cool and appealing atmosphere. To my designer's eye, the space is luxurious yet not intimidating.

I spot a heavyset man seated on one of the well-appointed cream sofas, scrolling through his phone. A woman sits next to him, placing a hand on his thigh. Okay, maybe not.

Next, my gaze lands on a nice-looking man with a lithe

build casually leaning against one of the pillars, hands in his pockets. Not bad, though he appears to be ten years my junior, and I happen to know from Maddie that the man I'm looking for is five years my senior.

Moving on.

Ah. There he is. I should have known he'd be surrounded by adoring fans.

The man stands tall and confident, his movie-star smile brighter than the crystal chandeliers overhead, as he graciously interacts with the women around him. I have an inkling of recognition. Maybe I'd caught a glimpse of him on TV somewhere—an interview on a morning show perhaps.

His hair, a beautiful blend of silver and charcoal that my husband, er, *ex*-husband, would never allow to happen to him, bore an expensive cut, combed back to reveal a lean face, square jaw, and high cheekbones. Movie-star looks. I shrug mentally. Okay, so he's good looking. Then again, so was my ex. Don't be fooled by pretty packaging, I tell myself—the box could still hold a snake.

One night, I remind myself. Then all of Paris will be mine for nine whole days.

Lifting my chin, I mutter, "Time to meet my so-called 'Dream Date.'"

Geoffrey

"Ladies, please excuse me. I believe my date has arrived."

I'd felt her eyes on me while I signed autographs and took selfies with a few diehard fans who still remember me but assumed at first she was another of the throng.

When I'd agreed to this idiocy dreamed up by my agent,

obviously, I had no idea who the winner would be. It could have been anyone from a self-absorbed twenty-something who just wanted a free trip to Paris (though given my own age, doubtful) to a blue-haired eighty-something with a walker and more replacement parts than my 1965 Shelby Mustang. Or a forty-something hipster who reads Murakami, drinks craft cocktails, and wears vintage band tees.

It hadn't mattered. It was one night of photo ops for social media, and then my "date" and I would part company. I've had worse nights. I can charm just about anyone for a couple of hours.

What I hadn't expected was a beautiful, mature woman with more style than most women in Hollywood. Funny, "striking" had been the first word to enter my mind. Then recognition dawns and a jolt of awareness shoots through me. *It's her!*

My grin widens. Sometimes the universe does provide.

Tall and graceful, she strides over to me on stilettos that put her height just under six feet. The purple dress fits like it'd been made for her, stopping just below the knee to reveal shapely legs with firm calves.

I do like a nice calf on a woman.

But, like this morning, her most notable feature is her hair. Even more brilliant under the light of the chandeliers, which spark the silver among the pewter strands that just brush her shoulders and frame a face with high cheekbones and that wide, full mouth. In my profession, few women would have been caught dead with a single strand of gray showing, much less their entire head of hair. But this woman rocks it, like the brilliant Helen Mirren.

As she nears, I notice violet eyes set off by full dark brows. Eyes that had been obscured by her sunglasses earlier. Did I say her hair was her most notable feature? No, her eyes take the top spot when it comes to her features.

That is, until she smiles. Be still, my heart. If she'd smiled like that this afternoon, I would have melted into a puddle at her feet.

That smile freezes on her face as recognition flares in her violet eyes.

I can't help the chuckle that escapes. "We meet again. You must be Eleanor Marshall."

She regained her composure. "And you're obviously Geoffrey Harrison."

I take her warm hand in mine and have the absurd urge to raise it to my lips for a kiss. I settle for a brief handshake. "Well, if I wasn't, I would be now," I say, pouring on the charm.

I hesitate beneath her violet gaze, and she continues, "If you were expecting a young beautiful, twenty-something, sorry to disappoint."

I hate her apology. I hate that she feels the *need* to apologize.

"Younger women don't interest me. A life lived adds depth to a woman. Eleanor, you are quite simply stunning." The faint blush that tinges her cheeks pleases me beyond measure.

"Thank you, but flattery isn't necessary."

"Truth isn't flattery."

A camera shutter clicks, and she turns in surprise.

"I apologize for the photography, but—"

She waves me off. "The contract I signed included a photo release that covers God and everybody. I'm just not used to being the target of photographers."

I'd be willing to bet the camera loves her. Sighing, she turns back to me, an expectant expression on her face.

"Right. Shall we?"

Eleanor

. . .

Geoffrey holds his arm out to me like a gentleman from another era. I slip my hand into the crook of his arm and encounter a well-muscled bicep beneath the fine wool of his jacket. Not that I should be surprised. After all, he earns his living on his looks.

"We're dining at Le Cinq here in the Four Seasons."

I admit I am more excited about dining at the Michelin three-star restaurant than I am about meeting my, er, companion. I wouldn't call myself a foodie, but I do appreciate fine dining.

"Yes, the itinerary was quite specific, including the time and place of our dinner, along with the duration—three hours, followed by after-dinner drinks in the bar, with photo ops sprinkled among the evening's activities."

"Activities?"

We leave the voluminous marble-floored lobby behind for a quieter corridor, stopping at the maître d' stand, where we are met by a stiff, yet polite man with a Parisian nose, a delicate mouth, and a heavy French accent. "Ah, Monsieur Harrison, your table is ready." He delivers the words in English like he has a mouthful of marbles.

He bows formally and leads the way through a gilded feast for the eyes, that is both sophisticated and comfortable. Brocade carpet muffles the voices of the diners, while gold-leaf Louis XVI chairs, crystal chandeliers, Phillipe Starck-designed cutlery, and fine china scream, "Let them eat cake!" For a country that cast off the yoke of the monarchy over two hundred years ago, Paris hasn't cast off the décor.

I notice the double-takes and the open-mouth stares of some of the diners as we pass, and I glance up at Geoffrey. What must it be like to be recognized everywhere you go? But he appears to take it all in stride, nodding to gawkers along the way.

The maître d' seats us at a secluded table, away from the prying eyes of the other patrons, for which I am grateful. While Geoffrey may be used to being the center of attention, I am not. And even though *I'm* not on social media, I know how judgy people can be. I don't want an image of my face to end up on someone's Instagram with a recalcitrant piece of lettuce hanging from my mouth.

Geoffrey treats me to another custom of a bygone era—he holds my chair out for me, before moving to the other side of the table for two. Once the maître d' has us situated, with our white linen napkins draped across our laps, he bows and leaves us.

An awkward silence descends, and I resist the urge to fidget with the expensive cutlery. This isn't a date. It isn't. And yet . . . it certainly *feels* like one. A *first* date—the worst kind of date. I haven't been on a first date since my first date with my ex-husband back in college, some thirty-three years ago.

To my utter relief, a tall gentleman in waiter attire introduces himself as Henri. "Monsieur Harrison, your bottle of Veuve Clicquot will arrive shortly."

"Madame." I sit back as he proffers the dinner menu, which gives me an excellent excuse to study something besides the awkwardness of the situation.

After a few moments, Geoffrey interrupts my thoughts, "What appeals to you?"

Generally a decisive person, I rattle off my choices. "The prawns to start, followed by the turbot, and the seasonal green salad."

His brows lift in surprise. "I like a woman who knows what she wants."

Why does that comment send a thrill through me?

After our glasses are filled with bubbly, and we've placed

our orders, Geoffrey lifts his glass in a toast. I follow suit, wondering what on earth he would toast to. "To ten days in Paris! May they be filled with delight."

That I can toast to. A camera shutter clicks, and I do my best not to flinch, now aware of the photographer behind me. I take a sip of the excellent champagne—Geoffrey certainly knows how to entertain—and search for a safe topic of discussion. I've never seen his movies, so that's out. Preferring to avoid any personal questions, I don't want to ask about family. Before I can come up with something, he speaks.

"So, Eleanor, you're here on a date with me—"

"This isn't a date," I interject.

His blue-gray gaze sweeps over me as tangible as a touch, before taking in the glass of champagne in my hand, the elegant table setting, and then the alcove in which we dine. "Looks like a date. Feels like a date."

"It's not a date," I insist. "It's a publicity stunt."

He sets his glass on the table and leans forward. "I'm curious. What made you enter the contest? Is it the charity? The free trip? Because it clearly isn't me."

The last statement held a note of pique. The "entry fee" for the contest was a contribution to the charity—an international food bank—to which all proceeds were directed.

"I'm sorry to disappoint you, but I didn't enter the contest. My best friend entered me. I'm not a fan—I didn't even know who you were before now. So while I appreciate all this," I wave my hand to take in the sumptuous atmosphere of the restaurant, "at the end of the evening, we'll part ways. You can go back to your life, and I can go back to mine." Such as it is.

"Ouch," he says with a sardonic grin. "You wound me." He holds a hand over his heart in dramatic fashion, and I can't help but smile in response. He is a charmer, for sure. So like my ex.

The appearance of our beautifully presented first course interrupts our debate momentarily.

As he settles into his potato gnocchi and I my prawns, he eyes me speculatively. "You either have a very understanding husband," his gaze drops to my bare left ring finger, "or you are single."

Geoffrey

That soft smile—however brief—had felt like a victory. I'd like to make her smile more, relax that firm grip she has on her emotions. Unravel the beautiful woman sitting across from me. But instead, my comment made her frown again, and a flash of pain had crossed her face.

"Divorced. Recently." She doesn't look up as she forks a bite of prawn. I didn't think she would continue this topic of conversation, but she surprises me.

"Since you are here on what you call a 'date,' you either have a very understanding significant other or you, too, are single."

Touché. "Divorced. Many years ago."

"And no one since?" She closes her stunning violet eyes, then opens them. "I apologize. It's none of my business."

"Eleanor, we do need to carry on some form of conversation to pass the evening."

"Yes, but since we are parting ways, I see no need to get personal. Let's just . . . keep it superficial."

Disappointed by her pronouncement, I lift the glass of champagne to my lips. Eleanor Marshall intrigues me. I want to learn her deepest secrets. Learn what made her so stern. So serious. So . . . unhappy.

Yet, I can't say her lack of familiarity with my acting career doesn't pinch a little. Well, a lot. She doesn't even know who I am. Talk about a knife wound to the ego. An ego that's been feeling more than a little fragile lately.

"All right. What do you do, Eleanor, or is that too personal?" I wait, hoping she will answer.

"I own a successful upscale boutique called Ellie's on San Sebastian Island, a barrier island off the coast of North Florida."

The pride in her voice is evident and she continues. "It's an eclectic shop, offering upscale resort wear, including bathing suits, cover-ups, beach shoes, and accessories, as well as active wear and dresses catering to the affluent resort guests. It also offers small antiques and home accessories for those with second homes on the island. In the winter, I sell fine, lightweight cashmere, scarves, hats, and gloves for chilly winter days and brisk nor'easters, along with sunglasses and jewelry." She blushes and shakes her head. "Sorry. I'm sure you didn't want an inventory."

I eye her again, taking in her appearance. I could just imagine, with her taste level, the clothing and accessories she offers. I have no doubt when she said "successful" she'd meant it, but it is another bit of information that intrigues me. "Ellie's? Is that what people call you?" Such a relaxed name for someone who, by all appearances, doesn't allow herself much time for fun.

She sets her knife and fork on her plate and wipes those luscious lips with her napkin before answering. "My friends call me that."

Ah. Point taken. Another barrier she places between herself and others. Message received. We will not be friends, and I will not be calling her Ellie.

Eleanor

Before he can ask more questions, I offer up one of my own. Not that I'm interested, I tell myself. Just to be polite. "And where do you live?"

"I have an apartment in New York, as well as a home in England, and a flat here in Paris."

"Of course you do."

He shrugs. "I travel a great deal between the three countries. I prefer to stay in my own place, rather than in a hotel."

Okay, I'll grant him that. "Makes sense."

"Why is this your first trip to Paris?"

"I'm sorry?"

"You speak French, you appear to love French cuisine." He nods to my empty plate. "You sell antiques in your boutique. Paris seems like a compulsory destination for an apparent Francophile."

"How do you know this is my first visit?"

"Your entry. One of the questions asked whether the entrant had been to Paris before."

Maddie knew me well enough to answer that question truthfully. I wave a hand. "Raising a child, starting and growing a business . . . life." *What a lame excuse.*

"You have a child?"

Of course he would latch onto that. So much for avoiding personal subjects. "I have a daughter."

He lifts a brow, clearly expecting more information.

"She's pursuing her master's in architecture at UVA—the University of Virginia. She graduates next year."

"Congratulations to her. And to you. She sounds as driven as her mother."

"How would you know whether I'm driven or not?" My response is a bit harsh, but that word—"driven." When used in the context of my ex-husband and his drive to build a highly successful plastic surgery practice, it's intended as a compliment. When used in the context of my desire to build a successful business—a criticism.

His brows shoot up at my affronted question. "It was intended as a compliment, Eleanor. You have a successful business. That doesn't happen without drive."

"I apologize." I shift in my seat, uncomfortable with my defensive reaction to his comment. I can't explain it without delving into unwanted territory. "Perhaps jet lag is setting in, making me grumpy." I offer up a smile with the subterfuge to make it more palatable.

He nods, though he clearly sees through the excuse. He's just too much of a gentleman to challenge it. "I will take that as a hint and allow you to return to your room immediately following dinner."

"Oh, but I thought the evening's supposed to include after-dinner drinks and 'photo ops.'" I use air quotes around "photo ops." Why had I reminded him when he was offering me an out?

"You're tired. You should get some sleep. At least allow me to take you to breakfast before we bid one another adieu."

"Breakfast is included in the prize package, so there's no need for you to *take me*." Heat creeps into my face at what those words imply, having nothing to do with breakfast. *Take me.* Ugh.

He sighs in exasperation. "Don't be obtuse. I'd like to see you at breakfast."

It's the least I can do, given his willingness to cut the evening short. Holding back my own exasperated sigh, I say, with all the politeness my grandmother instilled in me, "That would be nice. Thank you."

Geoffrey

After a superb meal, the waiter brings our desserts. A *mille-feuille* with roasted strawberries and mascarpone, with a dark chocolate drizzle for Eleanor. I went with the classic crème brûlée.

Her choice of the decadent dessert surprises me. I expected just a cup of black coffee.

Just as I'm about to crack the hard caramel layer, a moan, deep and throaty, comes from the direction of my dinner companion. That can't be. My spoon still poised above the dish, I lift my gaze to Eleanor. Her eyes are closed, the fork still in her mouth, a look of total bliss on her face. She slowly draws the fork from her mouth, and my groin tightens at the action, as I wonder if this is what she sounds like during sex.

She chews slowly and swallows before opening her eyes to find me staring at her. A pretty blush steals across her cheeks.

"Sorry." She lifts a shoulder. "I don't often indulge in sweets, so when I do, I take the time to savor every bite." She forks another bite of the cream-filled puff pastry into her mouth and wraps her lips around the fork.

Dear lord. I shift in my seat, my own dessert forgotten as I watch her "savor" her dessert. She comes off as so restrained, so proper—so this side of her is . . . delicious. And seductive.

She points at my own untouched crème brûlée with her now-empty fork. "Aren't you going to eat your dessert?"

Oh yeah. My own sweet and creamy treat. The one that pales in comparison to watching her suck every morsel from her fork. "Yeah." I crack the sugary crust and take a spoonful into my mouth. I barely taste the sweetness, my mouth dry as another forkful makes its way to her lips. Her tongue darts out and licks a bit of the cream from the corner of her mouth. I lick my own lips, wishing they were hers. They'd be sweet and soft. As tempting as even the most decadent French dessert.

Who knew watching a woman eat dessert could be a form of sexual torture? She stabs a strawberry and swipes it through the dark chocolate pool on her plate. My dirty little mind goes straight to the gutter, and I imagine a rosy taut nipple covered in dark chocolate, just aching to be suckled.

Hell, I've got to put a stop to this, otherwise I won't be able to get up from this table. I inhale the remainder of my dessert, while I turn my thoughts to my flagging career. That ought to deflate my erection in short order.

Blessedly, she's devoured everything on her plate and is sipping from her glass of sherry. I wipe my mouth on my linen napkin, glad I offered to cut this evening short. I couldn't take much more of this woman's hidden sensual side.

Eleanor

"I'll escort you to your room," Geoffrey says as he presses the call button for the elevator.

"Oh, that's not necessary."

"Well, since my suite is next to yours, it seems silly to take separate elevators."

"You're staying here? In the hotel? But you said you have a flat here."

"Since I didn't know how late our evening would be, I took a room," he said, matter-of-factly.

My surprise must have been evident, because he continues, "Don't read anything into it, Eleanor. It wasn't done with nefarious intent. I had no plans to seduce the winner."

I shake my head as a flush rises in my cheeks. "I didn't—"

"Never mind."

The elevator door opens, and he presses his fingertips to my lower back, indicating I should enter first. Ever the gentleman. I have to admit, I miss the feel of a man's warm hand there, making me feel both protected and respected.

The crew makes to follow us, but Geoffrey holds up a hand. "No. This is where the filming ends. Thank you, and good night." The elevator door closes on their dismayed faces.

"Thank you."

"This may only increase speculation that we ended up together for the night," he warns. "But you're tired, so I see no reason to prolong the evening with additional photos, etc."

The doors open on the eighth floor, the hotel's top floor, and Geoffrey guides me out and down the hall to my door. I steel myself against the delicious feel of his warm hand on my lower back. My nerves jangle when we stop outside my suite. Will he try to kiss me? Surely not. After all, this is just a publicity stunt, and there are no longer cameras here to capture it.

He touches my arm and leans forward, and my breath catches. He *is* going to kiss me. What do I do? My stomach flips at the thought.

"Good night, Eleanor." He presses a kiss to my cheek, quick, light, and warm. "Sleep well." Then he strides down the hall to his door. Before going in, he turns and says, "Nine a.m. work for you?"

"Yes." I rush to enter my own suite, heart hammering in my chest. Closing the door behind me, I lean back against it and hold my hand to my cheek like a lovesick girl. Is that . . . disappointment I feel? Disappointment that he *didn't* kiss me on the lips?

"Ridiculous." Pushing off the door, I slip out of my shoes, and pad across the thick carpet to the luxurious bathroom, enjoying the relief my sore, tired feet craved.

The elegant marble tub calls to me. A hot bath would ease the jet lag and help me fall asleep. As I run the water and go through my evening beauty routine, I recall the feel of his lips on my cheek, however brief.

As I step into the lavender-scented bubble bath, I recall the touch of his warm hand on my lower back. And as I lay back with a groan of pleasure, I recall the heat and strength of him through his jacket sleeve when I placed my hand there.

It's been decades since I've been attracted to another man, and I've forgotten how that felt. Am I attracted to Geoffrey? Perhaps. I suppose most women would be. But after our agreed-upon breakfast, my obligations will be fulfilled. Then all of Paris would be mine to enjoy.

Alone.

I lean my head back against the tub with a sigh. Somehow, that no longer appeals to me.

Geoffrey

Loosening my tie, I cross the room to the bar and pour myself two fingers of fine French brandy. As I let the warmth of the liquor glide down my throat, I stare out at the Eiffel Tower and think of the woman in the suite next door. I wonder what she's doing. Is she as rattled as I am? It's difficult to tell. She always seems to be in total control. Until dessert.

What had I gotten myself into? I sure as hell never expected such a beautiful, intriguing woman to win the contest. Someone who would make me question my self-imposed celibacy. Someone who would make me want to return to the days of whirlwind romances with plenty of sex and not much else.

I grimace. No. Eleanor isn't the type of woman you love and then leave. She possesses too many layers—too much depth to welcome a superficial relationship. I have the feeling that the more I learn about her, the more I'd want to learn. And the more I discover, the more there would be left to be discovered. She would offer an unending supply of surprises. And a challenge. She didn't fawn over me, and I doubt she ever would. To her, I am any other man. And oddly, I like that.

It's a good thing the contest only included the one dinner. And now, breakfast. What had I been thinking, drawing this out? It would've been best to end it tonight.

And yet . . .

When I pressed my lips to her warm, smooth skin, her silky hair caressed my cheek, and I caught a whiff of her perfume—something familiar, but I can't put my finger on it. Something floral, yet sophisticated.

After the sexual tension of dessert, it was all I could do not to bury my face in her neck and nibble my way to her ear. To fill my hand with a plump breast. To see if I could elicit the same throaty moan as a bite of *mille-feuille* with roasted strawberries, mascarpone, and a dark chocolate drizzle.

Desire pools in my belly once more. Dammit. It had been far too long since I'd been with a woman—casual encounter or relationship. I toss back the rest of the brandy and head for the shower—a cold one.

Chapter Two

DAY TWO

Geoffrey

"Oh, good. I've caught you both together."

"Malcolm, what are you doing here?" The unexpected arrival of my agent was never a good thing.

"Social media is blowing up. In a good way!" he adds.

I shake my head. "Over what?"

"Over you and Ms. Marshall." He nods a greeting toward Eleanor, and I'm compelled to introduce them.

"Eleanor, my agent, Malcolm Butterworth. Malcolm, Eleanor Marshall."

"Pleasure," he says, then tugs his phone from his back pocket and thrusts it in my face.

We'd been enjoying a polite, though superficial conversation, accompanied by a delicious breakfast of perfectly poached eggs, thick house-made yogurt with fresh berries, and a basket of flaky croissants.

With a glance at Eleanor's shocked face, I take it from him.

"What am I looking at?" While I know social media is important, I couldn't really care less about engagement and other social media indicators. After all, that's what I pay my agent and PR team for.

"The images and videos of you two are trending. You're a viral sensation!" Malcolm pulls out a chair and sits, uninvited, a satisfied and shocked grin on his face.

I hand the phone back to him and look up and into Eleanor's now-pale face. "Wonderful," I say distractedly.

"Don't you see? This plan is working out better than I ever expected. You're relevant—more than relevant—again. We can use this to go back to the studios that have written you off."

I wince at the term, not a little embarrassed that Eleanor heard it.

"That's wonderful, Malcolm. Great work." I reach out and clap him on the shoulder and resume my breakfast, urging Eleanor to do the same.

"We can't stop now." Malcolm looks between me and Eleanor, and I have a feeling she is not going to like what comes next. "We have to keep the momentum."

Eleanor sets her fork down with a clatter. "What are you saying?"

"Geoffrey's followers are clamoring for more of the two of you. Together." His head bounces back and forth between the two of us like he's watching a match at The French Open.

"No." Eleanor's reply is quiet but firm.

"I have commitments this week, Malcolm," I add with a meaningful look in his direction.

"Yes, yes." He waves away my concerns. "But we can work around that. We need to keep the trend going."

I am going to throttle him if he doesn't make himself clear. "Malcolm, I'm begging you, spell it out for me because I'm clearly not getting it."

He sighs and says, "We send you out with a film crew to capture the two of you enjoying the sights of Paris. The Eiffel Tower, the Louvre, Versailles."

"You do know Versailles isn't technically in Paris," I say, just to irritate him.

Malcolm rolls his eyes at me, then looks to Eleanor, whose head is swinging back and forth like a metronome, clearly signaling her denial. But Malcolm isn't one to take no for an answer. "You're here for nine more days. Geoffrey can show you Paris, from the main tourist attractions to the hidden cafés only the locals know."

"No," Eleanor repeats. "My contract only obligated me to last night's dinner and photos. I am now free to see Paris on my own. Alone."

"But what's the fun in that?" Malcolm presses. "Paris isn't meant to be seen alone. It's the City of Love!"

The more Malcolm says, the more Eleanor digs her heels in, and the more I begin to see his point. The whole goal of this scheme is to boost my presence on social media and to make the studios see I still have a following. If we drop this now, some other hot new social media sensation will take over, and I'll be irrelevant again. The problem is, Eleanor will be hard to convince. Then an idea occurs to me.

"What's your favorite charity?"

She blinks. "I'm sorry?"

"What charity do you support above any others?" Out of the corner of my eye, I can see Malcolm's knowing grin. I might be struggling to capture new roles, but I've amassed a small fortune in my career. This isn't about the money—it's about continuing in a career I love.

"A Step Up. Why?" she asks with narrowed eyes, skepticism clear in her voice.

"What is A Step Up?"

"It teaches etiquette to underserved populations."

My eyebrows shoot up. "Really?"

"People don't realize the impact learning etiquette—or the social graces, as my grandmother would have said—has on people trying to improve their job opportunities, especially those in underserved communities. It's not just about learning which fork to use." She waves a hand at the table setting. "It's about learning to look someone in the eye and shake their hand. To speak directly to them with poise and confidence."

Huh. I never thought about it like that. "I'm convinced. I'll give fifty thousand U.S. dollars to A Step Up if you do this."

Eleanor

My breath escapes me in a whoosh. *Fifty thousand dollars!* Is he insane? That kind of money would allow thousands of young people and single moms and dads to take etiquette classes for free! The director of the organization would faint if she received that much money.

And then there's my ex. And his paramour. Some part of me wants him to see the woman he discarded living it up in Paris with a famous actor and trending on social media. He doesn't follow social media himself, but his practice has a social media coordinator who would likely see it. And I have no doubt my daughter Abby would tell her father. And it could only boost my business.

I chew my lower lip. But could I do it? Could I stand up to the world's scrutiny—to the trolls I know are out there waiting to tear a woman down, especially an older woman? Could I handle being followed by a film crew, recording my every move? And more importantly, could I spend the next nine days with Geoffrey Harrison and not fall prey to his charm, just like I had my ex-husband's?

I look up to see Malcolm and Geoffrey staring at me, practically on the edge of their seats.

I draw in a deep breath, still not sure what I'm going to say. Then, it just pops out. "I'll do it."

A grin splits Geoffrey's handsome face, while Malcolm hoots with excitement, drawing the attention of nearby diners.

"But—" I hold up a finger. "I have some conditions."

"Of course," Geoffrey said. "Shoot."

"I still have designated time to myself. I don't want to spend twelve hours a day in front of a camera."

"Done," Malcolm says.

Geoffrey interjects, "I have a commitment Friday evening, and an all-day engagement on Saturday, so you'll have that time to yourself. And I have a couple of appointments this week, where you'll have free time as well."

I nod. "I have a few business-related errands to run, and I don't want—or need—company for those. I might be able to take care of them during your appointments."

Geoffrey raises a brow, but nods. "Anything else?"

"Yes. No romance. No holding hands, no romantic gestures, and definitely no kissing. I won't be party to a fake romance for the sake of your popularity."

Geoffrey sits back, looking a little deflated, and he and Malcolm share a look. Malcolm shrugs. "Fine."

"And at the end of nine days, you transfer fifty thousand dollars to A Step Up, and we go our separate ways."

He sticks out his right hand.

I hesitate a moment, but take it in a firm grip, and we shake on it.

"Done."

Geoffrey

It took a couple of hours for Malcolm to secure a film crew. He lucked out with a crew that was supposed to be shooting B-roll at the Palais Royal for an upcoming movie this week, but a pipe burst and the venue was closed for repairs. I eye the two-person crew, Hélène and Stéphane, standing outside the hotel, and check my watch. Eleanor agreed to meet me in the hotel lobby at 11 a.m.

So much for parting ways. Can I do this? Can I spend another nine days with this woman and not want more? More of something I can't have. Then a wry smile lifts the corner of my mouth. I have no doubt she will ensure the necessary physical and emotional distance.

The soft ding of the elevator draws my attention, and Eleanor exits wearing a chic, wide-brimmed hat, her broad sunglasses already in place, as if she were incognito. And the wry smile turns into a full grin.

She looks like a breath of spring, in the same emerald green dress she'd worn to breakfast, breezy flats on her feet. She's chic. Classic. A mature Audrey Hepburn in *Sabrina*—ready to take on Paris.

Unlike yesterday, when I wanted to carry out my business unimpeded, today I want to be recognizable to my fans. No billed cap, no dark sunglasses—just my graying hair and standard aviators.

Eleanor looks past me to the film crew outside, and her mouth flattens.

A flash of guilt sweeps over me. I should call this off. My career isn't Eleanor's concern, and she deserves to enjoy the rest of her trip out of the spotlight. But I plan to make it up to her by showing her the city I love with its famous tourist attractions and secret gems. Hopefully, she will look back on this trip and smile.

"Ready?" I asked.

"*Plus prête que jamais.*" As ready as I'll ever be.

I chuckle in response. "Eleanor, we're not going to the guillotine. It will be fun. I promise."

She slides her sunglasses down her nose and flashes those violet eyes at me, her disdain clear. "Where to first?"

"It's April in Paris. The Eiffel Tower, of course!"

Eleanor

We shook out a blanket on the huge grassy lawn of Parc du Champ de Mars, the Eiffel Tower looming large in front of us.

The Four Seasons packed a sumptuous picnic basket for us, including fresh crusty French bread, succulent Jambon de Paris, fig jam, creamy brie and camembert cheeses, and red grapes. A chilled bottle of chardonnay completed the meal. I try my best to ignore Hélène and Stéphane, who were assigned to photograph and film our activities.

Clearly, the cameras don't affect Geoffrey, as he lies back on the blanket, propped on one elbow, munching on a slice of bread with brie. He looks the epitome of the cosmopolitan gentleman, his graying hair ruffled by the breeze, a light scruff covering his jaw, his sunglasses covering just enough of his face to create an air of mystery. Relaxed Geoffrey is even sexier than dressed-up Geoffrey. Rolled up shirtsleeves reveal tanned and corded forearms. The same forearms I had beneath my hand last night. The thought gives me a chill even in the warm sunshine. Who knew forearms could be so sexy?

"What a day!" His pronouncement startles me out of my forearm musings.

"It *is* beautiful. Not a cloud in the sky." I sigh with . . . contentment? A feeling I almost fail to recognize, it's been so long since I last encountered it.

Geoffrey hands me a slice of bread spread with fig jam, topped with a slab of ham and a slice of camembert. "Thank you." I take a hearty bite and nearly moan with the pleasure of it. A sip of the crisp chardonnay rounds out the salty ham, sweet figs, and buttery cheese. Perfection.

"Did you know," I ask, gesturing with my wineglass, "the Eiffel Tower was once yellow?"

Geoffrey looks up at the tower, then rolls onto his side, facing me, propping his head in his hand. "I did not."

"It was also once yellow-brown, and then chestnut. Now, it's painted every seven years with "'Eiffel Tower Brown.'"

He gazes at me thoughtfully for a moment. "Tell me again why this is the first time you've visited Paris."

I delay my response under the pretense of slicing more bread. Just when I think he's dropped it, he prods, "Eleanor, we are spending at least a few hours a day in each other's company. We have to discuss *something*."

True. It's just . . . I don't *want* to like him. And despite myself, he's *very* likable. And the more we talk, the more I'm going to like him. "Life." I shrug.

He rolls onto his back with a groan, and I feel a twinge of guilt. He's right, of course. We can't speak of nothing but Paris attractions. Why my reticence to reveal innocuous facts about my life?

I draw in a breath and give him the Cliff's Notes version of my life with Barry. "My ex-husband is a plastic surgeon. We met when he was in medical school at Columbia University, and I was at Parsons School of Design."

Geoffrey rolls onto his side again, removing his sunglasses and looking at me as I speak. Attentive. Interested.

"I graduated, he entered his residency at NYU, and we got married. I went to work for a boutique in SoHo. Then it was on to his fellowship, which he also did at NYU. Travel wasn't an option—we had neither the time nor the money."

I gaze out at the "Iron Lady" recalling those days when our busy calendars required us to schedule "quality time" and our lack of funds required us to get creative with our entertainment budget. Free concerts or plays in Central Park. Picnics in Bryant Park. Window shopping on Fifth Avenue. They were some of the happiest days of our marriage. Before we lost each other to business and social obligations. Before he took me for granted.

"Then he joined a practice in Manhattan for a few years. He had dreams of establishing his own practice, but New York was prohibitively expensive, so we moved to Florida. Our focus for the first five years was establishing and growing the practice. Then we had Abby, and she became my focus." I smile and glance over at him to see if his eyes are glazed over with boredom. Instead, his blue-gray gaze holds mine with such an intensity, my breath catches.

"And what of you? You graduated from one of best design schools in the U.S. What did you do for *you*?"

No one has ever asked me that. First, I was Dr. Barry Marshall's wife. Then Abby's mother. It would be many years before I would become "Ellie."

"When Abby started middle school, I opened my boutique," I say it as if it were simple. As if it hadn't required struggle, as if it didn't entail feelings of guilt or frustration over Barry's lack of support for me and my dream—after I dedicated so much of my adult life to his dream. "The boutique became my focus, second only to Abby."

"And then?" He plucks a grape from the bunch and pops it into his mouth.

"And then, what?" I don't understand the question.

"Well, you said Abby is in graduate school. What of the time since she graduated from high school and went to college? Wouldn't that have been the time for you and your husband to travel?"

It would have been, at least for me, if not for my workaholic husband. Ex-husband. But I'm not going to share with this man why my much-anticipated girls' trip to France was canceled over three years ago. "I guess time just got away from me."

He narrows his eyes, and I think he's going to push for more. Instead, he nods and says, "Thank you."

"For what?" I ask, confused.

"For sharing with me."

This man is *thanking* me for talking about myself?

He rises and holds out his hand to me, nodding in the direction of the tower. "Let's see Paris from the top."

Geoffrey

"I should have told you to bring a jacket." The wind at the top of the tower holds a chill more akin to winter than spring, and Eleanor is shivering.

"I'm fine. Really."

"You're not fine. Your jaw is clenched, and your arms are covered with gooseflesh. If I had a jacket, I would offer it to you, but since I don't," I reach out and pull her into my arms, clasping her close against me.

She's stiff as a board. I'd like to think it's the cold, but I know it's the wall she's built around herself like a physical barrier.

"Don't."

"Don't what?"

"Don't play the romantic hero."

I can't help but laugh at her crustiness. "I'm not playing the romantic hero."

"Then what *are* you doing?" Her voice contains a note of alarm.

"I'm saving you from costly dental bills when you crack a tooth with your teeth-chattering." The camera shutter clicks in rapid succession.

Just as I think she's going to pull away, she finally melts—just a tad—against me, and I'm lost. Lost to the feel of her, lost to the scent of her, lost to the knowledge that she's found even the tiniest degree of warmth from my body. God, how am I to resist this woman over the next nine days?

And then she sighs, and my pulse quickens. *What else would make her sigh?* I wonder. To prevent myself from going down that same dangerous road as last night, I indicate the view from the top, turning our bodies, my arms still wrapped around her.

The tower offers a magnificent vantage point to view the sprawling cityscape of Paris. It's no wonder it's a favorite spot to pop the question. The Seine meanders gracefully through the heart of the city, slicing through the urban landscape like a silver serpentine chain. On the river's banks are some of Paris's iconic landmarks like the Louvre, Notre-Dame Cathedral, and the Grand Palais.

"If you look north, you'll see the wide expanse of

Champs-Élysées. Further in the distance is the Arc de Triomphe." I nod my head to the view directly in front of us. "To the east, in the distance, are the historic neighborhoods of Montmartre and Sacré-Cœur. Of course, there is the Basilica of the Sacré-Cœur." I lift my hand and point at the prominent white dome perched atop Montmartre Hill. "If you look to the south," I turn us both in that direction, "you'll see modern Paris, with its high-rise buildings dotting the skyline. I love the juxtaposition of the futuristic skyscrapers against the classic architecture of the older parts of Paris." I look down, "And of course, the Seine, below us."

"It's breathtaking," she murmurs, her gaze scanning the city's landmarks.

You're breathtaking, I want to say, but she'd think it was cheesy. And maybe it is, but it isn't any less true. This woman makes me want things I haven't wanted in a very long time. Like to have a special someone in my life—other than my daughter.

"But not only does this view allow you to appreciate the city's architectural elegance, but you can also see the symmetrical layout of the city, with its carefully designed squares and parks, and the rooftops adorned with chimneys and intricate details."

"I see what my daughter meant," Eleanor says.

I shake my head, trying to clear my thoughts and focus on her comment.

"What your daughter meant about what?"

"That travel opens your heart and your mind." She shrugs. "Abby studied abroad several semesters. France, Spain, Italy, and England—studying architecture."

"And you never thought about joining her?"

"I told you—" She shrugs again. "Life."

There is a sadness behind her smile. A sadness I want to explore, but she takes that moment to step away from me, effectively raising the barrier she's built once more.

"What's next on your list for today?"

I nod to the view. "Why don't we see what the Eiffel Tower looks like from the top of the Arc? But first . . ."

Eleanor

Once we're back on solid ground, Geoffrey takes my hand and pulls me through the crowd. "What about the picnic? Shouldn't we clean that up?"

"The hotel's driver will handle it."

I realize he's taking me underneath the pillars of the tower.

"Look up."

Complying, my breath catches at the sight. "Oh my." I'm looking up through the delicate latticework of the tower, against the backdrop of an azure sky.

"Pretty amazing, right?"

"I'll say." I'm so mesmerized by the image that I don't realize he's still holding my hand until I feel his fingers clench mine. Just as I'm about to pull my hand away, he releases mine and takes me by the elbow.

"Let's go."

As we cross the Pont de'léna over the Seine to the Jardins du Trocadéro, the film crew following closely behind, Geoffrey points out areas of interest, like the Sacré-Cœur off in the distance. I admit I am too distracted to notice. I'm too busy checking the flying text messages about a screw-up with an order for beach cover-ups for the coming summer season. The order is from one of the Husband-stealer's preferred wholesalers, one I haven't personally dealt with before, so I have no contacts with the company.

The distraction is a double-edged sword. I hate that it's

interfering with my tour of Paris, but I also welcome the distraction from the memory of Geoffrey's arms around me, so warm and solid. And I do mean solid. When I placed my hand on his chest, it was like touching a marble statue. A *warm* marble statue. I had to resist the urge to glide my hand over the rest of his torso, to learn its ridges and valleys beneath his button-down shirt.

As I'm typing out a quick message to my manager, I run into something solid, nearly knocking my hat off and causing me to lose my grip on the phone. The solid object is Geoffrey, an irritated look on his face. "What?"

He scowls at my phone, then lifts his gaze to my face. "Is that necessary?" He lifts his arms as if to encompass all of Paris. "You're in one of the most beautiful cities in the world, a place you've never visited, and you're like a teenager with her nose stuck to her telephone screen."

He gives me an annoyed look, and I give him an angry one. Holding up my phone, I say, "I'm not doom-scrolling social media. I have a business to run."

"And you don't deserve a vacation?"

I stare off into the distance. I don't owe him any explanation. I seem to recall *I'm* doing *him* a favor by spending the next nine days with him.

"Eleanor, don't you have people who can take care of things for nine measly days?"

"I did, but she had an affair with my husband." I can't believe I just blurted that out. The surprised look on his face confirms that I did, indeed, say that out loud.

"I'm sorry? Did you just say one of your employees had an *affair* with your husband?"

So we're going to unpack this now on a bridge over the Seine? "Let me clarify for you. My *business partner* had an affair with my then-husband. I am trying to make her my *former* business partner, and he is now my *ex*-husband."

His mouth works, as if trying to figure out what to say, and then the look I hate more than anything crosses his face—pity.

"No." I slash my hand through the air, just as my phone buzzes with another incoming text. "Do not go there. *Do not* pity me."

His expression changes into an emotionless mask. "Eleanor, I don't even know what to say to that."

I huff out a humorless laugh. "Join the club." My phone buzzes again like an angry bee. "I have to resolve this issue. I promise, I'll enjoy the gardens more if I can take care of this."

His mouth sets in a grim line, but he nods. "But can it wait until we get across the bridge and out of the way of other pedestrians?"

I suddenly realize the flow of people on the sidewalk is parting around us like a river around a boulder. "Yes. Sorry."

About ten text messages later, we reach the other side of the bridge. "Isn't it early there for business?"

I look at the time. "It's eight-fifteen there. The boutique opens at nine."

"Okay, here's a bench. Sit and take care of your . . . issue." Geoffrey thrusts his hands into his pockets.

A few more text messages fly between me and my manager, Naomi. She believes she's found the name of the company rep the Husband-stealer worked with to place the order and is going to reach out.

"Fire's out for now," I say as I look up at his face from under the brim of my hat.

"Good. There's the Warsaw Fountain," he nods his head to indicate the large fountain in front of us. "Let's go."

He places his hand on my lower back to guide me as he describes the fountain. "It was created for the Universal Exposition in 1937 and is the centerpiece of the gardens. The water cannons offer an incredible water display—when they're working. In the summer, there are lights around the fountains at night, creating a stunning visual. There are also a number of sculptures—gilded bronze animal statues and the two stone statues, 'L'Homme' by Pierre Traverse and 'La Femme' by Daniel Bacqué."

We stop at the edge of the fountain.

"Now turn around," Geoffrey urges.

I turn as requested, and my breath catches at the sight before me. The Eiffel Tower stands in stunning splendor, piercing the painfully blue sky with its intricate latticework. "Incredible," I breathe.

"It's amazing what you see when you put your phone away," Geoffrey points out.

A flush creeps into my cheeks. He's right. Of course, he's right. There's nothing worse than having a companion who is more focused on a six-inch screen than they are on you. I know that feeling all too well.

"It's not that I'm not interested." I attempt to defend my behavior. "I'm just trying to unravel a business partnership, and it's getting . . . complicated."

"You said you were trying to make her your *former* business partner. Why isn't that already a done deal?"

"Turns out unraveling a five-year business partnership is more difficult than unraveling a thirty-year marriage with copious assets."

He touches my arm, and the zing of pleasure catches me off-guard. "I'm sorry, Eleanor. Truly. But isn't that all the more reason to enjoy what Paris has to offer?"

Geoffrey

. . .

I'm going to make it my mission to entertain Eleanor during our time together so that she doesn't have time to think about her ex-husband and her soon-to-be-former business partner. Her ex-husband had an affair with her business partner and, one would assume, her friend? It's appalling!

Who does that to someone? Especially someone like Eleanor.

I long to ask her questions but settle for distracting her instead. "To the right is the Aquarium de Paris, or we can visit the Palais de Chaillot, which houses the naval museum and the anthropology museum. Do either of those interest you?"

She glances around at the manicured lawns, colorful flowerbeds, and tree-lined pathways, then up at the sky. "No. It's too beautiful to be indoors."

I agree. "Then let's just walk. On the weekends, the park is filled with street performers, artists, and musicians, and during the summer months, temporary carousels and amusement rides make it a popular spot for locals and tourists." I point out bits of statuary here and there, but otherwise I'm content to have this woman by my side. Remembering my goal to distract her, I ask, "If you could go anywhere in the world, where would you go?" At her lifted brow, I say, "Other than Paris, of course."

She appears to consider for a moment before saying, "Scotland."

"Really? I wasn't expecting that."

She shrugged. "I may be a bit of a Francophile, but I have Scottish ancestry."

I put on my best Scots accent. "Aye, lass. I have a wee bit of Scots in me too."

My heart leaps when she laughs at my antics. That laugh. It's throaty and bubbly, and from what I've seen so far, rare. I'd gladly give up my career if I could make her laugh like that more. That thought surprised the hell out of me.

"And what about you? I'm sure you're probably well-traveled, but where would you go that you haven't been?"

"That's easy. Hawaii."

"Hawaii?" She stops and gazes up at me. "You've never been?"

I can't see those gorgeous violet eyes behind her sunglasses, but I can feel them on my face, studying me. "No. Have you?"

She gives me a "get real" look, then continues down the path. "I haven't traveled, remember?"

"Well, I know you haven't been abroad before now. But I didn't know you hadn't traveled in your own country."

"I've traveled. I used to live in New York. And I've traveled a fair bit in the eastern U.S., especially for market."

"For market?"

"Yes. To buy for the boutique."

"Ah. But that's for business. Not for pleasure."

"It still counts as travel."

"But we're talking about pleasure here. Where have you been in the U.S.?"

"Does Disney World count?"

"I don't know. Was it pleasurable?"

"It was summer, so it was hot and crowded. I wouldn't say it was *pleasurable*. But it was for Abby's seventh birthday, and the memories of her joy when she saw her first Disney princess —well, you can't put a price on that." She wears a soft smile, as she stares unseeing, her mind clearly recalling those happy times.

I feel a twinge of guilt at the missed opportunity. But as my therapist says, "Water under the bridge." I can't do anything about that now. I just have to move forward.

We'd crossed the gardens and were exiting at Magdebourg.

"Where to next?" Eleanor asks, as she adjusts the hat on her head.

"We can walk to the Champs-Élysées. It's about twenty

minutes from here. You up for that? Or we could take a car if you're tired."

"A walk suits me."

I guide her to take a left out of the gardens to walk up Rue de Lübeck to les Champs, as the Parisians call it—the most beautiful avenue in the world.

Eleanor

My phone buzzes with another text. I cut a glance at Geoffrey.

"Again?" he asks on a heavy sigh.

"Just let me check." I pull out the phone and see another text from Naomi. My pulse ratchets up, wondering if it's a new problem or the resolution of the current problem. All the text says is "problem solved." I release a breath and put my phone back in my cross-body bag.

"Well?" The question surprises me. I thought he couldn't care less about my business issues.

"Problem solved."

"Good. Now can we enjoy the rest of the afternoon uninterrupted?"

"I can't make any such promise," I say, a chilly note in my tone. If he expects to spend nine more days together, he needs to understand there will likely be interruptions.

We walk in silence for a few minutes. I can feel the annoyance rolling off of him. I'd be willing to bet that if some movie studio called him with a part, he'd answer that call. *Hypocrite much?*

"If I looked at the photos on your phone, what would I see?"

"I'm sorry?" I ask in confusion.

"What photos would I find on your phone? Photos of you with your daughter, your friends? Or would I find images of ideas and items for your store?"

Well, that question hit home. And it makes me angry that it does. It does indeed have hundreds of photos from trips to market. Photos that have long since served their purpose and should have been deleted. Note to self: Clean out photos. It also includes before-and-after photos of the boutique when we made some upgrades to the décor.

But in my defense, sprinkled among those market photos, there are photos of Abby at her graduation, photos of us at a house we rented in the mountains for a quick mother-daughter getaway between semesters, and some silly photos of me and Maddie trying on hats. Okay, so those photos were taken at market when she came with me a few seasons ago, but still. And now I have a few photos here in Paris.

"I'm going to take your silence as tacit confirmation of the latter."

I cross my arms in annoyance that he has me pegged. "And what about your phone?" I shoot back. "What would the photos on your phone tell me about you?"

Instead of reacting to my sharp tone, he seems to consider the question. "You'd see a few photos of my Montmartre flat that I texted to an art dealer who was shopping the galleries for some pieces, and there are also a few photos with friends I had dinner with a couple of weeks ago. Then there's a photo of one of Cédric Grolet's desserts I had at The Berkeley in Knightsbridge that was insane." He shakes his head and laughs. "It was almost too beautiful to eat. Oh!" He snaps his fingers. "And there's a photo of me with my neighbor's adorable dog. He's a cock-a-poodle. Never saw myself as a small-dog person, but Samson's all kinds of cute." He wears a goofy grin.

Okay, first, he doesn't strike me as someone who collects

art. Second, he doesn't strike me as someone who feels compelled to photograph food. But third, and most surprising, is the photo of his neighbor's dog and his gushing description.

"All right. You win."

"I didn't know this was a contest."

"Well, clearly you were trying to make a point with your question about the photos on my phone."

"I was. But it wasn't a contest. I only wanted to bring to your attention that you need to relax and enjoy life and not work so hard."

"Maybe I enjoy working."

He shrugs. "I enjoy working too. Not everyone can say they love what they do for a living. But I also know breaks are important. It's those breaks that prevent burnout and allow me to take on new projects with renewed energy and focus."

Gah. This man! How does he manage to poke at all the little sore spots I'd rather ignore? But some of those sore spots have become more akin to a toothache that never goes away.

"Fine," I say, resigned. What's the point in arguing? What's the point in telling him that my business filled the hole left when my daughter—seemingly the only reason for my marriage—went off to live her own life?

We stop at an intersection with a wide, grand boulevard lined with trees, elegant buildings, and luxurious shops, and I know we've reached the Champs-Élysées.

"By the way, what happened on June 5, 1989?"

"What?"

"When we both went for the taxi the other day, I asked when the last time you'd smiled was, and you said June 5, 1989."

I try to remember the offhand comment. "Oh. Nothing happened on that date. At least nothing memorable." I shrug.

"So, you pulled that date out of thin air?"

"I must have."

He shakes his head and gives a rueful laugh. "And here I thought something wonderful happened to make you smile that day."

"Sorry to disappoint you."

"I'm sure I'll survive. Now, we can go left to the Arc de Triomphe or right to the Place de la Concorde. Do you have a preference?"

"Arc de Triomphe," I say. Despite all the walking we've done today, I want to climb to the top of the arch and take in the view."

He makes a formal bow and indicates the direction with an outstretched arm. "Your wish is my command."

Geoffrey

Breathing a little hard from the two hundred eighty-four steps to the top, I escort Eleanor out to the *terrasse* for another panoramic view of Paris. I note the rapid rise and fall of her chest, but she's clearly no stranger to aerobic exercise. I find that sexy. I love a woman who takes care of herself. It's not about size or weight—it's about health and fitness. From what I can tell, despite her busy schedule, she makes time for fitness.

I also note the sweat pouring from the red faces of the camera crew. "*Désolé*," I mutter in apology. There's an elevator, but it's only for those with mobility issues.

"Oh my," she breathes, and I feel a sense of pride in her awe. Pride that I can show her this, and pride in the fact that she enjoys it—that she's engaged, despite the day's business (and marriage) issues. Her wide-eyed wonder makes the climb worth it.

I was serious when I told her breaks were important. She deserves to treat herself every now and then. I always need a break between movies. Though lately, I seem to be on a permanent break.

I step up behind her, and my hand automatically goes to her hip. She doesn't seem to notice as she gazes out at the magnificent view of Paris, similar to the view from the Eiffel Tower, yet different in its perspective.

I hear the camera shutter click in rapid succession.

I point past her and say, "To the north is Notre-Dame." I indicate the twin towers of the cathedral, still under renovation after the devastating fire. "Then there's the Louvre along the Seine." This close to her, I can smell her perfume and the faintest whiff from her exertion. It's a delicious combination of sweet fragrance and earthy woman.

"To the east, you can see down the Champs-Élysées all the way to the Place de la Concorde." Below us, traffic whirs along les Champs and around the twelve-lane roundabout that encircles the arch, looking for all the world like ants on a collision course.

Eleanor gazes down. "Do they ever crash?"

"Of course, but most of the time, the result is a fender-bender and a few choice French curses. I'm man enough to admit I won't drive through that, but for many Parisians it's another emblem of Paris's greatness."

I shift her slightly with a gentle nudge of my hand, still resting all too comfortably on her hip. "To the southeast . . . the Eiffel Tower."

"Oh! It's beautiful!" She leans back into my chest, and my breath hitches. I don't think she's even aware of the intimate position.

The camera shutter clicks again. I wonder if, when she sees the photo on social media, she'll regret it.

"Beyond that, to the south, you can see Montmartre Hill. My flat isn't far from there."

"Really? I don't see you living in such a bohemian neighborhood."

"Why not? I am an artist of sorts."

"I pictured you in, say, Neuilly-sur-Seine." She indicates north, toward the La Défense.

"Near the business district? And how does someone who has never been to Paris know so much about it?"

She shrugged. "Reading."

I tsk and shake my head.

"What's wrong with reading?"

"Nothing. But why read about it when you can live it?"

She lifts her chin and gazes up into my face, and my breath catches at the soft smile on her lips. It's all I can do not to kiss her right there at the top of the Arc, with all of Paris at our feet.

Eleanor

"I hate to admit it, but I think jet lag is catching up with me again." After taking the two hundred eighty-four steps down from the top of the arch, we walked another half hour down les Champs, as Geoffrey calls it, to the Place de la Concorde, and my legs feel like dead weights by the time we arrive.

"We've covered a lot in one day. I should have kept the itinerary light, especially when you're still adjusting to the time difference."

"No, I've had a wonderful day. Truly." I smile up at him. "If you ever decide to give up acting, you'd make an excellent tour guide."

"I'll keep that in mind." His mouth widens with a grin.

His grin is . . . devastating. It makes my stomach do little somersaults, which is ridiculous at this stage of my life. With all that I've had to deal with the last few years, you'd think I'd be inured to such charm. Clearly, I'm not, because when we stood on the *terrasse* at the Arc and he placed his hand on my hip, I felt an odd mix of excitement and peace. Excitement because his hand was large and firm against my body, and peace because it felt so right.

I scoff to myself. So right that I leaned back against his solid chest without conscious thought. It just seemed natural.

"We can call it a day and return to the hotel."

"We're here, so we might as well look around."

"If you're sure." He frowns down at me.

"I'm sure. Then I'll be ready to return to the hotel. I hope you don't mind, but I think I'd rather order room service, take a hot bath, and crawl into bed."

"Eleanor, this is your trip. You can do whatever you want —as long as you enjoy yourself."

At the heart of the square stands the remarkable Obelisk of Luxor, a soaring ancient monument gifted to France in the nineteenth century by Muhammad Ali Pasha, Ottoman ruler of Egypt. I take out my phone and, with a smirk at Geoffrey, I take a few photos of the obelisk, then of the elegant buildings that form the backdrop of the square. "There. Now I have something on my phone besides work-related pictures."

Geoffrey grins and nods approvingly.

Tucking my phone away, I say, "If I recall my French history, the Place de la Concorde served as the site of many beheadings during the French Revolution."

"It did. Louis XVI and Marie-Antoinette, among others, were guillotined here."

I shudder. "How gruesome."

"Indeed. But on a happier note, there are some of Paris's

most famous museums nearby." He stopped short. "How about we come back to the Place de la Concorde the day we visit the museums?"

"And what day will that be?"

"I don't know yet." He winks. "My tour itineraries are impromptu and subject to change without prior notice."

"But we'll come back?"

"Of course! What is a visit to Paris if you don't see the Tuileries or L'Orangerie?"

I nod. "Then I like that plan."

He turns to Hélène and Stéphane and explains the plan for today. They clearly look like they're up for that idea as well.

"All right, let's hire a taxi."

We walk to the corner of les Champs and Rue de Bassano, and Geoffrey hails a taxi. As the driver stops, Geoffrey reaches for the door handle. "We're sharing this cab, right? After all, we aren't strangers any longer."

I laugh and shake my head. Who would have believed three days ago I'd be sharing a cab with the same man who tried to steal my taxi?

Eleanor

"Mom, what's going on there? Are you . . . having an *affair* with Geoffrey Harrison?"

Those are the first words out of my daughter's mouth when I answer my phone. Not "Hi, Mom," or "How are you, Mom?"

"Abby! Nice to hear from you. I'm fine, and you? How's school?" I collapse onto my hotel bed. I hadn't been lying to Geoffrey when I'd said I was exhausted.

"No, no. Don't avoid my question. Are you having an affair?"

"How do you even know who Geoffrey Harrison is?" How can my daughter know him when I didn't? He's almost thirty years older than her.

"Mom, he was only the biggest romantic lead when I was in high school. I had such a crush on him!"

Since when had my brainy daughter turned into such a romantic?

"Especially after the movie *From Paris, With Love.* When he took the heroine to the top of the Eiffel Tower, and it was cold, and he pulled her into his arms, and they kissed for the first time. Le sigh." She releases a breathy sigh to punctuate her words. "And stop avoiding the question."

I stiffen at the description. Isn't that what he did today? Well, without the kiss. Was he playing the romantic lead for his fans when he did that, reminding them of his movie, even after I told him no romance, fake or otherwise? Anger shoots through me at the thought of being used for his own ends.

But wasn't that what I'd agreed to? Wasn't that the bargain we'd struck? Minus the romance.

Irrational disappointment chases away the anger. If he *was* playing a role, why *didn't* he kiss me? Or at least try to. Not that I would've let him, but . . . dammit, am I not attractive enough for him to even try? He probably goes for younger women, like so many men his age. Like Barry.

"And Mom—when you were standing on the top of the arch and you leaned back into his chest? You looked like . . . a couple in love!"

She'd noticed that? I wonder if anyone else had noticed.

"Dad's head is going to explode," Abby was saying.

"What? Why?"

"Mom, you're a social media sensation. At first, everyone

was wondering who the lucky woman was, then someone outed you. Now the posts have gone viral."

I try to swallow, but my mouth has suddenly gone dry. "What?"

"The picture of you with Geoffrey's arms around you at the top of the Eiffel Tower, your head nestled under his chin—like the scene in *From Paris, With Love*—has over a million likes!"

I collapse onto the bed in my hotel room, staring out at said tower.

". . . and Dad is going to flip out."

I shake my head at this turn of events. I guess I knew there would be activity on social media, but a million likes? I don't have any personal social media—just the boutique accounts run by my marketing department—aka a local high schooler. I'd have to take Abby's word for it.

"So, I'll ask you once again, are you and Geoffrey a thing?"

I sigh and scrub my forehead. "No, sweetie, we're not."

"Bummer."

I bark out a laugh at her disappointment. "Sorry to burst your bubble. We just agreed to spend the nine days in Paris together. He's going to show me the popular tourist sights, as well as some not-so-touristy areas of Paris."

"Like his flat?" she teases.

"Definitely not."

"Why not, Mom? Have some fun! A fling with Geoffrey Harrison, rom-com heartthrob, would definitely fit the bill!"

"Abigail Marshall, I am not going to have a fling with this man." Besides, the man doesn't *want* to have an affair with me.

"Mom, you have sacrificed so much for me, and watching you fight breast cancer and then go through the divorce," she pauses, and I hear a sniffle, "I just want to see you happy. I want to see you let go—do something just for you and have fun for once. Please."

My daughter. My heart. I blink away tears at her words. This has become a recurring phrase from her. "I *am* having fun." Wasn't I? I'd only checked my phone a few times today for those business texts and emails. That was something.

"Have *more* fun. You deserve it for everything you've had to put up with."

Abby and Barry were on decent terms, though Abby had been horrified by her father's actions and had taken my side on the issue. Part of me didn't want the divorce—and the reason for it—to taint their relationship. I know Barry loves Abby. But sometimes, in my darker moments, Abby's support for me felt like vindication. Not a feeling I'm proud of.

"I love you, Abby, my girl."

"I love you to, Mom. Promise me you'll have some fun."

"I promise." After all, I plan to visit the antique flea market while I'm here. That would be fun.

I end the call, then notice I have over a dozen more text messages. Had something else gone wrong at the boutique? That's what I get for not paying closer attention. There were texts from Naomi (my boutique manager), Lakshmi (my best salesperson), and even Tabitha—my, er, marketing manager. What the hell?

Scrolling through the texts, my heart in my throat, I start pacing the room.

Naomi: The phones are ringing off the hook!

Lakshmi: Everyone wants the dress you were wearing today. Can we order more?

Tabitha: Get u Ellieee 🤩 ur going viral! 📱💖 ur a social media star.

I return to my seat on the bed and blow out a breath. I thought my agreement with Geoffrey might lead to an uptick in my boutique's popularity, even if only temporarily, but I hadn't expected the phones to ring off the hook! And as for the dress, I suppose I could get the manufacturer to make another run. It was one of my own designs.

Every season, I included a few styles of my own to complement the other clothing items I offered. They were usually popular, but now . . . I glance over at the gilded mirror on the opposite wall and smile.

What was it Tabitha said? *Get me. I'm a social media star.* Oh yeah, Barry's head is going to explode. Too bad I'm not going to be there to see it.

Chapter Three

DAY THREE

Geoffrey

I wake to gray skies and drizzle. But I guess even Paris in April has to have rain to make all those flowers grow. Today calls for indoor activities. Good thing the city has a few museums, I think wryly.

I reach for my phone to see several texts from Malcolm. What now?

> Malcolm: The Plan is working! One million likes!

> "Holy shit!" When he'd hatched this extended crazy plan, I'd never expected that. A few thousand, maybe. But one million?

> Malcolm: Keep it up!

I plan to. Aside from the fact that people were taking notice of me again, I enjoyed the hell out of yesterday with Eleanor. She continues to intrigue me. Makes me want to drill down, unpack her emotions, and discover what makes her tick. As an actor, understanding motivations is key. And there is more to Eleanor's motivations than she divulges.

> Malcolm: Peter Cassel called. He want to talk about a movie.

I sit up. Peter Cassel was only one of the top producers and directors in Hollywood. His movie *Endless Blue Sky* had been an Oscar nominee and his leading man, Carson Birdsong, had been up for best actor. He didn't win, but still. This could be the role I've been hoping for. Something I can sink my teeth into.

Don't get me wrong. I have nothing against rom-coms. After all, I'd made over a dozen of them, and they'd proven *very* lucrative. As I told Eleanor at dinner, I have an apartment in New York on Fifth Avenue. I have a flat here in Montmartre, and I have a smallish country estate in the Cotswolds for when I need to get away from everything. Yes, the movies had made me rich. The role of romantic lead was practically made for me. I had looks. I had charm. Not a boast, just the truth. And I'm a nice guy. No leading ladies had ever had any reason to accuse me of untoward behavior.

But I'd been typecast into roles I'd aged out of, and finding work—the work I wanted, the work I'd earned—had become difficult. The last thing I want to become is a has-been. The roles open to me now are father-of-the-groom, rather than groom, or the dirty old man instead of the boy next door.

I want to play juicy leads, or at the very least, supporting roles with depth.

My phone buzzes with another text.

> Malcolm: The film crew will be there at 10 am.

I glance at the time and wonder if it's too early to text Eleanor.

Me: Morning. How did you sleep.

I wait a few minutes, but about the time I think she isn't going to reply, I see the three dots.

Eleanor: Very well. And you?

Me: Same. I was afraid I would wake you with my text.

Eleanor: I've already been to the fitness center and had my first cup of coffee.

The fitness center? No wonder she looks so fit. A twinge of guilt threads through me. I should have been in the fitness center myself. My trainer would be disappointed. That guilt proves short-lived, as I begin to wonder what Eleanor wore for her workout. Was it those tight workout pants and a sports bra? My imagination went into overdrive. Eleanor bending over to stretch. Or maybe in one of those yoga poses, like downward dog, her skin glistening with sweat. My phone buzzes impatiently again, reminding me I have a text.

Me: Good for you. An early riser, then?

Eleanor: Always.

Then thinking of Eleanor in bed made me wonder what she wears to bed. A lacy negligee? Or is she more of a pajama bottoms and T-shirt kind of gal? Or maybe nothing at all.

My phone buzzes again.

Eleanor: It's raining. What are the plans for today?

Hmm. Was she eager to see me? I allow myself that illusion, then give a thought or two to the day's itinerary. With a plan in mind, I text back.

Me: It's a surprise. Just dress for indoors and meet me in the lobby 10.

Eleanor: 👍

Geoffrey

I glance at my watch and, as if on cue, the elevator dings. The doors open and a few guests pile out. Behind them is Eleanor, and as usual, she looks as if she's stepped off the cover of *Vogue* or *Elle*. A vivid turquoise tunic sweater skims her body's subtle curves. Snug denim ankle pants hug a pair of shapely legs. On her feet, a pair of fashion sneakers. Absent are the bold sunglasses she'd been wearing the last two days. Her pewter and silver hair is pulled back into a ponytail, revealing darker strands along the nape of her neck, and draped over her arm is a hot pink hooded rain jacket. I love a woman who's prepared.

She looks up and those violet eyes connect with mine. A thrill of anticipation courses through me. I grin, enjoying the feeling. I haven't experienced it in . . . well, I can't remember the last time I experienced it. Her smile in return ratchets up my heart rate, leaving me a little breathless. Damn. What this woman does to me.

"Morning." She beams.

"Morning. You ready?"

"Yes. Where to?"

"I'll tell you when we're on our way."

Once we're ensconced in the dry, warm private car I hired

and we pull out into traffic, I settle back and let my gaze travel from the top of her head, along her profile, then down her firm breasts, and finally her long legs. Her attention is on the rain-soaked streets of Paris, its visitors and inhabitants shrouded against the chilly drizzle, so I drink my fill, taking full advantage of her distraction.

An elegant hand rests on her thigh, the trim, polished nails, part and parcel of her understated style. I resist the urge to reach over and take her hand in mine. To connect with her in a physical way.

"Do you want to hear today's itinerary?"

She turns her attention to me, eyebrows lifted. "Yes."

"I thought we would start with the Paris Opera House, then the Musée d'Orsay, then back to the Place de la Concorde for a visit to L'Orangerie to see Monet's *Water Lilies*. After that, I thought perhaps afternoon tea at Angelina. Then, last but certainly not least, the Louvre, where we'll hit the highlights. It would take days to see everything in the Louvre. It will all be a quick tour, but if there's anything you wish to spend more time with, we can come back another day. And, if you're not too tired, we can end the day with an early dinner at a lovely café near the museum."

She shakes her head.

"What is it? If you don't like the itinerary, I'm not married to it. We can change it up."

"No. It's . . . perfect. Truly."

Perfect. My joy reigns supreme.

When we arrive outside the Opera House, the weather has resolved to blanket the city in a steady days-long drizzle, obscuring some of the taller buildings in the distance and leaving a chill in the air. Not ideal weather for viewing the Corinthian columns and elaborate sculptures that adorn the Beaux-Arts exterior façade of the Opera House.

I step out of the car and extend my hand to Eleanor. She

flips up the hood of her jacket and covers her head as she slips her hand in mine and steps from the car.

I had already given instructions to the driver to pick us up out front in an hour.

"Let's go," I say, tugging her alongside me as we dash to the entrance.

Once inside, she lowers her hood, and she's laughing, a blush painting her cheekbones, her eyes alight with joy. I am momentarily struck speechless, which is saying something for someone who makes his living speaking.

Completely unaware of my predicament, she spins in a circle, her head tilted to admire the painted ceiling of the Rotonde des Abonnés. "My god, it's beautiful!"

"Yes . . . beautiful." But I'm not looking at the ceiling. Giving myself a mental shake, I say, "Wait until you see the Galerie du Glacier and the salon, . . . or the auditorium. There are so many stunning visuals in this building."

While she wanders the lobby, I purchase our tickets for a self-guided tour, keeping in mind the one-hour time limit I set for us. The film crew did not join us this morning, as we were unable to obtain permission from the Opera House, but they will join us later at the Orsay. I rather like the thought of having Eleanor all to myself for an hour, without the pressure to create "Instagrammable" moments.

She's standing beneath the rotunda, taking photos of the ceiling with her camera, her back arched for a better view. I'm happy to see she'll have photos she can look back on with fondness, and I'd like to think I had a little something to do with that.

I slip my hand around her elbow, and she turns with a warm smile. "This is spectacular. I had no idea."

"Let's walk over to the grand staircase. I'll take your picture and you can send it to Abby."

"That would be nice. Thank you."

We walk toward the massive double marble staircase that leads to the upper floors of the Opera House, and she hands her phone to me. I note her screensaver is of a young woman with blond hair, a mortarboard with a graduation tassel on her head, and a smile that radiates joy.

"Abby's graduation photo."

"She's beautiful." I enlarge the image, then glance from mother to daughter. "She looks like you. She has your stunning violet eyes."

Her gaze shoots to mine as a flush rises up her face and into her cheeks. "You think my eyes are stunning?"

"I can't imagine anyone who wouldn't." I stare a moment longer into their depths, then blink and clear my throat. "Now go stand on the steps and look appropriately awed by your surroundings."

I can see wheels turning in her mind, trying to come up with a suitable pose. She places a hand on the rail and the other on her hip. I sigh. Eleanor is clearly not a woman who lets loose.

"Come on, you can do better than that. Look awed!"

"I feel silly," she says in protest, then glances around at the other tourists milling around the venue.

"Who cares?"

Her brow furrows, then she lifts her hands in the air as if conducting an orchestra, and her lips part in an expression of amazement. "That's it!" I take a few photos to ensure one of them is to her liking. I hand her camera back to her. "Was that so hard?"

She's scrolling through the photos, a soft smile on her lips. "No, I suppose not."

"Good. Now let's see the rest of the Opera House."

Eleanor

Geoffrey is right—there are so many breathtaking spaces in this building. After visiting the gallery and salon, we took in the library. It's hard to believe anything could rival the Baroque opulence and grandeur of the Paris Opera House. Then again, we haven't visited Versailles yet.

"I saved the best for last," Geoffrey says, as we approach the doors to the auditorium. He is a patient and attentive tour guide, and I can't imagine seeing Paris without his knowledge of, and pride in, this city. I'd like to learn more about his obvious connection to Paris.

He opens the heavy door, and we enter a world of red and gold opulence. And at its heart is the central dome. We walk in near-reverence to sit beneath it, enthralled.

"Marc Chagall painted the dome in the 1960s. It was quite controversial at the time. But according to the booklet, the original painting remains. Chagall's work is suspended from the ceiling in a lightweight frame."

The painting is radically different from the surrounding gilded decorative accents, corpulent cherubs, and riot of red velvet.

"The chandelier is made of bronze and crystal and weighs seven tons," Geoffrey continues. After a pause, he says, "Are you a fan of *Phantom of the Opera*?"

I turn to look at him. "Oh yes! When Abby graduated from high school, I took her to New York for a mother-daughter trip. We went to a few shows, *Phantom* being one of them."

Geoffrey gestures to the massive chandelier in the center of the dome. "The Paris Opera House is the setting for it. Gaston Leroux used a rumor about the Opera House being haunted to create his story. That's the chandelier that crashes during a performance. Leroux also wove the underground lake into his story."

I lift my head and look at him, eyes wide. "There's actually an underground lake?"

"Yes. But don't get too excited. It's nothing like the lake in the musical. It's really just a cistern used to manage the groundwater below the building's foundation."

"Oh." I sigh. I wouldn't consider myself a romantic person, but this is oddly disappointing.

Eleanor

"Why do you think she's the only one who's naked?" I ask.

We're standing before Édouard Manet's *Le Déjeuner sur l'herbe*, or *Luncheon on the Grass*, one of the Orsay Museum's many masterpieces. The painting depicts four people in the woods: two men and two women. The woman in the background appears to be clothed in only a shift, but it's the woman in the foreground who shocks the viewer, as she is completely naked. Her eyes are boldly turned to the viewer, as if daring them to be scandalized.

Geoffrey shrugs and says, "Because no one wants to see the men naked? Or maybe she's a naturist—or an exhibitionist." He leans over and murmurs in my ear, "Or maybe she wants to be tupped."

I push him away with a laugh. "Stop."

Housed in a stunning former railway station on the left bank of the Seine, the Orsay Museum, or Musée d'Orsay, is small compared to its larger sister museum, the Louvre. Once a train station, the Gare d'Orsay was a major transportation hub in Paris in the early 1900s. Today, it holds some of the world's most renowned works of art from the Impressionist and Post-Impressionist era, featuring works from artists including Claude Monet, Auguste Renoir, Vincent van Gogh, Paul Cézanne, and Edgar Degas.

The breathtaking Beaux-Arts-style building—with its grandiose and ornate features, its symmetry and proportion, and the glass roof and ceiling rosettes in the arched bays—is the perfect location for an art museum, and it has long been on my list of Paris must-sees. And here I am, thanks to Maddie's interference. And yes, I should send her flowers.

Geoffrey is still considering the painting. "Could you ever do that?"

"What? Sit naked in the woods with two lechers? No."

"No. I mean, could you be comfortable enough in your own skin to just . . . be naked?"

Since his question seems in earnest, I give it some thought. Could I? "Maybe when I was twenty," I finally say. "But now, no."

His mood has turned pensive. Without taking his eyes off the painting, he muses, "Why do we value the beauty of youth, rather than the wisdom of age?"

I shrug and say, "Because we're shallow creatures?"

He offers me a sad smile, then appears to give himself a mental shake. "Come. We have more art to see. "

In front of Degas's bronze statue, *Little Dancer Aged Fourteen*, my phone buzzes. Frowning, I reach in my bag and pull it out to see a text from the last person I'd expected to hear from—except through my lawyer.

> Phoebe: You must not be too heartbroken over Barry—I see you've moved on, and with a movie star, no less. You're probably doing it just to get back at me. Trying to make me jealous that you can score Geoffrey Harrison.

I stare down at my phone, stupefied at her audacity. "That little b—"

"Eleanor, what is it?" Geoffrey grips my elbow, but I'm too pissed to respond.

She has a lot of nerve commenting on my life, when she's the one who stole Barry in the first place! How could I not have seen just how self-absorbed she is? Serves me right for looking at the text in the first place. I should have heeded Geoffrey's many admonitions to ignore my phone.

"Eleanor?"

"It's nothing." I shove the phone back in my purse. I'm not going to grace that text with a response. She's just trying to goad me into saying something she and her lawyer can use against me. When I told her our partnership was over, she had the unmitigated gall to be shocked. As if I would stay in business with the women who stole my husband!

Geoffrey turns me to face him. "It's not nothing. Something—or someone—has clearly upset you. Is it the boutique?"

"I'd really prefer not to talk about it." I glance over at the film crew. My phone buzzes again. *WTF?*

"Are you going to answer it?" Geoffrey nods toward my bag and the location of the buzzing smartphone.

"No."

"Well, that's a first."

I huff out a biting laugh and cut him a look. The look Barry always called "the scalpel" because it was razor-sharp and intended to cut the recipient to pieces. Didn't seem to faze Geoffrey though.

"Answer the text, Eleanor. That way you can take care of the problem and enjoy yourself."

"It's not that kind of text."

"What kind of text is it?" He folds his arms over his chest.

"The kind you don't respond to." I cut another glance at Hélène and Stéphane.

"Spam, then?"

"Yeah, you could call it that." To my surprise, the phone buzzes yet again. "Oh, for the love of Pete!" I reach into my bag again, yanking out my phone. Before I can look at it, Geoffrey takes it from me. "Hey!"

His lips move as he reads the texts then, frowning, he lifts his gaze to mine. "Who is this?"

"My ex-husband's hussy," I whisper.

His gaze returns to the screen. "Damn. The woman must have brass bullocks." Geoffrey signals to the film crew to give us some privacy. As if we have much privacy in the middle of a museum, but at least this moment won't end up on social media.

"She does. Now can I have my phone back?" I lock it as soon as he hands it to me.

"Aren't you going to read it?"

"No."

"Well, if you're not going to respond, at least block her. That woman should not be texting you."

"I know, but . . . it's complicated."

"Complicated how?"

"We still have joint control over the bank accounts. My lawyer advised against doing anything that could be seen as retaliatory until we dissolve the partnership."

"And how long will that take?"

"Months, maybe longer. I told you, dissolving this partnership has been more complicated than dissolving my marriage. At least both parties wanted the divorce."

"You mean one of you doesn't want to dissolve the partnership?"

"She doesn't."

"She sleeps with your then-husband, and thinks that's not a partnership-ending event?"

I lift a brow and his eyes widen. "That's—"

"Insane?"

"Yes." He glances up at the glass ceiling, then back at me. Then he reaches out and pulls me into his arms. "God, Eleanor, I don't even know what to say."

I'm not sure I would comprehend it if he did have something to say. His big, strong arms wrap around me and hold me close, right there in front of Degas's *Dancer* and everybody, and it feels so . . . right. Tears burn the back of my throat.

Dammit. I will not cry over this. I. Will. Not. Neither Phoebe nor Barry are worth my tears.

Geoffrey

The feel of Eleanor in my arms is bliss. This strong, beautiful woman doesn't deserve to be treated as if she's a discard.

An idea begins to take root, and I grasp her wrist and walk around a corner to a more private spot, tugging Eleanor behind me. I turn and take her by the shoulders so that I can look into her eyes that are swimming with unshed tears. Dammit. I could happily deck Barry right now. "I know you said you wouldn't fake a romance, but why not?"

She's already shaking her head no. A tear spills onto her cheek at the movement, and she angrily swipes it away. Good. I'd rather she be angry than sad.

"Hear me out. Your ex is a first-rate ass for what he did to you. And your business partner—she's . . ."

"A bitch?"

"Well, yeah. Why not get a little of yourself back? Make

them and the rest of the world think you're having a whirlwind romance? She already thinks we're a thing. Let me be your rebound, albeit a fake one."

"And how exactly will faking a romance help?"

"At least it would show him what he let get away from him, and that you don't give a flying fig about him. And it would show your ex-business partner too."

"But it's so . . . sordid. I couldn't let my daughter think I'm having a romance when it's actually fake. Nor would I let my best friend think that either."

"Then don't. Tell them the truth. But to the rest of the world, we're having an affair."

She narrows her eyes at me. "And why would you do this for me?"

I shrug and say, "You agreed to spend time with me in Paris to help my career. Why shouldn't you get something else out of it, besides a free trip to Paris?"

"And fifty grand for A Step Up," she reminds me.

"That too. But a little public fling won't hurt my career either. The more I'm in the public eye, and my name is on the public's lips, the better. So it's a win-win."

I can see her waffling, and I press my case further. "Come on, what have you got to lose? We pretend to be in lust, if not in love, for a week, then on the last day, you return to your life in Florida, and I'll return to . . ." What will I return to, with no movie prospects? Giving myself a mental shake, I continue, hoping she won't notice my incomplete sentence. "No harm, no foul."

She crosses her arms over her chest and lifts a suspicious brow. "And what would this entail? How would we pretend we're having an affair?"

I shrug. "Show each other affection. You were married. How did you and your husband show affection?"

She blinks.

I lift a brow, wondering if they ever showed each other affection, or if it had been so long she'd forgotten. At the pain in her violet eyes, I take pity on her. "The usual. Holding hands, embracing. Kissing."

"Kissing?" she asks, a slight squeak in her voice.

I swallow a laugh. "Yes, kissing. You know, when two people lock lips. Maybe some tongue is involved."

She looks up sharply. "No. There will be no tongues involved."

I sigh. "Fine."

She still looks dubious. "And how do we make it believable? I won a contest and suddenly we're in lust?"

"We build up to it, just like in my rom-coms."

"Since I don't watch rom-coms, that reference doesn't help me."

I sigh in exasperation. "And why is that?"

"Why is what?"

"Why don't you watch rom-coms, like millions of other women do?"

"Time. Plain and simple. That, and I'm not a romantic."

"You're a Francophile and you say you're not a romantic?"

She shrugs. "I like art and architecture. That doesn't make me a romantic."

I give her a skeptical look. I think she's fooling herself, but I let it go for now. "What do you do for fun then? To relax?"

"Design clothes."

"That's relaxing?"

"To me it is." She lifts a slender shoulder. "Some people knit. I design clothes."

"Okay, I can see that. I think. But still, you can't take two hours out of your day and watch a movie? One with a guaranteed happy ending?"

"I'm not into happy endings at the moment."

"Point taken. But isn't happiness the sweetest revenge?

Show your ex that you've moved on, and you're happier without him."

"I thought success was the sweetest revenge."

"That too."

"I repeat—how does this work?"

"I'll break it down for you." I tick the points off on my fingers. "First, there's the Meet-Cute."

"Wait. What's a meet-cute?"

"Are you serious right now?" At her look, I realize she is. "A meet-cute is when two people meet for the first time. It's usually a humorous or charming encounter. We had that in spades. I couldn't have written a better meet-cute than our taxi encounter," I say with a wink.

Eleanor just rolls her eyes.

"Even without that, I have to admit the Dream Date Contest makes a good meet-cute. Next is the No Way. This is where the hero and heroine say, 'I'm not falling in love, and I'm definitely not falling in love with you.' You definitely gave off that vibe the night of our dinner." I give her a sheepish grin.

"Now, to make the plot interesting, you have to add the next ingredient: Forced Togetherness. We've met that element. Between your contest win and our agreement, we've satisfied this plot point as well. We've agreed to spend a lot of time together."

"This brings us to Attraction. This is where we would pick up the story, with little touches, longing looks, and maybe shared experiences. Sharing food is a good way to show this. As our attraction grows—"

"*Fake* attraction," she interjects.

"Right. As our *fake* attraction grows, we move to the Maybe. This is where the hero and heroine think it might just work. Relationships are usually fun and easy at this stage. Nothing heavy to deal with yet."

"Then there's the Deeper Attraction phase. The hero and heroine grow closer emotionally and physically. This is where they're willing to give in to temptation." I waggle my brows at her, and she smirks.

She points her finger at me. "There will be no temptation, so we can skip that phase."

"If you say so," I reply, doubt heavy in my voice. "Before things can move forward, though, one or both characters begin to question whether this will really work. This is the Maybe Not phase. Inevitably, something happens that makes one or both of the characters choose fear over love. This is the Definitely Not, or the Black Moment. Everything comes crashing down. And that's it."

"What do you mean, that's it?" There's a note of longing in her voice, which tells me I've drawn her in. "I thought romances ended like Cinderella, with happily ever after."

"They do. But we needn't worry about the remaining plot points, because we'll end our fake affair there."

Her face falls a bit, then, as if giving herself a mental shake, she gives me a brisk nod. "Right. Of course."

Just when I think she's moved on, she says, "Just tell me. For my own edification."

The corner of my mouth lifts at her sudden interest in the plot points. "Okay, after the Black Moment, the hero and heroine become Lost Souls without one another. They question their decision to allow their fears to rule their lives, instead of allowing love in."

Her brow furrows, whether in thought or doubt, I don't know, but I continue. "Then, there's Realization. One or both of them realize they choose love, and they regret their decision. That brings up to the Grand Gesture, where one of them puts it all on the line for love or risks losing the love of their life. If the Grand Gesture pays off, it's Happily Ever After. The hero and heroine overcome their fears and ride off into the sunset together."

"Sounds very formulaic," says Eleanor the Skeptic.

"That's because it is—a bit. But that's also why it works. Now, the plot will need to move quickly from point to point, since we only have a few days—but we can make it work."

She looks behind me. "What about Hélène and Stéphane?"

"What about them?"

"Will they know it's fake?"

"No. The fewer people who know the truth, the better."

"And Malcolm?"

"He's my agent. He'll need to know the truth."

"Okay. For the sake of argument, if I say yes to this scheme of yours, I get to decide what . . . intimacies I'm agreeable to?"

"Of course. Before filming any movie involving physical intimacy, the actors involved meet with an intimacy director or coordinator. Actors agree to the level of physical intimacy they are comfortable with on set and ensure continued consent during the filming."

"Are you saying we need an intimacy advisor?"

"Well, no. I've been through enough interviews—I think I can use my experience here. We would agree on what physical intimacies we're comfortable with, and we can continue to check in with each other every day to see if we're still on the same page."

She bites her lower lip as her gaze meanders from my face to my chest, and lower, her expression telling me she is questioning whether any intimacies with me would be tolerable. Very humbling, I tell you. And yet, also very arousing.

She finally nods. "Okay."

Apparently, I meet her minimum acceptability standards. "Okay, you want to fake a romance? Or okay, you want to discuss agreed-upon intimacies before you decide?" At her frown, I continue, "If we're going to do this, we need to communicate clearly to avoid any misunderstandings."

"Right. I agree to a fake relationship . . . in public."

I nod. "And do you want to discuss the parameters?"

"I agree to hand-holding, hugging, and kissing on the cheeks and lips." She holds up a finger again. "No tongue," she reminds me.

"Agreed. Any other touching, like my hand on your lower back, or your shoulder?"

"Agree."

"I agree to the same, along with you taking my arm, wrapping your arm around my waist, or around my neck."

She looks perplexed for a moment.

"This isn't a one-way street, Eleanor. Men can feel sexualized too."

"Right. Of course. I apologize. Now, how do we build this relationship to make it believable?"

"If you're willing, you can just follow my lead."

She eyes me again, as if trying to decide whether she can trust me or not.

"Eleanor, in all the years I've been in Hollywood, there has never been an allegation of sexual misconduct made against me. And there never will be."

"Fine. I'll rely on you to take the lead."

"Do we begin tomorrow with Versailles?"

She sighs. "I suppose it's as good a time as any. And if we're going to make this convincing, I guess you should call me Ellie."

"All right, Ellie. Shall we go up to see the museum clock?" I hold out my elbow for her to take.

She eyes it dubiously for a moment, then places her hand in the crook of my arm.

We're really going to need to work on her public displays of affection.

Eleanor

Did I really just agree to a fake affair with Geoffrey Harrison, movie star and heartthrob, just to get back at my ex-husband and his hussy? What the hell was I thinking? It was a moment of weakness resulting from my hurt and anger over Phoebe's text.

Now, as we make our way to the Orsay's exit, I'm having second thoughts. No, not second thoughts—first thoughts. I'm finally thinking with my brain, instead of my heart, and I've changed my mind.

But as Geoffrey's large, warm hand rests on my lower back, my body says *reconsider*. Would it be so bad to hold his hand in mine, to feel his arms around me? His lips on mine? I shiver involuntarily.

"Are you cold?" He gazes down at me, concern in his eyes.

"No, no. I'm fine." My words come out breathy and nervous.

"I thought we'd dash over to the Musée de l'Orangerie to see Monet's *Water Lilies*. I'm afraid we won't have time for more than that if we're to have lunch and see the Louvre."

I nod in agreement. Seeing the *Water Lilies* has also been on my list of must-sees, but I'm too keyed up with thoughts of faking affection for this man to verbalize my enthusiasm for his suggestion.

We hop in the waiting car and, within a few minutes, we're outside L'Orangerie. Located in the Tuileries Gardens, the building was originally built by Napoleon III to protect citrus trees during the winter months. But in 1920, the building was transformed into a museum to house Monet's most iconic and influential bodies of work: *Les Nymphéas*, or *Water Lilies*.

After purchasing our tickets, we enter the hushed

atmosphere of the museum and make our way directly to the rooms where the murals are displayed.

My breath catches at the sight, and my doubt and recriminations fall away. Monet himself designed the two elliptical rooms that house the eight murals depicting his beloved garden at his residence in Giverny, creating a panorama in shades of greens, pinks, blues, and purples.

It's unlike anything I have ever seen. And for some reason, I feel the sting of tears and a deep appreciation for Maddie's interference and Geoffrey's persistence. Without these two people, I likely would never have seen this—this wonder. I blink away the tears that blur my view of these masterpieces.

"Beautiful, isn't it?" Geoffrey whispers near my ear, as if to speak any louder would shatter the peace and reverence of this space. His breath is warm and seductive, urging me to lean into him and feel his presence. "I never tire of seeing this," he continues.

"You come here often?" I ask, as I turn slowly to view each panel.

"Every time I'm in Paris."

"Do you have a favorite in this room?" Even though I don't think I could choose any single panel as my favorite.

"I'd say *Soleil Couchant.*" He points to the painting featuring swirls of blues and greens to pinks, yellows, and oranges. "*The Water Lilies—Setting Sun.*"

I stand before the painting. I can see why Geoffrey chose this one. The colors are peaceful, yet brilliant, and clearly evoke the work's title—the setting sun's rays reflected off the water of the lily pond.

Geoffrey touches my shoulder. "Come. We could stare at these all day, and we have another room to see."

I give the painting one last lingering look, then follow Geoffrey's lead. It's true. I could have stayed in that room with those paintings and let the world outside fade away.

If only it were that simple.

Geoffrey

"I'm famished," I say, as we take our seats at the coveted table 45, Coco Chanel's favorite table at Paris's famous Angelina.

Hélène and Stéphane will occupy the table next to us. I insist that, if they must spend their days with us, that in addition to their fees, they enjoy the same experiences—my treat. Plus, keeping them close by ensures they will capture some of the more candid moments between Eleanor—or rather Ellie—and me.

She's been pensive since visiting the Orsay Museum and my proposition to fake a romance. Perhaps she's having second thoughts. And although I said we could start tomorrow with Versailles, I may plant the seed here, in this romantic setting, with intimate conversation, delicate treats, and some of the world's finest teas.

I glance across the table at Ellie, who's looking over the menu.

"May I suggest we get the teatime set menu?"

"What?" Her gaze lifts to mine with a frown of surprise, as if she's forgotten I'm here. That won't do.

I pluck the menu from her hands and set it aside, just as the server comes to take our order. Perfect.

"Monsieur, Madame." The young woman nods to each of us. "What may I bring for you?"

"We'll have the set tea menu. One for each of us."

"Very good, Monsieur. And to drink?"

"*L'Africain*, of course." I flash my best smile at the young woman, who likely has no idea who I am.

"Oui, Monsieur."

I'm hoping to induce the almost-sexual moans that resulted from her indulgence at Le Cinq. If Angelina's signature hot chocolate doesn't do it, I don't know what will.

But right now, Eleanor is sitting back in her seat, arms crossed over her chest, her brow creased in annoyance. This is a very "Eleanor" posture. Unlike her "Ellie" posture when she's relaxed and enjoying herself.

"I am quite capable of ordering for myself."

"Of that, I have no doubt. But you have never been here, and since you haven't, I want to give you the full Angelina experience. Now, I invite you to get out of your own head and take in the timeless charm of this Paris establishment."

"I'm not—"

I hold up a hand. "Don't deny it. You're overthinking my proposition, and it's putting more of a damper on our day than the rain."

She sighs, looks out the window at the chilly drizzle, then back at me. Her gaze is steady and direct. "Okay." She nods and takes in the elegance of the tearoom. As her gaze lights on each exquisite detail of the sophisticated Belle Époque décor—from the ornate chandeliers to the plush velvet seating, the gilded mirrors to the paintings from Vincent Lorant-Heilbronn—I can see her shoulders relax, her frown lines disappear, and her lips soften. Soft classical music fills the air, creating a serene environment that relaxes and indulges.

I knew she would appreciate the attention to detail in every aspect of this experience.

"It really is quite beautiful," she murmurs before her gaze returns to me, a soft smile on her lips. "Thank you."

Now that I have Ellie back, it's time to instigate "The Plan."

Eleanor

"Another chocolate, Madame?"

I look up at the server and shake my head. "Oh no, I really shouldn't."

"She'll have another," Geoffrey says. "As will I."

I glower at him over the rim of my cup.

"Relax. You're on vacation," he cajoles.

Infuriating man.

Angelina's set tea menu consists of two delicate finger sandwiches of cucumber and watercress, a slice of French bread with melted brie, and an offering of mini sweets, including a delicate pastry, a strawberry macaroon, and a Madeleine. Geoffrey added the miniature version of their iconic Mont Blanc dessert—a delectable airy meringue topped with whipped cream and strips of hazelnut cream. Between that and the heavenly hot chocolate, or *L'Africain*, I know it will take more than an hour in the gym to burn off the calories.

Our server arrives with two more hot chocolates—make that *two* hours in the gym. To add insult to injury, Geoffrey holds out one of the mini Mont Blancs. Rolling my eyes at the indulgence, I reach out to take it from him, but he pulls his hand away.

"Uh-uh," he admonishes, like he's disciplining a naughty child. "I want you to take it from my fingers—with your mouth."

I snort. "You're insane."

"Feeding one another is a powerful symbolic gesture that conveys a deep sense of intimacy, affection, and emotional connection."

A laugh bubbles up at the absurdity, then I swallow it. "You're serious."

"Dead serious." He leans in and whispers, "Nothing says

romance like feeding one another."

"Even more than a kiss?"

He shrugs. "This act can be found across many cultures. People around the world recognize what it means."

In the mood to challenge him, I sit back in my chair. "What does it mean?"

"It means we trust one another. It's like a trust fall, only with food. It essentially says, 'I trust you to not accidentally poke my eye out with the fork.' Or in this case, a finger."

Despite myself, the corner of my mouth lifts. "What else?"

"It means sharing is caring. It's like saying, 'Hey, babe, I have this delectable morsel of food and I want you to experience its deliciousness too.'"

"Go on."

"It also shows culinary compatibility. It's like a taste test for relationships."

"Hmm. That's a stretch. Just because a couple doesn't like the same food doesn't mean they're incompatible."

"True. But it's a lot more fun when they do."

"What else you got?"

"Feeding each other can sometimes lead to moments of laughter as you navigate the fine art of aiming the spoonful into your partner's mouth or trying not to spill food on their favorite shirt."

"I suppose," I say, dubious. "Anything else?"

"Yes. I saved the best for last."

"Do tell." I cross my arms over my chest and lean forward.

"Feeding each other can be incredibly sensual and can serve as foreplay." He waggles his brows at me, making me laugh. Then he glances around the room at the full tables. "Unfortunately, we'll have to keep it PG."

"Fine." I sigh with feigned annoyance. "You can feed me."

He lifts the morsel once more, and as I lean forward to take it into my mouth, my pulse quickens. His gaze drops to my mouth, and he licks his lips. He hasn't even touched me, and I can feel the flush creep up my neck and into my face. Time slows down as I wait with an anticipation I haven't experienced in a very long time. It's as if I'm back in high school waiting for Dean Lyman to give me my first kiss.

When his fingers brush my lips, I nearly moan with need. His gaze lifts to mine, his eyes hot, pupils dilated. I close my mouth around the sweet, and he sucks in a breath. The decadent treat itself is anticlimactic after the anticipation. As I chew, I sit back, still a little dazed from the sheer sensuality of the experience.

He smiles. "Good?"

"So good. So much more than I expected." And I'm not talking about the Mont Blanc.

He pops one into his mouth, chews, and washes it down with a sip of chocolate. "Show me a photo on your phone and tell me about it."

"What?" His abrupt change in demeanor throws me off. It's as if he isn't affected at all by that bit of food foreplay. For my part, if he suggested we go back to the hotel room for a quickie, I'd probably jump at the chance.

Geoffrey slides his chair around next to mine, bringing his cup of chocolate with him. "Show me a picture." At my hesitation, he bumps his shoulder against mine and flashes me a grin certain to leave women swooning. "Come on. Show me yours and I'll show you mine."

I must admit, his grin is convincing. "Fine." I reach into my bag and wake up my phone, trying to think of a photo to show him that isn't work-related. Holding my phone so he can't see the screen, I scroll through until I find the photo of me and Abby at a girls' dinner when she was home for Christmas break.

When I shift the screen so he can see it, he leans in close, so close that I can feel his warmth and smell the bergamot and citrus notes of his cologne. "Ah, Abby."

"Yes." I look at the image and try to see what he sees in my daughter. Her blond hair is set off with subtle highlights that capture the glow from the fairy lights strung around the restaurant. Her broad grin is her father's, but her eyes are mine—almond-shaped, and a unique combination of Barry's deep blue and my violet, topped off with delicate arching brows. Her high cheekbones add definition to what is an otherwise round face.

"She's beautiful, Ellie." He turns to look at me, and I can feel the fan of his warm breath against my cheek. I shiver at the sensation. "Like you," he murmurs.

A camera shutter goes off, and I blink. The next thing I know, his lips graze my cheek, just as the camera clicks again. I freeze, both aghast and enthralled by the feel of his warm, soft lips on my skin. This image is sure to make his Instagram feed, and then, as my grandfather used to say, "We're off to the races" on the whole fake romance scheme.

"Thank you for sharing that with me, Ellie." His gaze locks onto mine, and my heart stutters in my chest. We're so close. It wouldn't take more than a subtle lean to press my lips to his. His eyes drop to my lips, and without thinking, I wet my lips, readying for his kiss. Maybe he isn't as unaffected as I'd thought.

"Can I have your autograph?"

We both look up to see an American woman standing at the table, a paper menu in her hand.

And just like that, the spell is broken.

Geoffrey

"The Louvre is another of my favorite haunts when I'm in Paris." I guide Ellie through the doors of I. M. Pei's glass pyramid. "The sheer scale of the museum and its thirty-five-thousand-plus works of art ensures there's always something new to discover with each visit."

Still shaken from our almost-kiss, I'm babbling a bit to release the tension created by the moment. I have no doubt the photo with my lips pressed to Ellie's cheek will be all over social media by tomorrow.

I could have lingered there, close to her, breathing in her elusive floral scent, reveling in the warmth of her skin. God, she is so alluring. I really thought she was going to kiss me. Imagine my disappointment when she didn't. Imagine my frustration at the interruption.

As for her, she's said very little since we left the café. Just giving me uncomfortable smiles in response to my inane comments. I'm not even sure she's heard anything I've said.

"You probably know the museum is housed in what was the Louvre Palace, a former royal residence." My babbling continues as we walk to the ticket counter. "The museum houses masterpieces by Rembrandt, Vermeer, Michelangelo, and of course, Leonardo da Vinci, and classical sculptures like the *Winged Victory of Samothrace* and the *Venus de Milo*."

I take a breath as I buy the tickets and accept the museum map from the attendant. I don't really need the map to locate the museum's most famous works, but I'm happy to have something in my hand to keep me from fidgeting.

I have never been so out of sorts with a woman before. Even when filming the first intimate scenes with my co-stars on the set.

I take a deep, calming breath. "Shall we see the most famous resident of the museum?"

Ellie looks at me as if she's just awakened from a deep sleep. Good, maybe she didn't notice my rambling. "Who?"

"You know—the *Mona Lisa*."

After waiting patiently to make our way to the front of the throngs viewing the painting, we exit the heavily guarded room and head for one of my favorite sculptures—the *Winged Victory*, mainly for its role in the movie *Funny Face*, starring the iconic Fred Astaire and a young Audrey Hepburn.

Ellie has begun to come out of the shell she'd closed around herself since the almost-kiss, and I have an idea to recreate the iconic scene from the movie. It's almost closing time, so the crowds have thinned out, making this a good time to carry out my plan.

The Greek statue stands at the top of the monumental Daru Staircase, the perfect location to showcase the magnificent work.

"Oh!" Ellie gasps when we reach the bottom of the staircase and gaze up at the massive statue. "She's beautiful."

"While the staircase is empty, I want you to climb to the top and stand behind the statue until I give the signal." She's still wearing her rain jacket. Perfect. "Then I want you to walk down the stairs holding your jacket out like wings."

"What? Why?"

"I'll show you later. Just trust me."

"But I'll feel ridiculous."

I make a show of looking around at the empty corridors and staircase. "The only people here are you, me, and Hélène and Stéphane. It's perfect."

She releases a sigh of the put-upon and trudges up the stairs. I have to say, I don't mind watching the subtle sway of her hips beneath her jacket as she climbs.

When she reaches the top, I say, "Okay, stand behind the statue so we can't see you. And take your hair down and shake it out."

"This is silly," she grumbles, but she complies.

"Perfect." I nod at Stéphane and Hélène. "*Prêts*?" I ask, and they both nod.

"Now. Walk down the stairs. Don't forget to hold out your jacket."

She steps out, lifting her jacket out, and descends the stairs.

"Quickly. Deliberately. And smile."

She flashes a grin and gets into the action. She is an awesome sight with her silver hair, violet eyes alight with pleasure. Damn.

"*Brillante*!" Stéphane shouts.

Brilliant, indeed.

Eleanor

Still feeling the high from Geoffrey's staged photographs, adrenaline buzzes through my veins. It may sound silly, but as I strode down those stairs, my rain jacket forming wings behind me, my hair loose and a little wild, I'd felt . . . beautiful. Powerful. Confident. Things I haven't felt in a very long time.

Afterward, Geoffrey pulled me aside and showed me a video on YouTube of Audrey Hepburn descending those same stairs in a beautiful red evening gown, her sheer red scarf forming her wings. It's a breathtaking image.

I find I'm looking forward to dinner with Geoffrey. He still owes me a photo and description from his phone, and I'm anxious for a glimpse into his private life.

We're heading to the museum exit when my phone buzzes in my purse. Ignoring the admonishing look from Geoffrey, I remove it from my purse and almost stumble when I see the name on the screen. Barry Marshall. We haven't spoken in months.

Is something wrong with Abby?

Panic grips me as I accept the call. "What is it? What's wrong?"

Geoffrey steps toward me and places his hand on my arm, a look of concern on his face.

Barry sighs on the other end, then in his familiar calming (patronizing?) voice says, "Eleanor, there is nothing wrong."

I glance up at Geoffrey, wary of having any kind of personal conversation with Barry while he looks on. The frustration triggers anger. "What is it then?"

"I want you to hear it first from me."

I scoff. "Unlike the news of your affair. How very magnanimous of you."

I feel Geoffrey's sharp gaze on me. When I look up, though, he's turned to Hélène and Stéphane, making the cut sign for them to stop filming and photographing.

"Eleanor, it's important."

At his serious tone, my heart plummets into my stomach, like a drop on a roller coaster. "What?" I croak out.

"Phoebe is pregnant."

I can't even . . . Words have left me. My entire vocabulary—both English and French—is eluding me. My fifty-eight-year-old ex-husband is going to be a father. A father! To the child of my former friend and business partner, no less. My eyes burn with tears I refuse to shed. He has clearly moved on with this life, while I'm left still untangling the mess his affair has created in mine.

"Eleanor?"

"Go on," I choke out.

"I know this is a surprise. It was for me as well. God knows becoming a father at almost sixty was not in my plan."

A harsh laugh escapes me. "'You play, you pay.' Isn't that what you used to warn Abby and her boyfriends?"

"Yes. Thank you for that little reminder." His voice is low

and exasperated. "I don't expect you to be happy for us, it's just . . . I wanted you to know." He pauses, then says, "Looks like you're having a good time. Is Geoffrey Harrison your rebound?"

Fury floods my veins. How dare he!

"That is *none* of your damn business." I glance up at Geoffrey, who's leaning against the wall, his arms crossed, a frown marring his brow. Abby had said Barry's head was going to explode. She'd been right.

Abby! Oh god. What will this do to her? "Abby. Does she know?"

There's yet another pause on the other end, and it's my turn to poke. "Barry?"

"No. She doesn't know yet."

"You'd better tell her. Soon."

"I will. I just want to tell her in person."

Good luck with that, I think. Abby is going to be . . . furious? Stunned? Maybe a little jealous?

"You do that, Barry. And don't break her heart, while you're at it."

"What's that supposed to mean?"

Memories of past arguments over Barry breaking his promises to Abby wash over me. Promising to be at her dance recital, her soccer games, her first prom, only to have work interfere. A Broadway actress who needs a facelift ASAP for an upcoming role. Another surgeon's botched procedure that Barry had to correct. It was always something.

"I'm not going to argue with you. Tell her. Soon." I end the call and squeeze my eyes shut. I don't know how long I stand there before I feel a warm hand on my shoulder.

"Ellie? Is everything all right?" Geoffrey's voice is warm with concern.

I draw in a deep breath and open my eyes to find his blue-gray ones staring back at me. My face heats with embarrassment. "It's fine. I'm sorry you had to hear my dirty laundry."

"What can I do?"

"Nothing. Thank you." I touch my temple where a tension headache is building. "Would you mind terribly if we skipped dinner?"

"No, of course not. We can go back to the hotel. Maybe you can order room service later if you feel up to it."

"Thank you."

Geoffrey

I should stay away. I should give Eleanor the space she needs to sort out whatever bombshell her ex-husband dropped on her with that phone call. Catching only one side of the conversation hadn't offered many clues, other than it came as a shock to her, that her daughter doesn't know, and that it was bad enough to give her a headache.

I could guess. He's marrying her former business partner mere months after their divorce. That would be enough to upset her. Or he's ill. But she was too angry for that to be the case. Maybe he's moving away. No. From what I'd learned of Dr. Barry Marshall, he wouldn't leave a thriving surgical practice of his own making.

I find myself standing outside her hotel room door, listening for sounds of what? Crying? Breaking glass? Silence? Could she be asleep? Will I wake her if I knock? Then I hear a curse and smile. I have not heard Eleanor curse, and I find it . . . charming. The proper lady has a hidden side.

I knock softly on her door. Just when I think she's not going to answer, the door swings open. "Geoffrey! What are you doing here?"

And that's when one very important question is answered. What Eleanor wears to bed. Or at least what she wears before climbing into bed. I'm still hoping she sleeps au naturel.

She looks like she's starring in an old 1940s film. One with Katharine Hepburn and Spencer Tracy. Or Katharine Hepburn and Cary Grant—*The Philadelphia Story.* Peeking out from beneath a deep purple silk robe is a pair of paisley silk pajamas. On her feet, slippers. She's as elegant before bed as she is during the rest of the day.

Her face is devoid of makeup and her hair is pulled back into a sleek twist, though a few tendrils of silver have escaped the clip. She is the most beautiful woman I've ever seen. Truly.

Say something, idiot. "I was worried. Clearly you received some shocking news this afternoon." I hold up my hands. "You don't have to tell me what it is, I just wanted to check on you." I glance behind her into the room and see a room service cart, the dish still covered by the fancy silver cloche. "Good. I see you ordered dinner."

"It arrived just a few minutes ago. I thought you were room service with something they'd forgotten."

"I should let you get to it then, before it gets cold." I take a reluctant step back from the door, hoping she'll invite me in. But I am disappointed.

Eleanor

I hesitate before swinging the door open again. I don't want to be alone tonight after all. "Would you like to come in?"

His face lights up, but he says, "I don't want to impose."

"You're not. I ordered a comforting bouillabaisse, and they sent up enough for four. Along with plenty of warm, crusty French bread. Please." I indicate the white-linen-draped cart.

I'd ordered a bottle of wine as well. I hadn't planned to drink the entire bottle alone, but I knew one glass was not going to be enough.

Geoffrey pulls up one of the elegant armchairs, then waits while I seat myself and lift the cloche from the tureen-sized bowl of seafood stew. A fragrant steam rises between us, and he sniffs the air in approval.

"Smells delicious. One problem, though. There's only one bowl."

I look up at him, the corners of my mouth lifting. "Why is that a problem?" I stand and slide my chair alongside his and lift the bowl toward us. The coziness of the scene settles into my chest, releasing some of the tension present there, and I give him what I think (hope?) is a flirtatious grin. "Unless you mind sharing."

His gaze locks onto mine and the smile on his face warms me to my toes. "Not at all." God, he *is* a handsome man.

We settle into dinner, passing the spoon back and forth, using the seafood fork to remove the succulent mussels from their shells, savoring the tender fish, and the rich broth. We pass the wineglass filled with the oaky chardonnay between us. Oh, there were water glasses in the room we could have used, but the intimacy of sharing the glass fills an emptiness in me.

After demolishing the meal, we sit back, eye each other, and sigh in mutual satisfaction.

"You appear to feel better. Your headache?"

"Gone."

"Good." He glances around the room as if looking for a topic of discussion. But I don't want to make idle chit-chat.

"My ex-husband is going to be a father," I blurt out.

Geoffrey sits up in his seat and stares at me. "Well." He pauses. "How does that make you feel?"

I wince, and fiddle with the stem of the now-empty wineglass. "You sound like a therapist."

"You don't have to answer the question, but I am genuinely interested in your feelings about this revelation."

"My feelings . . . my feelings are—in no particular order—shock, anger, hurt, and maybe a bit of—"

"Jealousy?"

"No. I'm not jealous."

Geoffrey gives me a look that says, *Get real*.

"Okay, maybe I'm a little jealous, but not for the reasons you might think."

He doesn't prod me to answer, which gives me room to take a deep breath and decide whether I want to share this with him or not.

"We didn't plan for Abby to be an only child. I had two miscarriages before Abby. And my pregnancy with Abby was . . . difficult. Morning sickness that lasted all day, every day, for almost my entire pregnancy. I say almost because I didn't carry Abby to term. She was born six weeks early and spent the first two weeks of her life in the NICU." The sadness of those days still lingers. The loss, the fear, but also the joy at Abby's birth and eventual discharge from the hospital. She began to thrive after her third month, and began gaining on other babies in her percentile, so the story had a happy ending.

Geoffrey sits quietly during my story, listening intently. Just like he seems to do whenever I speak to him.

I smile reassuringly. "Anyway, Abby overcame her premature birth and grew to be a healthy child, teenager, and now woman. But Barry swore he never wanted to see me go through that again. And frankly, I didn't want to either. So, we decided Abby would be it for us."

"And now he's going to be a father again," Geoffrey says, tenderness in his voice.

"Yes. He's going to get another opportunity. With someone else." My heart aches at the thought. "And Abby is going to have a half-sibling who will be almost twenty-five years younger. I don't know how she is going to feel about that, given the circumstances." I set my napkin on the table. "I should be there when he tells her."

Geoffrey reaches out and takes my hand in his. The warmth is so reassuring, so comforting. "I'm sure you do. But Eleanor, *he* needs to tell her. She needs to hear it from *him*, not you."

"I know. Truly, I do. It's just—"

"You want to be there for her."

I look up into Geoffrey's eyes and I see compassion. Empathy. Understanding. "Yes."

He gazes down at our entwined fingers. "If you want to go home, I'll understand. All you have to do is say the word. Don't worry, I'll still give the money to A Step Up."

It strikes me that I don't want to leave. In fact, I never even considered leaving after Barry broke the news. I'm actually enjoying myself. I love Abby—more than she will ever know—but I also know she is going to face hurdles and heartaches in her life, and she is going to have to learn how to overcome them. If I want Barry and Abby to repair their relationship, I know they are going to have to work through this together. I can't run interference. I will be there when she needs me to offer guidance when she airs out her feelings, but I can't tell her *how* to feel.

"No. I want to stay."

The grin that splits his face sends my heart racing. "Good."

Geoffrey

"I should let you get some sleep. Remember, I have an appointment in the morning, but I'll see you at one o'clock for the drive to Versailles."

Eleanor walks me to the door, but before she opens it, I place a hand on each shoulder and turn her toward me. "I had a wonderful day today, and shocking news notwithstanding, I hope you did too."

She nods, her eyes wide. And then she gives the universal signal—she licks her lips as her gaze drops to my mouth, and I'm sunk.

I lean in, holding my breath, giving her time to pull away, but instead, she draws closer, her luscious lips parted. We are but an inch apart now. I wait, drawing out the anticipation as my breath backs up into my lungs. She closes the distance, touching her lips to mine in a tentative kiss. Her lips are warm and soft, and I groan. I drop my hands to her waist and pull her in close, taking over the kiss, claiming her mouth. She gasps, and I take advantage of the moment to tease her open lips with mine. Remembering her admonition, I keep my tongue to myself.

She leans into me, her lush breasts pressed to my chest. God, she feels amazing!

Her grasp tightens, holding my mouth to hers, and I will my hands to stay at her waist. She's vulnerable. I don't want to do anything she might regret later. Exercising a level of willpower that should earn me sainthood, I break the kiss and step back, breathing hard.

She raises a hand to her lips, and I'm gratified to see she's as shaken as I am. "What the hell was that?"

"Call it . . . rehearsal. Good night, Eleanor. Get some sleep." I leave while I still can, before my libido takes over. Another cold shower will be in order.

Eleanor

The door closes behind Geoffrey with a quiet *snick*. "Oh my," I breathe. I lift my hand to my lips again and close my eyes, leaning against the solid door behind me for support. Geoffrey is the first man I've kissed other than Barry in over thirty years. And it was *wonderful*!

I push off from the door and walk in a semi-daze to the room service cart where the remains of our cozy shared meal make me smile. That was *some* rehearsal!

Screw Barry and his news. I have a kind, gorgeous flesh-and-blood man to share Paris with. Maybe I should give Maddie's idea some serious thought.

A romantic fling might be just what I need. Even if it *is* fake. After all, my heart is safe. I'm not going to fall in love with the man in a matter of days.

Not long after I settle into bed, my phone buzzes with an incoming call. Maddie. Perfect, I can tell her about Phoebe.

"*Bonsoir*," I say.

"Hello, dahling," she says in reply, drawing out "darling" like she's some New York City socialite.

"So, what are you doing?" She hesitates, then gasps. "I'm not interrupting, . . ." she drops her voice to a whisper, "sexy times, am I?"

I laugh. "No!"

"You're alone then?"

"I am."

"Where's your lover boy?"

I snort. "He's not my lover boy."

"Why the hell not? You two are looking pretty cozy on Instagram." She pauses, then says in a throaty voice, "Have you done the deed?"

"We're not—that's to say, he's not—and, and you sound like one of our kids asking a question like that."

"Well, why not? Have a fling! In Paris! With *Geoffrey*

Harrison, for God's sake! Something you can tell your grandchildren."

"Right. That's exactly what I'm going to tell my grandchildren. That I had a sordid affair with a movie star."

"Okay, I see your point. Then write about it in your memoir." After a brief pause, she continues, her voice soft and caring, "Ellie, you've put yourself on the back burner for so long, you don't know *how* to do something just for you. First Barry, then Abby, then your business—"

"My business *is* for me," I protest.

"Yes, but . . . can it keep you warm at night? Or make you feel . . . like a woman? A *beautiful* woman who's still in the prime of her life?"

I snort again.

"Promise me you'll think about it at least? Now, tell me everything." The eagerness in her voice makes me laugh.

I give her a brief rundown of my day with Geoffrey. She *hmms* and *ahs* at all the right moments. Before I get to the Louvre, I pause.

"And that's it? That's all you got?"

Well, not exactly, but I know that's not what she means.

"What more do you want?"

"Um, some heavy petting in the backseat? A passionate goodnight kiss at the door? Something. Anything."

I shake my head. Maddie and her one-track mind. If she only knew. "There is something else."

"I knew it. Tell me, tell me." I can practically hear Maddie rubbing her hands together in anticipation.

"Phoebe is pregnant."

Silence.

"Hello?"

"I'm sorry, did you say Philandering Phoebe is *pregnant*?" Never mind a philanderer is male—Maddie likes her alliterations.

"I did."

"Who's the father?"

"Who do you *think* is the father?"

Maddie gasps. "Bastard Barry," she mutters. "How'd you find out?"

See what I mean about the alliterations? "He called me to tell me."

"Shut up! He did not!"

"He did."

"Just wait 'til I see him again. I'm going to knee him in the nuts."

I laugh. She probably would too.

"How are you feeling about that?"

"Raw. Angry. Jealous."

"Oh, honey. I know. I wish I was there to give you a hug." The warmth in her voice is a balm to my still tender nerves.

"Me too." Maddie was there through my miscarriages, my difficult pregnancy, and Abby's premature birth. She knows more than anyone how this news would make me feel.

"What can I do? Besides kick the bastard in his baby-maker?"

"Nothing. Just knowing you're there for me is enough."

"Well, I know it's easier said than done, but try to put it out of your mind, and enjoy Paris. And Geoffrey. This gives you more reason to have a fling with him. And make it public."

"What? I couldn't have a fling with him." Not an actual one anyway. "Besides, it takes two to tango, and he may not be interested in me as a dance partner." At least not a real one anyway.

"Pfft. Look in the mirror, Ellie. You're a beautiful, strong woman. Where's your confidence?"

Gone. It went up in smoke when Barry left me for a younger—more fertile woman.

"I'd like to kill Barry for that reason alone," Maddie was saying. "His illicit affair pulled the rug right out from under you, just as you were getting your feet back. You need to get your mojo back. And some good ol'-fashioned payback could be just the thing."

"What do you mean?"

"You and Geoffrey are burning up the social media. Why not spice things up a bit? Even if you don't want to have a fling, make it look like you are."

"Funny you should mention that." Here goes nothing. "You cannot tell a soul what I am about to tell you," I warn.

"Ooh! I'm drawing an X over my heart. Now, give me the scoop."

"Geoffrey suggested we fake a fling."

"Really?" She sounds skeptical. "I'm not knocking his idea, but I'm curious. Why?"

I explain Geoffrey's reasons, and then my own . . . petty ones.

"Ooh là là, that's delicious! Look at you getting back at Barry the Bastard."

"It feels rather . . . sordid and immature. Something a high school girl would do."

"Pfft. Does said fake fling involve real sex?"

"No. I don't think Geoffrey is interested in me that way. And I'm not sure I'm ready to go there yet anyway. But I could use some advice. It's been a very long time since I've, um, *dated* anyone. How do I make it *look* like I'm into him?"

"You've definitely been out of the game far too long if you can't remember *that*. Okay, here's what you do. Lean in close for the photos. Hold hands. Take his arm. Laugh at his jokes. Gaze lovingly into his eyes for the cameras."

"I can't do that—I'm no actress."

"Honey, if Geoffrey Harrison doesn't inspire a little flirtation, I don't know who does."

Chapter Four

DAY FOUR

Eleanor

Cranking up music I never thought I'd listen to, I pump up the speed on the treadmill in the hotel gym. This playlist, these songs, have become my anthems since I discovered Barry and Phoebe's affair. Songs like "Numb" by Linkin Park, "Uninvited" by Alanis Morissette, "Going Under" by Evanescence—they speak to my angst, to my anger and hurt. And playing them at hearing-damage levels feels so damn good. Especially after Barry's latest bomb.

As my heart rate rises, and a fine sheen of sweat covers my body, I exorcise my demons as I exercise my body to the sounds of Fall Out Boy and Fuel.

After last night, maybe I should add Evanescence's "Bring Me to Life" to the mix. Geoffrey's kiss certainly brought me back to life, showing me what I'd been missing. Every cell in my body came to life last night in an exhilarating, all-consuming way.

His last words to me, "Get some sleep," taunted me late

into the night, even after Maddie's call. If he only knew how impossible that had been. I lay awake last night reliving that kiss, like some silly teenager. But I'd also let my imagination run with what could have happened if he hadn't left when he did. Would we still be in bed this morning?

Returning my attention to my workout in the hotel's fitness center, I check my heart rate on the monitor. My radiation oncologist told me when I started my treatment that my physical fitness would go a long way in keeping me healthy during my treatments. If what I felt was healthy during those treatments, I'd hate to think what unhealthy would feel like. Even so, I took her message to heart and continued my routine when I could, and since my remission, I'd kept up a consistent fitness regimen. When the anger and the hurt over Barry's infidelity threatened to consume me, running became a means to deal with it. I always felt better about myself and the situation after a well-paced run.

The situation with the business was my biggest aggravation now. Phoebe came to me after her own divorce, looking for a way to put her interest in fashion to work. She started as a sales associate, then became an assistant manager, before we entered into a partnership agreement when she bought forty percent of the business.

Her eye for trends complemented my eye for classic, clean lines and lush fabrics. Our pairings worked. When I was sick, having her as my partner was such a blessing. She managed the business, so I could focus on getting well. Which makes what she's done that much harder to bear.

And now she's pregnant.

I worry about Abby and how she will react. But I also worry about our little community. I don't want to be "Poor Eleanor," whose husband left her for a younger, more beautiful, more *fertile* woman. Being the subject of gossip is revolting to me.

But isn't it a little late for that revelation? After all, I am apparently an internet sensation thanks to Geoffrey. And now, with the beginning of our fake romance today, I'll be in an even brighter spotlight.

My stomach lurches at that thought.

Eleanor

Later, with no particular destination in mind other than the Paris streets, I exit the elevator. The last few days with Geoffrey have been amazing, but somewhat exhausting. A couple of hours to myself this morning to relax and find a quintessential Paris café for some people-watching, a croissant, and a café au lait sounds like just the thing.

I step into the lobby and freeze. Geoffrey stands in profile, beside him a beautiful young woman—too young in my opinion—smiles up at him, standing close. The kind of close you only see between two people who know each other *very* well. He reaches up and cups her cheek before placing a tender kiss to her forehead.

Fury roars through me. How dare he! He *lied* to me. He told me he was single. That there was no woman in his life. And he was the one who'd suggested a fake romance! The philandering bastard!

"Remember," he'd said last night, "I have an appointment in the morning." And that kiss! What a load of BS. Not to mention pretty ballsy, meeting her in the lobby where I could see them. Or maybe that's what he'd intended. Maybe after he'd kissed me, he'd had enough of our agreement and wanted out, only he was too cowardly to just say it to my face. Just like Barry.

Barry hadn't had the guts to tell me about his affair with Phoebe—and neither had she, for that matter—so she'd orchestrated their discovery instead. There they were, the two of them, in a cozy booth in what had been our favorite restaurant, when Maddie and I had walked in for our weekly dinner. She'd *known* they'd be discovered. Apparently, she thought my public humiliation would be easier than owning up to their infidelity in private.

I spin on my heel, seeking refuge in the hotel boutique, wondering why I feel the need to run when Geoffrey is the one who's wrong.

"Ellie!"

Damn. He'd seen me.

"Eleanor, wait!"

I can feel the eyes of the hotel guests and staff on me, and heat suffuses my body from head to toe.

Geoffrey touches my arm, and I spin on him, fueled by fury. "Don't touch me."

His eyes widen, then a variety of emotions cross his face. Guilt. Chagrin. Then . . . humor. *Humor*? How dare he think this is funny! And what must the other woman think about him chasing me down? I glance over his shoulder, where the beautiful blonde stands, staring at us, confusion on her face.

"Go back to your . . ." I wave my hand in the woman's direction.

"Daughter."

"And leave me alone." Then his words sink in. "Your . . . daughter?" I narrow my eyes at him. "You never told me you had a daughter."

Guilt flashes across his face again. "You're right. I didn't. It's a long story, and I'll tell you about it. But first, come meet her."

When I don't respond, he reaches to touch my arm again, then drops his hand, as if thinking better of it. "Please."

Geoffrey

I never intended for Ellie to learn about Ava this way. Well, if I were truly honest with myself, I hadn't intended for Ellie to learn about Ava at all. Protecting Ava supersedes everything.

Eleanor is fairly vibrating with suppressed anger. Clearly, she thought Ava was a lover or girlfriend. But even though she now knows that is not the case, her anger over my lie of omission is palpable.

And yet. I can't deny that the idea she might have been jealous makes me feel . . . pleased? Happy? Maybe a little cocky? Was it possible? Had Eleanor been jealous? Guilt hits, then. Given her husband's infidelity, I shouldn't feel pleased.

Ava gives us a tentative smile as we approach, still confused. As soon as I saw Eleanor turn away in a fury, I chased after her, leaving Ava alone to draw her own conclusions.

"Eleanor, may I introduce my daughter, Ava Allard?" Surprise crosses Eleanor's face, likely at the different surname. "Soon to be Ava Gagnon."

"Ava this is Eleanor Marshall, the winner of the Dream Date Contest." Understanding dawns on Ava's face.

"Very pleased to meet you, Ms. Marshall. My father has told me about you."

Eleanor lifts a brow and gives me a look that says I have some explaining to do. "I wish I could say the same," she mutters. "But it is a pleasure to meet you." She shoots me another questioning look. "And please, call me Ellie."

"Ava is getting married on Friday. We have an appointment to finalize the reception plans, in the Salon Vendôme, here at the hotel, on Saturday evening."

"Ah, I see." A blush colors Eleanor's cheeks. "Well, I, uh, I won't keep you from your appointment."

"You're welcome to join us," Ava said.

"Oh no. I wouldn't want to intrude on your father-daughter time." She cuts me a narrowed eye look. "I was just going out for a walk." She gestures toward the street outside.

"I'll meet you back here at one, then?" I ask, hoping she won't use this whole episode as an excuse to say no.

She nods, then asks, "Ava, will you be joining us for the tour of Versailles?"

"*Non.* Thank you, though. I have an appointment at the bridal shop for my final fitting."

"Well, I hope all goes well. I'll see you later, Geoffrey." She gives me a pointed look.

I follow her exit with my gaze, intrigued by a flustered Eleanor. She always seems so poised. So in control. It is refreshing to see the person behind the façade.

"Shall we?" I ask my daughter as I wrap an arm around her waist. I find myself looking forward to my trip out to Versailles, where no doubt Ellie will expect nothing less than the whole truth, and nothing but the truth.

Geoffrey

I lead Ellie out of the hotel to a waiting BMW, where our driver, Maurice, stands outside the back passenger door. The film crew will follow in another car. If I am going to tell her about Ava, I want privacy.

"Monsieur Harrison." He nods, before opening the door for us.

I extend my hand to Ellie to help her into the car.

Once we're ensconced in the backseat, Eleanor turns to me —for that's who I am currently facing—her arms crossed, ready for battle. "All right. Spill it. With the conversations we've had about Abby, why didn't you tell me?"

I reach out and press the button to close the glass between us and the driver. No sense in prevaricating.

"I have a daughter," I say with a wry smile.

"Yes." She lifts a brow. "And?"

I sigh, run a hand through my hair, and lean back into the plush leather seat.

"Her whole life, I have tried to protect Ava. Kids of celebrities and politicians have no privacy, through no fault of their own, and can be subjected to cruelty, especially on social media and in the tabloids. I never wanted that for her—to the point that I, at one time, thought it best if I weren't part of her life."

I risk a glance at Eleanor, and I see understanding there. Understanding that I don't deserve. Even if my intentions were good, cutting myself from my daughter's life had been a mistake I can never atone for.

"But there was also danger."

Eleanor shifts in her seat to face me. "What do you mean 'danger'?"

"When Ava was about two years old, the four-year-old daughter of French film star Louisa Toussaint was kidnapped and held for ransom."

Eleanor gasps, her eyes wide.

"It scared me to death. That's when Iris and I agreed it would be best to keep Ava's existence a secret."

"The last name," Eleanor said.

"Yes. She took her maternal grandmother's last name. Another layer of protection."

"Tell me the other child was unharmed," Eleanor asks, her voice barely a whisper.

"She was found and her captors tried. But of course, even at four years old, she will live with the memories of that for the rest of her life."

"And so you left. How long were you estranged from one another?"

"I was gone much of her life, from the time she was five until she started university." My throat grows tight at that confession. The truth shames me to my core.

"I see." There was no judgment in that statement, but there should have been. From what I know of Eleanor, she would never be separated from her daughter. "You had no contact with her?"

"I did. First through my ex-wife, then directly with letters, and then emails. Eventually phone and video."

"And your ex-wife? She's still in the picture?"

"Iris lives in Sweden, and she and Ava are still close. Iris and her husband will be here for the wedding."

"And how did Ava handle all of this?"

I rub the ache in my chest that always appears when I think about Ava and our separation. "Let's just say it's taken several years to rebuild our relationship. But I'm doing everything I can to earn her love again."

"And she lives in Paris?"

"Yes."

Well, that explains his connection to the city. "And is what you are doing working?"

Eleanor

I wait, breath backing up in my lungs, for Geoffrey's answer. I don't know why I am so invested in his response, but I want the lovely young woman I met to love her father. I want her to see the love I saw he clearly has for her. The love that, if I were honest with myself, had sent me into a jealous snit.

He blows out a breath. "I think so. She's made me part of the wedding planning. Not a typical role for the father of the bride, but it's my best role to date." He gives me a smile so genuine, I blink in wonder, momentarily disarmed by the transformation. This isn't a pour-on-the-charm smile. This is real. And it's dazzling!

Then I remember what he'd said the morning we negotiated our agreement. "These are the commitments you spoke of."

"Yes. I've let my daughter down most of her life. I won't do it anymore. It's too important to her. And to me."

I couldn't imagine leaving Abby without a mother for all those years. But I guess I could understand Geoffrey's reasoning, and he seems determined to make up for lost time. "I would never want to stand in the way of your commitments. Ava comes first."

His big warm hand enfolds mine. "Thank you. This is my life's deepest regret, and not something I'm proud of, but I am trying to make it right, and I appreciate your understanding."

"Is there anything else you're hiding from me—like a wife?" Seems like whether he has a wife or not would be public, but after this conversation, who knows?

"No, Ellie. There is no other woman. I'm not a man-whore, and I'm not an asshole."

I nod. "And does she know?" I look down at our clasped hands, then back up at him.

"She does now. She didn't know before this morning."

A wash of heat suffuses my face. What must his daughter think of me that I would fake a relationship with her father? "And how does she feel about it?"

He shrugs. "She's fine. She knows to keep it to herself."

"But—"

"Ellie, Ava has one thing on her mind this week, and that's her wedding. Don't give it another thought."

"Monsieur," Maurice's voice comes over the intercom, "we will be arriving at Versailles shortly."

Geoffrey

"Wow, it's crowded today," Eleanor says offhandedly.

I sit up and look at the crowd waiting outside the Palace of Versailles. Odd. It's a weekday before tourist season. Versailles shouldn't be this crowded, especially later in the day. As the car pulls up, the crowd inexplicably shifts toward the car. A ripple of excitement is almost palpable, and smartphones turn in our direction, as people rush forward, held back only by three security guards.

Bloody hell. They're here for us.

Eleanor shoots a gimlet eye toward me. "Geoffrey?" Clearly, she's figured it out too. "Did you . . . ?" She licks her lips before continuing, "Did you do this? Did you post where we were going today to broadcast our fake romance?" Her pitch rises with each word, signaling her discomposure.

No. *I* didn't. But I can guess who did. And it had nothing to do with our fake romance. I hold up a finger as I take out my phone and dial Malcolm.

"Malcolm, tell me you didn't," I growl, gazing into Eleanor's troubled face.

"Ah, so you've arrived. Is there a good crowd?"

I look out the window once more. "You could say that. But why?"

"This will get even more social media attention. A crowd posting their own photos and videos—it's genius!"

"No, it's not genius. It's a mob. I don't have any security. How the hell are we to get through that horde?"

"No worries. I've thought of that. Two bodyguards are waiting to escort you in."

Two large men in black slacks and black polos approach our driver, who rolls down the window to speak to them.

"We're going to talk later," I warn Malcolm before I end the call.

"What's going on?" Eleanor asks.

"Malcolm leaked where we were going today. He thought it would bring more publicity."

She leaned past me to look out at the crowd. "I'll say," she mutters, a catch in her voice.

"Listen, we don't have to do this today. I can have a come-to-Jesus talk with Malcolm, and we can come back another day."

She gnaws on her lower lip, then nods.

"Okay." I lower the interior window to tell the driver to return to the hotel, but she lays a hand on my arm.

"No. I didn't mean we should return to Paris. First, I want to see Versailles, and second, these are your fans. You can't let them down."

"You're sure?"

"Yes. I'm sure. After all, it's what I signed up for."

Eleanor

I'm shaking like a leaf when Geoffrey steps from the car and offers me his hand. This is insane. The crowd is yelling, and people are jostling for position, smartphones raised. I have to remind myself that it's all for Geoffrey. It has nothing to do with me.

Taking his hand, I get out of the car, and he pulls me close, wrapping an arm around my waist. He bends to speak into my ear. "Just smile. Wave if you like, but you don't have to say anything to the crowd."

I can just imagine how his actions look to everyone gathered outside the Palace. We look like two people in lust, if not in love. All part of the plan, right?

The two burly men take up positions on either side of us and, as we make our way through the open palace gates, they part the crowd, like Anna Wintour at Fashion Week. Geoffrey's arm remains wrapped around my waist, and I'm thankful for the warmth and security.

I glance back to see the camera crew shooting footage of the crowd. I assume they will join us inside once they get the footage they're looking for.

Amid shouts of Geoffrey's name, I'm startled to hear people yell my name as well. Then the questions fly like bullets in French, English, even German.

"Madame Marshall! Are you enjoying Paris?"

"Eleanor, how does it feel to be Geoffrey's *saveur du jour?*"

I cringe at being called his flavor of the day, but Geoffrey just smiles, nods, and waves, all while allowing the bodyguards to escort us to the entrance and, hopefully, peace and quiet. It's all a bit overwhelming.

Geoffrey's warm breath caresses my ear, and I shiver. "You're doing great. You okay?"

I nod, a little dazed by all the attention.

We are escorted to the Palace via the middle door of the Dufour Pavilion.

Once inside the entrance, I breathe a sigh of relief. The two security guards take a step back, giving me some breathing room. Even though they are clearly there to protect us, they are a little intimidating.

"Monsieur Harrison, welcome."

I look up and see a debonair gentleman striding toward us, his long legs devouring the parquet floor. "We will take you and Madame Marshall through a back corridor. You will still see the Palais, but we have coordinated the crowds so that you will see the rooms in private before they do."

"Monsieur Claude, thank you for accommodating us. I apologize for the crowd." He lifts a hand, gesturing toward the mob scene we just left. "It was unexpected."

"*Ce n'est pas un problème.*"

Geoffrey, ever the gentleman, introduces me to Monsieur Claude and explains that he is the director of communications for Versailles and that he has arranged a special tour for us.

Monsieur Claude looks behind us where Hélène and Stéphane stand. "Your agent also arranged permission for photos and filming."

Geoffrey hadn't mentioned anything about a special tour, so I assumed we would be part of the general crowd. I should have realized that would not be the case. Even without the crowd outside, Geoffrey's presence may have posed a distraction to the sightseers.

Up until this point, we'd been pretty anonymous. There had been a few people who approached us at museums for selfies and autographs, and of course, the one at Angelina that interrupted what I'm calling "the moment." I can't help but wonder if we'll face crowds like this the rest of the trip. The thought is a little terrifying.

Geoffrey

. . .

The hush of Versailles is a pleasant contrast to the cheering crowds. Of course, I've faced such crowds at red carpet events, award ceremonies, and film festivals like Cannes, but I was not expecting this. And I'm sure Ellie wasn't either.

"A group entered a few moments ago, so you will start your tour in the Apartments of the Dauphin, which recently reopened after a ten-year restoration. Then you will return to the main rooms on the first floor." Monsieur Claude spoke softly, as if loath to penetrate the hush with anything above a whisper.

"Merci, Monsieur Claude."

I pull Ellie close and whisper in her ear, "You okay?"

She nods and gives me a tentative smile, then asks, "Is this what the rest of the itinerary will be like? Dodging crowds?"

I see the trepidation on her face. "Not if I can help it. I plan to give Malcolm a dressing-down later."

"Monsieur Harrison," Monsieur Claude interrupts our conversation, "this is Céline. She will be your private guide for your tour."

A chic young woman dressed in a black pencil skirt and white blouse, her sleek blond hair pulled back in a chignon, stands before us.

"Madame, Monsieur," Céline nods at Ellie and me. "This way, *s'il vous plaît.*" She extends an elegant hand in the direction behind us. "I am not sure what you know about the Palace, but I will give you a brief history. Please feel free to ask questions."

As we proceed to the Dauphin's rooms, Céline offers a succinct history in a cultured French accent.

"The history of Versailles dates back to ancient times when it was a small village. However, it was during the reign of King Louis XIV that Versailles became one of the most famous and influential places in European history.

"In the early seventeenth century, Louis XIII built a

hunting lodge in Versailles. It was his son, Louis XIV, also known as the Sun King, who transformed the lodge into a magnificent palace and made it the center of political power in France. Louis XIV moved the French court and government to Versailles in 1682, and the Palace became the official residence of the king."

I reach out and take Ellie's hand, not for the film crew, but because I want to touch her. She glances down at our clasped hands, then up at me, but she doesn't pull away.

"The palace complex of Versailles included not only the main palace building but also the expansive gardens, the Grand Trianon, the Petit Trianon, and the Queen's Hamlet, which I hope you can take time to visit while you are here," Céline says with a smile.

Céline interrupts her history lesson to point out the sculpted woodwork in the Dauphin's library, then the paintings of his sisters in the Grand Apartment.

"This way, *s'il vous plaît*, to the Princesses' Apartments."

I lean over and whisper in Ellie's ear, "Are you duly impressed with the opulence of Versailles?"

She shrugs, "Pfft. This is nothing compared to *my* house."

I chuckle in response to this lighter side of Ellie. I like it. And I realize she hasn't used her phone today for anything other than photographs.

"Versailles became the stage for elaborate court rituals, ceremonies, and entertainment. The Palace was home to thousands of courtiers, nobles, and servants who attended to the needs of the royal family. It was a center of art, culture, and politics, attracting intellectuals, artists, and diplomats from all over Europe."

I find it interesting that the French now take pride in what had at one time been the symbol of oppression and decadence the revolutionaries so despised.

As if on cue, Céline said, "The reign of Louis XIV and the

grandeur of Versailles lasted until the French Revolution in 1789. The revolutionaries attacked the Palace and forced the royal family to leave Versailles. The French government later transformed the Palace into a museum dedicated to the history of France. Over the years, Versailles has undergone various restorations and renovations to preserve its historical and architectural significance. Today, it remains a major tourist attraction, drawing millions of visitors each year—"

Ellie mutters, "All of whom are waiting outside."

"Excusez-moi, Madame?"

"Oh, I was saying that is a lot of visitors," she says, her face completely deadpan.

I cough to hide my laugh.

"Oui, Madame."

Eleanor

After touring the luxurious interior of Versailles—including the various rooms in the King's and Queen's apartments, and the iconic Hall of Mirrors—we exit to view the sprawling gardens. I draw in a deep breath. To be honest, it was all a bit overwhelming. The ornate woodwork, the lavish fabrics, the crystal chandeliers, and the acres of sumptuous wall coverings were overstimulating.

And then there was the feel of Geoffrey's large, warm hand clasping mine as we wandered the Palace. I know we agreed that we would give an outward appearance of our fake romance, but I wasn't expecting such a sweet gesture—holding hands like high school sweethearts. Barry and I rarely held hands, even when we first started dating, and later in the honeymoon period of our marriage. He had never been one for public displays of affection.

Geoffrey steps up next to me and slips an arm around my waist, and to my chagrin, I lean into him. "It is a beautiful sight."

"It is indeed."

"I thanked Céline for her time. I thought we could tour the gardens at our leisure."

"I'd like that. But what about the mob?"

"They're still out front. All the ticket times have been taken for today, so they can't get in. Monsieur Claude is scrounging up hats for both of us." He points to my face. "Between our sunglasses and hats, we should be able to enjoy the gardens unmolested."

"Thank you," I breathe in relief.

"Again, I'm sorry, Ellie."

I gaze up at his chiseled face, a slight scruff softening his jaw. He is a beautiful human being. "It's fine."

Céline arrives with a billed cap that reads CHÂTEAU DE VERSAILLES for Geoffrey, and a straw floppy-brim hat trimmed with a floral ribbon for me.

"Perfect," Geoffrey says to Céline. "We'll return them when we leave."

"Non, Monsieur. They are our gift."

"Merci."

"Enjoy the gardens. Madame, Monsieur." She nods before leaving us.

The gardens stretch as far as the eye can see, with perfectly manicured lawns, symmetrical flower beds, elegant fountains, and gravel pathways.

After we don our "disguises," Geoffrey guides me past the Water Parterre, two symmetrical pools, to the Latona Fountain and beside two ornamental beds. The symmetry of the garden is soothing and peaceful, a refreshing contrast to the opulence of the Palace.

When we reach the "Green Carpet," the Grand Canal sparkling in the sunlight in the distance, Geoffrey touches my straw brim and says, "That hat suits you. It's very . . . Audrey Hepburn."

"You like her."

"I do. She was a wonderful actress, a tireless humanitarian, and a beautiful woman. You remind me a lot of her classic beauty."

I stop and look up at him, surprised by his comment.

"What? It's the truth." He reaches up and touches my cheek. "You're a beautiful woman, Ellie."

Before I know what's happening, his lips touch mine in a gentle caress. They're sun-warmed and soft, and a long-forgotten heat flares in my core. Before I can even think about returning the kiss, he pulls back and, taking my hand, leads me toward the Apollo Fountain.

What just happened? I can still feel the heat of his lips, and my tongue darts out to see if I can taste him. A faint hint of mint lingers on my lips, and I resist the urge to reach up and touch them with my fingertips. It was such a tender kiss, one you might expect two people in love to share. Or at least two people who are attracted to each other. Is that why he kissed me? Is he attracted to me? Or is it all an act, and he's playing for the cameras, selling the story of our "romance"?

"—probably the most recognized fountain in the garden."

I realize I hadn't been listening to him. "I'm sorry?"

He gives me a smirk, as if he knows I zoned out—and why. "I said, the Apollo Fountain is probably the most recognized fountain in the garden."

I try to give my attention to the fountain featuring who I assume is the fountain's namesake, Apollo, riding a chariot pulled by four rearing horses. The fountain is surrounded by a large circular basin made of stone and decorated with intricate sculptures and relief work. Water spouts from the mouths of various mythical sea creatures and flows into the basin, creating a dramatic display. The water then cascades down a series of steps and channels before ultimately reaching the Grand Canal.

"The Apollo Fountain is not only a stunning work of art but also a functional water feature. It was designed to supply water to the gardens and to fill the numerous water features in the surrounding area, including the Grand Canal."

"How do you know that?"

Geoffrey shrugs, "I've been here several times. I remember things."

"Why did you kiss me?" I ask abruptly.

His gaze meets mine. "I thought we agreed we would start displaying our fake romance today."

Right. Of course he didn't kiss me because he felt the urge—the pull of attraction. It's all an act, performed by a rom-com heartthrob. *Be sure you remember that, Ellie.*

"You okay?" He reaches up to touch my shoulder.

"I'm fine." I give him a smile I'm sure doesn't reach my eyes, but the sunglasses hide this fact.

He gazes at me a moment more, and my traitorous body wants him to kiss me again, but he doesn't.

"Now, turn around."

I turn back toward the Château, and my breath halts in my throat. In contrast to the busy, opulent interior, the exterior is subdued and elegant, its golden façade glimmers in the sunlight, exuding an aura of grandeur and history. I reach into my purse and get my phone out for a photo. *This* is something I want to remember for the rest of my life—even if the memory is attached to Geoffrey's "fake" kiss.

Geoffrey

My phone buzzes in my pocket, and I pull it out to see Malcolm's name on the screen. *Damn.* I want to give him the lambasting he deserves, but I also want to spend the last few minutes I have with Ellie relishing her warmth and her scent, as she sits next to me in the car.

"Aren't you going to answer it?" Ellie prods.

Accepting the call, I light into Malcolm. "Funny you should call. What was that stunt you pulled today? Your leak resulted in a security issue for Versailles and made Eleanor uncomfortable. I don't want that to happen again."

"I'm only thinking of your career! And all of this has paid off."

"What are you talking about?"

"Steven Cassel called again. He wants to talk to you about the lead in his latest movie."

I sit up from my position next to Ellie. "He does?"

"Yes. He wants to meet with you in L.A. on Friday!"

I slump back into my seat. "You know I can't do that." I glance over at Ellie, who's listening to the conversation with interest.

"Listen, if you want this part, you need to go to L.A."

"I can meet with him after the wedding, and after Ellie leaves."

Her eyebrows lift in alarm, and she touches my arm and shakes her head. "You go. Do what you need to do."

"Geoffrey, I've worked hard to get this meeting for you."

"No. My daughter is getting married, and unlike me, I hope it's her only wedding. I will not miss it. Surely Cassel will understand."

"He's on a timeline. He and his family leave Saturday for a three-week Mediterranean cruise. Your character is the last part to cast, and he wants filming to begin when he's back from the cruise."

"Why can't I meet him somewhere in the Mediterranean? I'll fly to meet him at his convenience after the wedding and Ellie's departure, or we can video chat."

"No-go. He's promised his wife there will be no work on this vacation."

"Well, dammit. I promised my daughter I would be here for her wedding. That should mean something to him if he's a family man." I lift my gaze to Ellie's. "And I promised Ellie I would show her Paris."

She shakes her head again.

Malcolm sighs heavily on the other end of the call. "I'll try. But I don't hold out much hope for him to change his mind."

I rub my temples. "Just try. That's all I ask. And, Malcolm, no more leaks." I end the call and toss my phone onto the seat in aggravation. A juicy part comes along, and I may have to pass it up. Who knows if, or when, another one will come along.

"Geoffrey, if this director will meet with you after your daughter's wedding, you need to go. Just as you were willing to let me out of our agreement, I'm willing to let you out of it. This is too important. Isn't the reason for all of this publicity to boost your career?"

I turn to face her and place my hands on her shoulders. "I spent most of my adult life breaking promises—to my then-wife, to my daughter, to myself, and others—all for the sake of my career. I'm not doing that anymore."

"But—"

I grasp her hand. "No. Hopefully it won't matter. Hopefully he'll understand that, just like him, I made promises I intend to keep." *Even at the cost of my career.*

Eleanor

Geoffrey left me at the door to my room, still brooding over the meeting with the director. He's having dinner with his daughter and future son-in-law, and his family. Maybe time with his daughter will bring him out of his funk.

If this director, whoever he is, is willing to meet with him before I leave, I'm going to insist he go, even if I have to book a flight home before my planned departure date to press the issue.

At the risk of sounding condescending, I was proud of him for keeping his promise to his daughter. I know he has a lot to atone for, but it looks like he's committed to that path.

I think of the many times Barry didn't keep his promises to Abby. The missed school plays, tennis matches, and dance recitals. He was there for the major life events—sweet sixteen, prom, graduation. But he'd missed so much.

And speaking of Abby, she had sent numerous texts and left a couple of voicemails while we were at Versailles. Nothing indicated it concerned Phoebe's pregnancy, but rather my fake *affaire de cœur*.

One text read: Mom! What's going on? Social media is blowing up with pictures of you and Geoffrey, his arm around your waist, his mouth near your ear. Call me!

Another read: You two look pretty cozy. Are you sure you're not having a fling?

Her last voicemail said, "Don't make me jump on a plane!" Reminiscent of my threats when she was an angsty teenager and wouldn't come down for dinner—"Don't make me come up there!"

So, I'm now faced with making a call I dread. For one thing, how do you tell your adult daughter you're having a very public *fake* relationship with a movie star? And worse, *why*? The idea of telling her that I'm doing it for an absurd and immature reason—to get back at her father—well, what kind of role model does that make me?

And for another, far more troubling reason I dread this phone call is, how do I withhold the news of Phoebe's pregnancy? It's clear Barry hasn't dropped that bomb, since I haven't heard from her about that. How do I keep such devastating news from her, pretending that I don't know she'll have a half-sibling seven months from now?

But dammit, it shouldn't be me to tell her. Barry needs to face the music and tell her himself. And now I must face my own music and tell her about Geoffrey's plan. What parents we have turned out to be! She may despise us both when this is all said and done.

"Abby!" I say when she picks up on the first ring.

"Mom! *What* is going on? Have you decided to take my advice and have a fling with Geoffrey?"

Her advice. I can't help but smile at that.

"Are you falling in love?"

What? How did she jump to that conclusion? Before I can say anything, she's off and running again.

"There's a picture of you two in a café, and he's staring into your eyes . . . omigod, it's soooo romantic!"

"The moment" at Angelina. Of course that made it onto Geoffrey's social media.

"Since when did you become such a romantic?" I ask my otherwise very practical daughter.

"Mom, have you *seen* that picture?"

No, but I experienced the heart-thumping connection of that stare. The feeling that he was looking deep into my soul. The yearning for his lips on mine. A yearning that had only intensified when he'd actually kissed me last night. And this afternoon.

"It's hard not to be when you see it," she continues. "And that kiss in the gardens at Versailles!"

It was time to put a stop to her romantic musings. "Abby, don't get your hopes up."

"But Mom—"

"Abby," I cut her off with my curt listen-to-your-mother voice. I try to soften the blow. "Sweetheart, it's fake."

A few heartbeats pass, and I look at my phone to make sure the call didn't drop.

"What's fake? The gardens?" came her feeble reply.

"Our relationship. Our fling. We're just . . . faking it."

"*Why*?"

And there's the question I dreaded most in this conversation. Here goes nothing. "Two reasons, really. One, Geoffrey thinks it would help with his career. He's apparently been having problems getting movie roles, and this keeps him trending on social media."

"And two?" she prods.

Right. "He knows about your father's . . . infidelity and our divorce." And Phoebe's pregnancy. "He thought it would do me some good to settle the score a little." I wince at my choice of words.

Silence. What must she be thinking of her mother at this moment—pretending to have an affair to get back at her father.

"Yes! You go, Mom! Way to show Dad what he's lost by sleeping with a bimbo almost half his age."

I can't hold back the startled laugh. "You aren't disappointed?"

"Only that it's not real, for your sake. But fake it till you make it! Who knows, you might actually fall in love. Just think, Geoffrey Harrison could be my stepfather!"

"Abby," I caution, "that's not going to happen, so don't get your hopes up. Besides, after what your father did, I don't think I'm ready for another relationship right now . . . if ever."

"You'll get there, Mom. You have too much to offer someone to spend your life alone."

I blink back tears at her sweet words.

"Speaking of my father, he's coming up to see me next week. I can't imagine why."

My stomach drops at the news. God, I should be there! I should get on a plane and be there to pick up the pieces of her broken heart.

"I couldn't care less about seeing him right now."

You may care even less when you find out why.

"I gotta run. I have a meeting with one of my professors. Have a good night. And Mom?"

"Yes, Abby, my girl?"

"Make the most of this, fake or not."

Eleanor

After my call with Abby and the day's activities, I should be tired, especially given the unexpected mob at Versailles, but I find myself restless instead. I'd said I didn't want to spend every waking moment with Geoffrey, but now I find myself missing him. Absurd. How do you miss someone you've only known for three days? I'm not missing *him*, I'm missing the company, that's all.

I spy the TV remote on the nightstand and, gnawing on my lower lip, pick it up. Would I find what I'm looking for?

Scrolling through the various streaming apps, I land on the one I signed up for months ago, thinking I'd actually have time to watch TV. After a few stumbles, I finally log in to my account and select the search option. And there it is: *From Paris, With Love*—the movie Abby had mentioned. And there's Geoffrey's handsome face, none of the current gray visible in his hair, smiling into the face of a beautiful blonde, the Eiffel Tower in the background. The man on the screen is handsome, but the flesh-and-blood version is even better.

The movie blurb read:

Step into the bustling streets of Paris, where love is always on the menu!

In this delightful romantic comedy, meet Emma March, a spirited American pastry chef with dreams as sweet as her creations. With Paris as her stage, she's determined to whisk up success in the culinary capital of the world. But with a demanding boss and a language barrier standing in her way, Emma's journey to the top of the pastry world might just crumble before her eyes.

Enter Alex Durand, a charming French tour guide whose heart beats to the rhythm of Parisian streets. Despite his love for the city, Alex can't shake the feeling that something is missing from his life—that is, until he crosses paths with the delightful Emma. Lost in more ways than one, Emma finds herself enchanted by Alex, guiding her through the labyrinth of Parisian life.

As sparks fly between them, Emma and Alex must navigate not only the winding streets of Paris but the complexities of cultural differences and the language of love itself. Will they find their happily ever after amid the croissants and cobblestones, or will the challenges of their romance prove too much to bear?

Indulge in a delectable tale of love, laughter, and the magic of Paris, where every moment is sweeter than the last.

Settling into my bed against the lush pillows to indulge in this guilty pleasure, I press play. Before I know it, I'm entranced. "Oh, he's a charmer," I murmur. He exudes charm even on the modest-sized television screen.

When Emma gets lost in the maze-like streets of Montmartre, Alex comes to her rescue and shows her the way to her intended destination. The so-called "meet-cute" Geoffrey mentioned.

Perfect, because tomorrow they plan to visit Montmartre. It will be fun to see in person what I'm seeing on the screen now.

The two main characters have great chemistry—I almost believe they have a real relationship, and I'm identifying the plot points Geoffrey explained as they relate to our fake relationship.

When Emma and Alex share their first kiss, I'm struck with the most irrational stab of jealousy. I wonder whether, if he can kiss like that on-screen, he was also faking it with me last night. Dammit. What's the matter with me? It's *all* fake! This *whole* blasted relationship is fake! Of course his heated kisses are fake. And I'd do well to remember that.

It's late when my phone buzzes with a text. I pause the movie, thinking Abby has some further advice. Instead, I see Geoffrey's name. *WTH?*

Geoffrey: What are you doing?

I'm certainly not going to confess to watching one of his movies.

Me: Reading.

Geoffrey: What re you reading?

Damn. What *am* I reading? I hastily glance around the room, and my gaze lands on a luxury lifestyle magazine.

Me: An article in l'Officiel.

Geoffrey: That makes sense.

The ellipsis appears again, then a new message appears.

Geoffrey: Are you in bed?

I'm leery of this question and gnaw on my lip for a moment before responding.

Me: Yes. Why?

Geoffrey: What are you wearing?

Is he . . . *flirting* with me? Do I flirt back, or do I just say my pajamas? Throwing my own recent advice out the window, I go with flirting.

Me: Is this part of the fake romance?

Geoffrey: Consider it getting into character.

Hmm. So, I should practice flirting, I guess. Looks like dinner lightened his mood.

Me: What do you think I'm wearing?

Geoffrey: It depends. In reality, you're likely wearing pajamas like the ones you were wearing the other night. Which were quite nice btw. But in my imagination, you're naked.

An unexpected thrill passes through me. He pictures me naked? Then I shudder at the thought. I'm a fifty-three-year-old woman, who admittedly still looks nice in clothes —but naked? I gnaw on my lower lip again, trying to come up with a witty reply. Before I do, another message comes in.

Geoffrey: No need to answer. A man can dream anyway.

Dream? Imagining me naked is a *dream*?

Me: I don't read in bed naked. Sorry. But I do sleep naked. Sometimes.

Now what on earth made me send that? I don't sleep naked! Old habits die hard. I gave up sleeping au naturel after Abby was born. The last thing I needed was my child climbing into bed with me and Barry in the middle of the night sans sleepwear.

Geoffrey: 😳

Oh dear. Do I come clean, or let him think otherwise?

Geoffrey: I can die a happy man. 😍

I laugh out loud at his response.

Me: Do you plan for this to be your last night on earth?

Geoffrey: No. I'm holding out to see this for myself. But if I slip the surly bonds of earth, I can go with that image in my head.

See for himself? Is he serious? I shake my head and giggle. No. Like me, he's just flirting.

Me: Good night, Geoffrey.

Geoffrey: Good night, Ellie.

Ellie. Why does that sound like an endearment coming from him?

So much for remembering this is all fake.

I click play again, determined to finish the movie. I'm struck by how the scene looks and feels familiar. Alex and Emma are seated at a café table with pastries she's made set out on delicate plates. Alex holds out a bite of croissant to Emma, and at her raised brow says in a lovely French accent, "Feeding one another is a powerful symbolic gesture that conveys a deep sense of intimacy, affection, and emotional connection."

At her skeptical look, he continues, "What? This act can be found across many cultures. It shows trust. It essentially says, 'I trust you not to accidentally poke my eye out with the fork.' Or in this case, my finger."

I sit up in bed as I remember the scene—*our* scene at Angelina. "Are you kidding me right now?" He took that whole scene from this movie?! Not word-for-word, but pretty damn close.

Fury rockets through me, and I wonder how many other scenes he's acted with me that come straight from one of his movies. Did the scene when he kissed me in my room the other night come from a movie too? Then I recall Abby's description of the two of us at the top of the Eiffel Tower and how similar it was to this movie. I guess I haven't reached that scene yet. I'm sure I would have recognized it if I had.

That jerk! I pace my bedroom as the movie continues playing, my heart pounding with . . . what? Indignation? Anger? Hurt? And unless I out myself, I can't confront him about it.

Then the devil's advocate inside my head asks, "What do you expect? He's an *actor*, for heaven's sake. He was playing a role for the cameras that day at Angelina and following the script."

I drop down onto the bed, suddenly deflated. Of course, the voice in my head is right. Geoffrey Harrison is first and foremost an actor. One who is pursuing a career revival and using our fake romance to do it.

Nothing like a bucket of ice water to the face to remind me I would do well to keep my emotional distance from him. I need to remember that every word out of his mouth is intended to charm and disarm his audience.

Clicking off the TV, I resolve not to be a member of that audience.

Chapter Five

DAY FIVE

Geoffrey

Montmartre, my home when I'm in Paris, is a historic and vibrant neighborhood located in the 18th arrondissement of Paris. I chose it for its bohemian atmosphere, rich artistic history, and stunning views of the city.

Montmartre's narrow, winding streets are lined with charming cafés, art studios, and unique shops, and galleries.

Now I get to show it to Ellie and see it through her eyes. The thought energizes me.

After the phone call with Malcolm yesterday, it took a glass of wine and a good meal with my daughter and her soon-to-be family to dispel the bad mood. Timing is everything in business and in life. If only the part had come two weeks from now. But I couldn't brood about it. I'd wait to hear back from Malcolm.

I'd been excited to have this beautiful woman next to me for the day, but Ellie had been a little distant this morning, offering only a cool smile and a lukewarm "good morning."

Maybe she hadn't slept well. She'd perked up a bit after a café au lait, but she's still reserved.

Once we began our drive, Eleanor seems to have transformed back into Ellie, her gaze swinging back and forth from one side of the street to another, as if afraid she'll miss something. It took a few days to break through her reserve and convince her to relax and enjoy her vacation, and now her enthusiasm is contagious, despite the somewhat rocky start to the morning.

"Tell me about Montmartre," she says, bringing me out of my thoughts.

"Well, it's been home to artists and writers. Pablo Picasso, Vincent van Gogh, and Henri de Toulouse-Lautrec were inspired by the neighborhood's scenery and frequented its many cafés and restaurants."

"Is that why you chose an apartment here?"

"One of the reasons. Like the Basilica, to me, it is the heart of Paris. And the heart of Montmartre is the Place du Tertre."

We pass a bustling square that has been a gathering place for artists and street performers for centuries. She leans over to get a better view. The scent of her perfume tickles my nose, and my brain briefly short-circuits. She eyes me expectantly, as if to say, "go on."

Uh, where was I? Oh yeah. "Visitors can watch talented painters and sketch artists create their masterpieces, or even commission a portrait or painting of their own. The square is also home to quintessential Parisian cafés and restaurants, where you can relax and soak in the ambiance.

"In addition to the art scene, the neighborhood is home to the famous Moulin Rouge, depicted in the movie of the same name." I look at her blank face and remember, she doesn't watch movies. We need to do something about that. "Then there's the Montmartre Cemetery, which is the final resting place of people like Edgar Degas, Alexandre Dumas, and the ballet dancer Nijinsky. We'll pay a visit to the Montmartre Vineyard, Le Clos Montmartre, this afternoon. It's one of the few remaining vineyards in Paris and produces its own wine.

"But our first stop is the most iconic landmark in Montmartre—the Basilica of Sacré-Cœur. We've seen the city from the Eiffel Tower and the Arc. It's time we saw it from atop the Basilica. You game?"

"Of course!"

Eleanor

As we climb the steps to the brilliant white Basilica, I realize for the first time in a very long time, I am happy to be where I am, despite my annoyance with Geoffrey. What is it called—mindfulness? I'm not thinking about tomorrow, or next month, or next season. I'm just happy to be here now.

That is, until I hear, "There they are!" followed by shouts and squeals.

"What the hell?" Geoffrey says, grasping me by the arm as we both realize there is a small mob waiting outside the church. "I'm going to murder him," he growls. In the short time I've known him, I've never seen him so angry. Agitation rolls off him in waves. Then his demeanor appears to change. He puts on a charming smile, wraps his arm around my waist, and heads to the church entrance, where the small mob is gathered. Actor Geoffrey on display.

He waves and pulls me in next to him to pose for the multitude of phones pointed in our direction. Cries of "We love you!" and "Can I have your autograph?" follow.

"Smile," he murmurs. "Look like you're happy to be here with me."

I paste a smile on my face, but like yesterday at Versailles, I'm overwhelmed by the attention.

After a few minutes of photos, Geoffrey says, "Let's go. They won't be able to follow us en masse into the church. Security will stop them."

As we walk past the crowd, a woman reaches out and grabs my arm. "Can I get your autograph, Ellie?"

Taken aback by her temerity, all I can utter is, "What?"

"Come," Geoffrey pulls me closer and ushers me into the church.

Once inside, he huddles me into a quiet corner and looks down into my face, his hands gliding up and down my stiff arms. "I'm so sorry. I am literally going to murder Malcolm. Probably shouldn't say that in a house of God," he mutters, looking around as if just realizing where he is. "I'll get to the bottom of this once we're back in the car."

"It's fine."

"It's not fine. That woman should not have put her hands on you."

I step back. "I'm fine," even though my heart is racing like I've had one too many cups of espresso. "Let's just . . . let's just see the cathedral." Drawing in a deep breath, I notice the interior of the cathedral for the first time since we entered. A beautiful mix of mosaics, stained glass windows, and decorative elements. The interior is cool and calming to my frayed nerves, the hushed, reverent tones of the visitors a soothing balm.

Taking Taylor Swift's sage advice, I "shake it off." I'm not going to let Geoffrey's deception or unwanted crowds tarnish the joy of Paris.

We wander to the centerpiece, a grand mosaic in the apse, depicting Christ in Majesty. It is breathtaking in its size and detail.

"It's one of the largest mosaics in the world," Geoffrey whispers in my ear. Though I know he is only trying to be respectful by whispering, his warm breath on my ear sends a shiver down my spine. Damn, traitorous spine.

Photography isn't allowed in the cathedral, so Hélène and Stéphane stayed outside.

After walking around the interior, Geoffrey places a hand low on my back. "Are you ready to tackle the two hundred thirty-four steps to the dome? I could use the exercise to shake off my anger."

"Sure." Though my legs are still trembling from my encounter with the crowd of fans.

We pay the fee to climb to the top.

Heart pounding, my breathing coming in harsh pants, we reach the top. And it is so worth the climb!

Geoffrey huffs out between breaths, "The Basilica sits atop the highest point in the city."

From the observation deck, we are greeted by an unobstructed view in every direction, the silver ribbon of the Seine meandering through the heart of the city. In the distance, the Eiffel Tower's latticework pierces the sky. The view from the Sacré-Cœur really puts the tower into perspective.

Geoffrey places his hands on my shoulders, and I resist the urge to shake them off. There are no cameras here, so why the gesture?

"Are you okay?"

Am I? I think so. "I'm fine. Really. It was just . . . a shock. Again."

"I'm sorry. I had no idea."

"I know." I reach up and place a hand over his, where they it still rests on my shoulders. And it feels so right.

"I'll have another come-to-Jesus with Malcolm. It won't happen again. But let's not spoil the day. I can take care of it later. In the meantime, I'll check with security about another less conspicuous exit from the cathedral."

Geoffrey

We made it out of the cathedral undetected, thanks to assistance from security, and after meeting up with Hélène and Stéphane, I say, "No visit to the Basilica would be complete without ice cream from Amorino Sacré-Cœur."

"Ice cream? Before lunch?"

Geoffrey chuckles, the tension from earlier having faded. "Come on, Ellie, live a little!"

She shakes her head and laughs, but from her expression, she's going to give in to temptation.

"After all, you just climbed the equivalent of seventeen flights of stairs, and that's not including the steps up to the cathedral."

The car pulls up and we climb in.

"It's not the closest ice cream to the church, but I think it's the best." A few short minutes later, the car drops us off and we queue up.

"Popular spot," she mutters, eyeing the line in front of us.

"Very."

A couple walks past with two beautiful ice cream cones.

"Are those . . . *flowers*?" The ice cream in the cone is in the shape of a rose.

"Yes. You can have as many flavors in the cone as you like. Each petal can be different."

"That's amazing! I've never seen anything like it."

"I have a theory about ice cream and people," I say, as we inch our way up the queue.

"Oh yeah? What's that?" she asks, folding her arms over her chest, a frown marring her brow. She looks . . . annoyed.

I decide to give her a pass after the unexpected crowd this

morning and continue, "You can tell a lot about a person based on the ice cream flavor they choose."

"Is that so?" There is definitely an edge to that question.

"Absolutely."

"Do tell."

"Take mint chocolate chip. People who choose this flavor tend to be adventurous, creative, and energetic. They like to try new things and enjoy unique flavor combinations."

"What about butter pecan?" she asks, a note of challenge in her voice, as if testing my theory.

"They tend to be warm, nurturing, and empathetic, and value family and relationships above all else."

"So ice cream choices not only reflect personality but also values?"

"Of course! One of the first questions on any job application should be 'What is your favorite ice cream flavor?' This one question could quickly winnow out anyone unsuitable for the job."

She nods, playing along now. "I can see how that would be more important than, say, education or skill level." A group of young women walks past with cones. "I suppose people who choose vanilla are boring sticks-in-the-mud who despise change."

We're next in line behind a family of four now.

"Not at all. People who prefer vanilla are classic, traditional, and reliable. They like things to be straightforward and uncomplicated."

"And what is your flavor of choice, Monsieur Harrison?"

"Chocolate, to be sure."

"Really?" She steps back in surprise. "I had you pegged for something more exotic, like say, pistachio or stracciatella. What does your choice of chocolate say about you?"

"Chocolate ice cream lovers tend to be passionate, romantic, and indulgent." I lean in close. "We enjoy the finer things in life and have a flair for luxury."

She giggles and nods her head. "I can see that about you."

That laugh just made my day. Maybe she's over whatever bee she had in her bonnet. "And you? What's yours?" I ask, but I already have her pegged.

She turns to the pretty young girl behind the counter, "*Un café, s'il vous plaît.*"

"Of course," I murmur, before placing my order for chocolate and two more cones for Hélène and Stéphane—one strawberry, one vanilla.

"All right, lay it on me. What does my flavor say about me?"

I grin. "And people who choose coffee are ambitious, hard-working, and practical, and often have a love for coffee and its energizing effects."

She looks at me, eyes wide.

Oh yeah. I'd nailed it.

Eleanor

"My daughter would like to invite you to the welcome dinner, as well as the wedding and reception."

"Oh, but . . ."

"Please. It would make her, and me, very happy."

"She shouldn't feel obligated."

After finishing the creamiest ice cream I've ever had, we are waiting at the corner for the car to take us to the Rue de l'Abreuvoir, a picturesque street in Montmartre. Geoffrey takes me by the shoulders and gazes down into my eyes. "Ellie, it's not out of obligation."

Much to my annoyance, his warm baritone washes over

me, kindling desire and taking me from zero to lust in 3.8 seconds. I can't stop myself—my gaze flickers to his mouth, and I wonder if it will taste of the chocolate ice cream he just had.

"Say you'll come."

My mind instantly goes to the gutter. "What?"

The corner of his mouth lifts as if he's read where my mind went. "To the wedding festivities. Say you'll come."

"Oh, right." I'd feel like a fish out of water, or in this case, an American wedding crasher. I quickly scroll through possible excuses, but I come up empty. "Okay, but only if you're sure it's not any trouble." I'm not sure what his aim here is, since there will be no cameras at the wedding.

"Ellie, I assure you, it's no trouble. After all, *I'm* paying for the wedding."

"Well, thank you for the invitation. I'm honored."

The car pulls up and, after climbing in, Geoffrey says, "Rue de l'Abreuvoir, *s'il vous plaît.*"

Street of the watering place, I muse. "What an interesting street name."

"There used to be a watering hole or trough for horses at the end of the street." He shrugs. "The name stuck. Even so, the street is one of the most iconic and frequently photographed streets in the city. We'll have lunch here."

"But we just had ice cream," I protest.

"We'll walk a bit first."

The car stops at a street at the bottom of a gentle incline, but barricades are blocking the entrance. "It looks like it's closed." I can't keep the disappointment from my voice. After Geoffrey's description, I was looking forward to walking this historic street.

"I know. It's closed for filming, but the director is a friend of mine."

"But won't we be in the way?"

"No. The filming won't start for a few more hours, but they had to close the street this morning. Come on." He climbs out of the car and holds his hand out. I place my hand in his, and he helps me out of the car.

A man in a security uniform holding a clipboard stops us. With a few words from Geoffrey and a check of his clipboard, the man lets us pass.

"The street would ordinarily be crowded with visitors. The best time to visit is in the early morning or early evening, when most of the crowds have dispersed."

It certainly isn't crowded now. There is the occasional person who I assume is part of the film crew, but otherwise, we, along with Hélène and Stéphane, are the only people on the street. The empty street has an eerie quality, as if I'd stepped back in time. The tranquil, romantic street is lined with picturesque buildings, many covered in trailing vines, as if time had forgotten them. Cobbled walks bordered the street in its gentle rise, with views of the Basilica perched atop its hill like a great sentinel.

"If you could live in any decade or year, when would it be? And you can't pick this one."

What an intriguing question. I mull over the answer as we stroll up the hill. "The 1950s."

"Why?"

"To meet Dior, Chanel, and Givenchy would be a dream. And the clothing aesthetic of the time period is one of my favorites. What about you?"

"That's easy. The 1930s—the golden age of Hollywood. When movies like *It Happened One Night*, *Bringing Up Baby*, and *The Philadelphia Story* were filmed, and featured stars like Clark Gable, Katharine Hepburn, and Cary Grant. Those were the classics I grew up watching. It's the decade that planted the seed of acting."

We stop in front of a pink building, its pastel color

standing out from the rest along the street, La Maison Rose painted in a contrasting sage green. "We'll have lunch here, but let's walk up the street first."

"Is the café open?" With the street closed, there didn't appear to be any reason for it to be open.

"It is for us," Geoffrey said with a grin and a wink. "Artists like van Gogh, Picasso, and Matisse frequented this neighborhood," Geoffrey continues, and we resume our leisurely pace. "In fact, at the end of the street is a bust of the French singer Dalida."

We stop for photos along our walk, finally ending at the famed bust of Dalida. The golden color of the breasts stands out in contrast to the darker bronze of the rest of the bust. "Interesting that the artist used a different color on her torso," I say.

"That's not why her breasts are a different color."

"What do you mean?"

"Apparently, rubbing her breasts brings good luck."

"You're kidding!"

"'Fraid not. Care to give them a rub?" he asks with a wink. "Maybe it will bring you luck."

My fingers twitch with the temptation to bring myself some luck, no matter how far-fetched the myth. "No." I laugh self-consciously.

"Well, I'm not above a little rubbing for luck." He walks over to the bust and places both hands over the golden breasts and turns with a cheeky smile for the camera.

Geoffrey

After dining on a light lunch of a variety of small plates, Ellie and I sit with glasses of an excellent Beaujolais. La Maison

Rose is one of my favorite cafés in Paris, and since it's not far from my flat, I'm a frequent visitor. The staff are friendly and remember my preferences. The cozy rustic interior with wooden beams, vintage décor, and a sense of history transports you back to the Bohemian days of Montmartre's artistic heyday.

The menu offers traditional French cuisine, with a focus on classic dishes and local ingredients. And the desserts are not to be missed.

Almost as if reading my mind, Laurent, our server, returns to the table, and I say, "A slice of the carrot cake, *s'il vous plaît.*"

"Oh, I couldn't." Ellie holds up her hand.

"Oh, but you must," I insist. "You won't find this carrot cake just anywhere. The secret ingredient is rosemary."

"Oui, Monsieur Harrison." Laurent ignores Ellie's protests and returns to the kitchen to fulfill my order.

Ellie sighs in exasperation, and I grin at her, making her roll her eyes.

"If you could eat the same meal every day for the rest of your life, what would it be?"

She props her chin in her hand and stares beyond me. "Hmm, that's a tough one."

"Take your time."

"If I could eat it without consequence, it would be pasta. Any kind of pasta. I just love it."

"What is the consequence?" I ask, curious.

"Weight gain, what else?"

"Ellie, you have a beautiful body." *A body I would desperately like to see more of.* "Why would you be worried about that?"

She snorts. "I work hard to maintain what you consider a 'beautiful body.'"

"What *I* consider? No. It's an empirical fact."

She laughs that beautiful throaty laugh of hers. The one that sends heat straight to my core every time. But I'm pleased to see the faint blush on her cheeks as she gazes down into her wineglass.

After a moment, she looks up. "Your turn. What would your meal be?"

"That's easy! My mum's beef stew. Melt-in-your-mouth beef, sweet carrots, and tender potatoes in a rich sauce made with a generous pour of Guinness."

"Sounds delicious."

"Is your mom still alive?"

"She is."

Our slice—or should I say slab?—of cake arrives, and Ellie's eyes grow round. "*Mon dieu,*" she breathes. Laurent carefully places two forks on the table in front of us and bows before leaving us to our decadent dessert.

Ellie lifts her fork and timidly slices into the cake, taking the tiniest of bites. Remembering her reaction to her dessert the first night we met, I brace myself. I watch as she slides the fork into her mouth and wait for the sweet cream cheese frosting and the moist, tender cake—with its rosemary, cinnamon, nutmeg, and ginger—to hit her tongue.

And there it is . . . that low hum of pleasure, the closed eyes, the look of pure bliss. And I wonder, once again, if that would be how she'd look if I were inside her.

I shift uncomfortably in my seat. *Mon dieu*, indeed.

Eleanor

A short walk from La Maison Rose, Le Clos Montmartre is a charming vineyard situated on Montmartre Hill.

My personal tour guide gives me a brief history on the

walk to the vineyard. "It is the last remaining vineyard in the city and dates back to the Roman era."

Not so much a connoisseur but someone who can appreciate a good glass of wine, I ask, "What grapes are grown here?"

"The vineyard grows Gamay, Pinot Noir, and Sauvignon Blanc. It fell into decline until the 1930s, when residents formed an association to revive it. The annual harvest is in October, and they hold a festival called Fête des Vendanges."

"Is the wine any good?"

"I'm not sure you could call it excellent, but it is highly sought after and has become a collector's item, especially given the limited production of around fifteen hundred bottles a year."

We approach the access gate and see that the handle is a charming metal wine bottle.

"We won't stay long, but I thought you'd like to enjoy the tranquility of the picturesque setting."

Content with his guidance, I walk alongside him down the brick paths surrounded by a riot of colorful flowers and limestone walls covered in trailing ivy. Rows of vines grow in exacting lines.

"In addition to the wine, they have olive, kiwi, cherry, and peach trees, as well as strawberries."

The air is fragrant with the scents of earth, decaying leaves, and the faint hints of vanilla, rose, and lilac from the remaining cherry blossoms. I draw in a deep cleansing breath. It's so peaceful that it's difficult to believe this green space is in the middle of Paris.

The scene at the Basilica had been tense. I'm not used to such attention, and being the focus of die-hard fans is a bit unnerving. It was such a pleasure to have the Rue de l'Abreuvoir to ourselves, without the fear that a crowd would be waiting to pounce.

"How do you do it?" I ask.

"Do what?" He stops to take a closer look as a butterfly floats by in search of nectar.

"Deal with all those people?"

"Ah." He shrugs. "You get used to it. But the first movie premiere I attended, I kept looking around to see who the fans were shouting at, until my co-star whispered, 'It's you.'" The corner of his mouth lifted in a rueful grin. "Now, I only *hope* I elicit that reaction."

Given this morning, I'd say there's no worry on that front. It's hard to believe studios don't see how popular he is with his fans.

"What drew you to acting?"

Another casual shrug. "I wasn't good at anything else. I'd been an incorrigible student, and my parents often despaired over my future. I went with a friend to an acting class in London, mainly because he said it was a good place to meet girls." He gave me a cheeky grin.

"And did you? Meet girls?"

"I did. But I also found my calling—and I'm not talking about being a *roué*."

"A *roué*? There's an old-fashioned word."

"Would you prefer man-whore?"

I laugh. "No. *Roué* sounds more . . . polite. So, this acting class?"

"Yes. My parents were classic movie buffs. They always had old black-and-whites on TV. I grew up with movies like *The Maltese Falcon*, *Casablanca*, and *Mr. Smith Goes to Washington.* But my favorites were the romantic comedies. *Bringing Up Baby*, *The Philadelphia Story*, and *My Favorite Wife*. I liked the lighthearted banter and the happy ending."

A group of people was heading toward us, and Geoffrey reached out and wrapped his arm around my waist, pulling me close to him, giving them room to pass.

"I never thought about being an actor. I never thought a career in movies was an option for a boy from Bristol."

Surprised by his comment, I step back. "Bristol? England? You said you were American."

"No. You *assumed* I was American."

"But . . . you have no accent."

"Oh, it's there."

I shake my head. The sentence ended with a rising inflection, as if he were asking a question. And he'd pronounced the 'th' in 'there' like 'v' and the 'r' sound at the end like 'ah.'

"I took diction lessons from an American. I thought if I was going to make it in Hollywood, I should learn American diction."

"And your French?"

"I learned when I filmed *From Paris, With Love*, and then I bought a flat here. If I was going to live here part-time, I wanted to be fluent in the language. But it also helped that my first wife was French."

"And what of a British accent?"

"I can also speak with the Oxbridge accent of the British royal family."

The last was said with the clear pronunciation one would recognize from Prince William or Prince Harry.

"You're a man of many talents."

He leaned in and whispered in my ear, "There are many more I'd like to show you."

The cheesy line should have left me cold. Instead, it left me with a warmth deep in my core.

Geoffrey

"There they are!"

Ellie gasps and freezes when we're met with a cacophony of shouts as we exit the vineyard. "What the actual fuck?" I mutter. How on earth had they found us here? "I'm going to kill Malcolm," I grind out.

I grab Ellie by the wrist. "Come on!"

This is my turf. I know the winding side streets and alleys of Montmartre like a born bohemian. If these are tourists, and given the American accents, they are, we could lose them easily.

Pulling her behind me, we turn left onto a narrow alley behind the vineyard, then run up the street to a hidden stairway that leads to some apartments. Ducking into the stairway, I wait to see if they've followed. I can't imagine they would pursue us, but you never know. There could be paparazzi in their midst.

Ellie leans against the wall, panting from the exertion of our mad dash. I tug her against me and press my lips to her hair. "I'm so sorry. Are you okay?"

I feel her nod against me. Then I feel her shaking uncontrollably. "Ellie? Don't be frightened." Worried, I rub my hand along her back in soothing strokes. "Ellie. Sweetheart."

She pushes away from me, resuming her posture against the wall. Instead of seeing a trail of tears, I see a wide smile, her shoulders not shaking with sobs, but with barely suppressed laughter. She covers her mouth with a hand, as a giggle threatens to erupt. "I'm sorry. I don't know what's come over me. There's nothing funny about any of this."

I can't help myself. I chuckle as well. Her laughter is infectious. I grip her by the shoulders and stare down into her face, and suddenly the air is charged with another emotion. Lust. The laughter dies, and my gaze is drawn to her mouth. Her softly parted lips waiting to be kissed. Who am I to deny them?

I lower my head and, cupping her face, press my lips to

hers. Just a gentle brush. Like the butterfly in the vineyard landing on a flower, I taste her. Her arms lift to my waist as I raise my head and pin those violet eyes with my gaze. "What's your deepest desire at this very moment?"

"Honestly? To run away. No adoring fans. No film crew."

"I can help you with that." We'd lost Hélène and Stéphane in the dash to hide. I'll text them later. I clasp her hand in mine. "Come on."

"Where are we going?" she asks, as I lead her from the seclusion of the stairway.

"To my flat."

The flat is nestled within a quiet alley in a beautiful limestone building adorned with thick ivy. The apartment is my refuge from the bustle of Paris. It's the perfect place to hide out until the coast is clear.

Geoffrey

A few minutes later, I throw open the door to my flat, Eleanor beside me laughing. The throaty sound of her laughter sends a jolt of pleasure down my spine.

Closing the door behind her, I still at the expression on her face. Her eyes are bright with shared amusement, her smile broad, and the color high on her cheeks from our dash down the alleys of Montmartre. It's like a veil of control has been lifted. She is ravishing!

Heat pools in my stomach. I want this woman—have wanted this woman since our first dinner. But does she want me?

She lifts a questioning brow at my look, then turns to take in my flat, and I am acutely aware of her distance.

I try to see it through Ellie's eyes as she wanders the space, lingering here and there to examine photos and other accessories. Does she find my flat appealing?

I love how the open concept floor plan seamlessly merges the tidy kitchen, dining area, and living room into one livable space. An open stairway along the far wall leads to the lofted bedroom suite nestled in the eaves of the building, adding an element of whimsy to the space.

Above, open beams stretch across the ceiling, a rustic contrast to the smooth, blond wood floors beneath. The apartment occupies the coveted top floor of the building, allowing for both privacy and the luxury of gazing at the world from a serene distance.

A focal point in the living area is the fireplace, graced by a white marble surround, a counterpoint to the casual French farmhouse-style interior.

Accessible through a set of tall French doors, an inviting balcony, with its wrought iron filigree railing, offers a vantage point that captures a breathtaking view of the Basilica. The balcony itself overlooks a quaint courtyard, creating a tranquil retreat from the streets beyond.

Ellie opens the French doors and steps out onto the balcony, and I follow, unable to resist any longer.

I stand close behind her, my hands resting on the railing next to hers, effectively caging her there.

She draws in a deep breath and releases it. "It's beautiful," she whispers.

I nuzzle close to her ear and murmur, "I want to kiss you."

She twists in the circle of my arms, her hands now braced on the railing behind her. "But . . . there's no camera crew."

"I want to kiss you for real, not for the cameras."

Her gaze flicks to my lips, and the moment she licks her own, I know she feels the same.

I slowly lower my head, giving her time to stop me, but then she lifts her mouth to me, and I close the distance. Her lips are soft and warm beneath mine, and I lightly brush my mouth back and forth over hers, reigning in my desire to crush her to me and plunder her mouth.

Recalling her admonition that there would be no tongue, I focus on her lips, tasting and teasing, nibbling at their delectable taste. Her arms wrap around my neck, her fingers combing through the hair at my nape, and I shiver involuntarily. She moans at my reaction, then opens her mouth to me, inviting me in. I enter with alacrity, my tongue sweeping hers, twisting and swirling.

Her tongue tangles with mine, taking the kiss deeper, and I want more. So much more. No, I want it all. I want to touch, and lick, and tease all of her. I want to see her beneath me, eyes glazed with passion, lips swollen from my kisses, as I drive into her.

I slide my hand up along her ribcage, then graze my thumb along the side of a luscious breast. She sighs into my mouth, and I take it as a sign that she's okay with my touch, so I palm her breast. She stiffens. I snatch my hand away as if I'd just touched a hot coal.

"I'm sorry, Ellie. I thought—"

She closes her eyes and shakes her head. "No. It's . . . I . . ." Then she does the unthinkable. She takes my hand and places it over her breast once more. "Please."

I will my hand to keep still, when all it wants is to squeeze and tempt and tease. "Only if you're certain."

Her heated gaze bores into mine, and I'm sunk. I claim her mouth once more and mold my palm to her breast, testing, teasing, reassuring myself she wants this as much as I do.

And god! Her breast is so firm and plump and . . . real! I've felt enough breasts in my life, on screen and off, to know. Everything about this woman is real. No breast implants, no lip filler, no hair color. My other hand glides down her back to cup and squeeze her ass. No implants there either. Her perky ass is real too. It's so damn refreshing.

And a lesson for me. Ellie has chosen to embrace aging with grace, while I've fought it tooth and nail. I've even gone under the knife once to correct sagging eyelids. It's just expected in show business. But Malcolm's recommended facelift? I can't bring myself to do it.

Ellie moans and presses her hips against my straining erection, reminding me I have this gorgeous, passionate woman in my arms. I want to feel her skin against mine. I want to taste her breasts. I want to plunge into her yielding wetness, sinking deep. I want to hear her cries of pleasure. I want to learn the sounds she makes when she comes.

I end the kiss before this can go any further, breathless and aching, and press my forehead to hers, my hands resting on her hips. "God, Ellie."

Her hot panting breath caresses my face, and a reluctant smile curves her kiss-swollen lips. "We should go."

My mind knows this to be true. But my body? Well, that's a whole different story.

Geoffrey

"I swear to you it wasn't me," Malcolm says. "It's brilliant! I wish I could take credit for it, but I can't."

I dropped Ellie off at her hotel room, and as soon as I entered my own, I called Malcolm to read him the riot act.

"Then how did they know where we were?" I grind out.

"A fan on social media. She's started a game of 'Where's Geoffrey?'—you know, like 'Where's Waldo?'—encouraging people to guess where you're going to be and showing up there. People who spot you are encouraged to post the location."

"Fuck."

"Don't tell me you're angry!"

"What do you think? I'm trying to show Ellie a good time in Paris, and these encounters disconcert her."

"I thought the whole reason for this escapade was to raise your status on social media?"

"It is," I insist. "I'd just like a little more control over the situation." *But I also want to enjoy my time with Ellie, and the lack of privacy with the film crew, and now the public, is starting to wear on me.* "It's also creating security issues. I don't think officials at the Basilica were too pleased about the obnoxious crowd outside."

"Do you want me to get a security detail for you?"

I sigh and scrub my free hand through my hair. I don't want to add more people to the retinue who are following us. It would feel even less like a vacation for Ellie than it already does. "No. With Ava's civil ceremony tomorrow afternoon, I'm taking Ellie to some of Paris's secret gems in the morning. It's doubtful anyone will figure that out." I pause, then say, "But I warn you, Malcolm, if there are people there waiting for us, I'll know you leaked it."

"There won't be!" he argues.

"And the wedding? It's under wraps?"

"Of course! I wouldn't let anyone ruin Ava's wedding."

I end the call and toss my phone on the bed, and gaze around the luxurious suite. The empty luxurious suite. I already miss Ellie's company, but I have plans for a quiet dinner with Ava and her fiancé, Gervais, before family and friends arrive for the big wedding ceremony on Saturday.

Ellie won't be at the civil ceremony. Ava wanted it to just be me and her mother, her mother's husband, and her future in-laws. I respect that. But Ellie will be joining for the family dinner afterward.

I'm looking forward to that part more than I should.

Eleanor

It has been an exhausting day. Stressful at times. Blissful at others. I unroll the parchment and set a book, a flower vase, my smartphone, and an empty water glass at the four corners to hold them open, and stare down at the portrait of myself.

After hiding out in Geoffrey's flat for a time, we ventured out again, stopping at the Place du Tertre, the square in Montmartre not far from the Basilica we passed on the way. Artists cover almost every square inch of the space, selling their art and drawing portraits for paying customers. Geoffrey had told me that since the space is limited, acquiring space is very competitive. Artists must submit portfolios to the town hall that controls access. But this also ensures that those lucky enough to acquire space are some of the best artists in the city. Spaces open up rarely—usually only when an artist dies or moves away. Apparently there's a ten-year waiting list!

Geoffrey had insisted on the portrait—a keepsake from my trip. But what do I want with a portrait of myself? Maybe I'll give it to Abby. I examine the portrait critically to determine if it looks like me. To determine if the artist accurately captured my likeness.

He'd certainly captured the crow's feet around my eyes, I think ruefully. But he'd also captured the odd violet color of my eyes, the gently arched eyebrows, the still high cheeks. He'd added a faint blush, I think. And perhaps a little more color to the lips. Because I didn't think I could hold a smile the whole time, I went with a soft, *Mona Lisa*-like expression. I tilt my head. It worked, I think. The face staring back at me is enigmatic. And perhaps a little unsure. Unsure of myself. Unsure of Geoffrey.

How much of this is for the camera? How much of this is real?

We ended the day at the Mur des Je t'aime, or The Wall of Love, in the Jehan Rictus Gardens. It features enameled lava tiles with "I love you" written in two hundred fifty languages. It's a popular spot for lovers and honeymooners, and for engagement and wedding photos. Geoffrey had pulled me into his arms and planted a kiss on me that made my toes curl. The perfect social media moment.

But it was the kiss in his flat that had left an imprint. The kiss that had led to more. Like his hands on my breast, my hips pressed to his, the ridge of his erection jutting against my stomach. How I had wanted him! I like to think I would have declined if he'd invited me upstairs to his bed, but I couldn't swear to it.

This public ruse cannot lead to more. I cannot let myself give in to the temptation that is Geoffrey Harrison and just be another notch on his proverbial bedpost.

But I *like* him. The man I see in private—away from the cameras. A lot. Too much, in fact.

My phone buzzes with an incoming call. Maddie. I answer with a French accent, "*Allô*?"

"*Bonjour, mon amie.*" Maddie's teasing voice makes me laugh.

"It's evening here."

"Oh, that's right. *Bonsoir*. And ooh là là!"

"What are you talking about?"

"The photo of you and Geoffrey in front of a wall with tiles. It's a wonder they didn't all melt. That looked like one passionate kiss!"

Not as passionate as the one in his flat.

"That Instagram post has a million views!"

I slump to the sofa and gaze out at the Eiffel Tower. If there had been any doubt to our "love affair," I suppose that image confirmed it.

"I told you—it's just for show."

"And why is that?"

"I told you—because he's trying to boost his image again."

"That's not what I mean. I mean why is it *just* for show? Why aren't you two hooking up?"

"Maybe he doesn't want me that way. Maybe we're not attracted to each other." Even as I say it, I know it's a lie. At least on my side.

"Bullshit. I could practically feel the heat from that kiss emanating from my phone. I'm surprised it didn't spontaneously combust. You need to go for it."

"But . . . how? How do I know it's not an act, because he *is* an actor, you know? How do I know if he's even interested for real?" I throw up my hands. "I haven't done this in thirty-three years! And god—the thought of coming onto him only to be rejected!" I could already feel the heat of rejection high in my cheeks.

"You'll know. Trust me."

"Will I? I know this is old-fashioned, but the only man I've ever been with is Barry. And that was after months of dating."

"Do we need to go over the signs of attraction?"

I release a nervous laugh. "Maybe." Maddie has been a self-professed serial monogamist since her divorce twenty years ago. She should know.

"One, if he holds your gaze."

I recall the hidden stairwell. The way he'd pinned me with those cool blue-gray eyes of his, staring into my own as if he could see into my soul.

"Two, if he looks for any excuse to touch you."

The warmth of his hand on my lower back as he guided

me to our table the first night we met. Taking my hand to help me into and out of the car. No, he was just being a gentleman. But then there were the times when he tucked my hair behind my ear. I couldn't count the public touches—the ones staged for public consumption.

"Three, stealing glances."

Earlier today, I turned to find him staring at me, a thoughtful expression on his face.

"Four, frequent communication."

Do text messages count?

"Five, he asks you a lot of questions. And six, he remembers your answers."

He does ask me a lot of questions. And not just small talk. Deep, probing questions. But has he remembered the answers? How would I know that? Quiz him on it?

"Seven, he introduces you to a family member, though that one may not apply in this case. The odds of him having a family member in Paris for this trip are slim."

If Maddie only knew he did have family here, and he *had* introduced me. Of course, I'd busted him, so he really had no choice. I don't want to reveal the secret he's carefully protected, so I don't mention this to Maddie. Nor do I mention the wedding invitation.

"Eight, if he wants to kiss you, he'll look at your mouth. But, clearly, that's already happened."

The kiss in front of the Love Wall was for the cameras. But the kiss in the stairway, the kiss in the apartment? He had looked at my lips. And there were no cameras. No film crew. No social media moment. Another little secret I don't intend to reveal to Maddie.

"If all the signs of physical attraction are there, you only have to act on it."

But the questions still lingered. Is Geoffrey Harrison *really* attracted to me? Or is he just displaying his acting skills?

"Girl," Maddie says, interrupting my thoughts, "you better go for it. Time is of the essence."

We chat a few more minutes about Abby and whether she knows about the baby (not likely), before we say good night.

No sooner had I ended the call with Maddie than my phone buzzes with a text, almost as if he knew we'd been talking about him.

> Don't eat breakfast in the morning. Meet me at 7:30 in the lobby, and wear comfortable shoes. 🩶

Heart emoji? What did *that* mean?

Maybe, just maybe, it's not an act. Maybe it means he really is into me.

Chapter Six

DAY SIX

Geoffrey

Right on time, Ellie strides into the lobby looking fresh and ready for our morning expedition. She'd chosen athleisure wear, which is perfect. The snug pants hug her beautiful form and turn my thoughts from walking to thoughts of . . . more pleasurable exercise.

"Morning." She eyes me with a raised eyebrow.

What must my expression be? Can she read my thoughts? If so, I need to work on my "blank face."

"Ready to see some of Paris's secret gems?"

"Where are we going? And I hope breakfast is involved."

I lift my hand in the direction of the front entrance to the hotel. "Breakfast awaits."

After settling into the car, Hélène and Stéphane behind us in a separate vehicle, I hand Ellie a café au lait.

"Mmm. Smells wonderful." She takes a sip and smiles. Seeing the joy on her face warms me. Making Ellie happy has become more important to me than the social media campaign.

"Are you going to tell me where we're going?" she prods.

"Have you ever been on the High Line in New York?"

"Yes, why?"

"Because before there was the High Line in New York, there was the Coulée verte René-Dumont, or Promenade plantée."

"You're taking me to a green stream?"

"Sort of. The Promenade is an elevated park built in 1993 and is considered the world's first. Like the High Line, it's built on an abandoned railway line. It can get quite busy later in the day, but this time of morning, it should be populated only with runners and walkers." I lift the box tucked onto the seat. "I thought we'd have a breakfast picnic then walk it off."

Her broad smile makes me blink. It's as if the sun suddenly rose above the city's surrounding buildings.

"Perfect." She settles back in her seat and gazes out the window at the passing scenery, the corners of her lips still lifted.

I could stare at her profile all day. When I urged her to get a portrait yesterday, I'd been foolishly hoping she would give it to me. I wanted something tangible to remember our time together. Ridiculous, I know. I'm sure she'll give it to her daughter, which is as it should be. What am I to her, after all? Just a fake love interest. And whose fault is that?

The car stops at the Place de la Bastille. I help Ellie from the car, then reach in and grab our breakfast. Taking her hand, I lead her around the building and up the stairs to the elevated part of the park. "The viaduct under the elevated area has been renovated into house galleries, artists' workshops, and small boutiques, as well as restaurants and bars," I explain, as we climb.

After reaching the top, I clasp her hand in mine. "Come. I know the perfect spot for breakfast."

Leading her to a bench beneath an arbor covered with fragrant climbing roses, I sigh in relief that no one had claimed it yet. "Here."

Before we sit, I hand a second box over to Hélène and Stéphane, eliciting broad smiles from both.

Ellie takes a seat, and I present her with the box of fragrant buttery croissants. Ellie may deny herself sweet treats, but I've learned beneath that reserved exterior she harbors a sweet tooth.

"You always consider Hélène and Stéphane." She eyes me, a tilt to her head.

I shrug. "They deserve it. They're doing a great job, and they're nice people."

She responds with an enigmatic, "Mmm," before she peers into the box and moans. I feel that moan down to my toes. "It's a good thing we're walking after this. What do we have?"

"There's apricot, almond paste, and of course, chocolate."

Looking up at me from beneath her lashes, she says, "I'm going to put on five pounds on this trip."

"That's what vacations are for," I say with a grin. She has nothing to worry about.

She takes a bite of the flaky treat and her eyes close in pleasure, the thick lashes forming lush curves. "God, this is so good." Her tongue darts out to lick some of the crust from her lips and I nearly groan. A dark smudge of chocolate sits at the corner of her mouth, taunting me. Begging me.

I lean forward and kiss the chocolate from her mouth, her lips sweet and buttery. "Delicious," I murmur. A blush rises to her cheeks, and warmth curls deep in my belly. She blinks a couple of times, then sits back against the bench, scanning the park.

"This is lovely. So tranquil and green."

"I often run here in the mornings, even though it's not close to my flat. At midday, the park is filled with people having lunch, and then later in the evening, people who work in the area come here to wind down before going home."

"I can see why."

We sit in silence for a few minutes, enjoying the sounds of nature—a bird calls from a tree overhead, and a light breeze creates a *shushing* among the bright green leaves.

"How was your dinner last night?"

"Nice. Quiet. It was good to spend time with Ava, Gervais, and his parents before the hectic day tomorrow."

"And her fiancé? You like him?"

"I do. I'll never think anyone is good enough for Ava—even me—but he loves her. That's the most important thing."

"What does he do? For that matter, what does Ava do?"

"Ava is an artist—painting, sculpture—and Gervais works in the financial industry."

"Sounds like a case of opposites attract."

"Yeah, you could say that. Ava is definitely the creative right-brain thinker, while Gervais is the analytical left-brain. But it works."

"And they'll settle in Paris?"

"Yes. For now, at least. I think Gervais is hoping for a transfer to New York or Brussels."

"Both good locations for an artist, I think." Ellie wipes her hands on a napkin and sighs. "I know Abby will marry someday, but I'll miss her when she does."

"Why will you miss her? Do you think she'll move away?"

"Not necessarily. It's just that . . . we're so close now, even though she's eight hundred miles away from where I live. I'm still a focal point in her life. Once she falls in love and marries, that focus will shift to him." A sad smile lifts her mouth. "But that's the way of it."

I reach out and take her hand in mine and squeeze

gently. "You'll always be her mother." She takes her hand from mine and makes a point of brushing the crumbs from her lap.

"Another?" I say, as I hand the box to her with one more croissant.

"No. They were delicious. But two's my limit." She drains her coffee cup. "How about that walk you promised?"

Eleanor

After completing the three-mile walk on the Promenade plantée, Geoffrey has one more stop planned before we return to the hotel so he can dress for Ava's civil ceremony. As we walk, hands clasped like a couple in love, Geoffrey explains the French marriage ceremony. Unlike in the U.S., and the U.K., for that matter, the official, legal wedding ceremony is not performed in a church or other venue. It must be performed at the local town hall officiated by a government official. The ceremony is typically attended by close friends and family and the couple's witnesses to the ceremony, in this case, Geoffrey, his ex-wife Iris, her husband, and the groom's parents. Two friends of the bride and groom would serve as the legal witnesses.

This ceremony would be followed by the dinner Ava had so graciously invited me to. The thought of meeting not only his daughter again, but her husband, his parents, and Iris makes my stomach flip. Ava knows the truth, but what of the groom and his family? What of Iris and her husband?

Many couples choose to have a separate religious or secular wedding ceremony with all the fanfare of the usual American ceremony, including a reception, after the civil ceremony.

Tomorrow's festivities would begin at 2 p.m. and last long into the night.

Tonight, I planned to wear the violet dress I wore to my first dinner with Geoffrey, which means I need a dress for tomorrow's ceremony. That is on my to-do list today.

"As charming as Rue de l'Abreuvoir is," Geoffrey says, breaking into my thoughts, "this street runs a close second for the most charming street in Paris. It is certainly the most colorful."

We turn the corner onto a picturesque cobbled street lined with row houses in different pastels: bright pink, aqua blue, peach, spring green, lilac, and butter yellow. The façades are adorned with colorful shutters, and the sidewalks lined with flowerpots, creating a whimsical, almost fairytale-like ambiance. I could instantly see a photoshoot here with spring's latest fashions.

"It's lovely!"

"I thought your artist's eye would appreciate it. There are thirty-five identical houses, all originally built as workers' housing. Unfortunately, it can be crowded with tourists in the summer, disrupting the peace and tranquility for the residents. But I suppose if you buy a home on Rue Cremieux, you have to expect visitors."

"Oh, I love that green one with the wisteria vine painted on the front. Would they mind a photo, do you think?"

"No. I'm sure the owners are used to seeing their home on social media."

I review the photos I took, pleased with the composition, then I feel Geoffrey's warmth as he steps close. I look up at him and draw in a breath at the expression on his face. His gaze pins mine, his blue-gray eyes now dark with desire—and something else. "Ellie." His eyes flick to my lips. "I'm so glad you're here." He lowers his head and his warm, supple mouth descends on mine. Even as the camera shutter clicks, I lift my arms, wrapping them around his neck, and pull him to me.

Despite the camera, this must be real. I have to believe, no matter how good an actor he is, he can't fake the passion in that kiss. Maybe it's time to take Maddie's advice.

Geoffrey

Later that afternoon, I stand next to Iris and Johannes, her husband of three years, while the *adjoint au maire*, or deputy mayor of Paris, reads the marriage laws. As Monsieur Aleu drones on, I gaze at my beautiful daughter standing tall and proud next to her groom. She wore an ivory dress that stopped about mid-calf. Gervais wore a charcoal gray suit with an ivory shirt and tie. Very classic and understated. Ava seemed to prefer that over the more flamboyant style of her mother, who wore a pink dress trimmed with feathers. In fact, Ava's style seemed closer to Ellie's taste.

Ellie. I miss her. My hand twitches with the need to reach out and take her hand. To feel its warmth as her fingers clasp mine. To experience this emotional moment in my life with her support. I glance down to see Iris take Johannes's hand and squeeze it, and an odd feeling settles over me. Not jealousy —I'd long since gotten over our divorce—but . . . longing. Longing for a special someone in my life.

The sound of Ava's voice saying "Oui" in response to Monsieur Aleu's question draws me back to the moment.

The French civil ceremony is about as warm as appearing before a judge for a moving violation. The *adjoint au maire* reads the marriage laws. And yes, it's as romantic as it sounds. The couple can also choose to exchange personal vows expressing their love and commitment to one another, but Ava and Gervais have decided to wait until what they considered the *real* ceremony, to exchange their heartfelt vows.

"*Je vous declare unis par les liens du mariage*," the *adjoint au maire* pronounces. I declare you united in matrimony.

Ava and Gervais share a brief kiss, and fifteen minutes from start to finish, they are married.

Probably the best part of the French civil ceremony is the *livret de famille*—a small book with their wedding information and plenty of pages to record future family events, including the births of their children.

"*Ma douce fille*," Iris says, taking Ava's face in her hands and kissing her—my sweet daughter. Ava had called her that since birth. A twinge of regret squeezes my heart. I still had to earn back the right to call Ava *mon petit rayon de soleil*. My little ray of sunshine.

Ava wraps an arm around my waist and presses a kiss to my cheek. "*Mon papa. Merci*." She lifts her own blue-gray gaze to mine, so much like my own. "I'm so glad you are here."

I feel tears burn the back of my throat. "So am I. I wouldn't miss it for the world." Or a part in a movie.

Eleanor

I've just stepped out of the shower when my phone rings. Wrapped in the hotel's plush terry robe, I reach my phone in two strides, thinking it's Geoffrey. It's not. It's Abby. Oh dear. I get the feeling Barry finally confessed.

"Hi, sweetheart."

"Mom! Did you know? Why didn't you tell me?" Her voice is rough, as if she's holding back a sob. Guilt washes over me. I should have told her. I should have softened the blow. But no. It was *Barry* who owed her the truth.

"Abby." I keep my voice calm and soothing. "It was your father's responsibility to tell you. I do hope he told you in person."

"He just left. How could he do this? How could you not tell me?" Her voice became more strident. "He's way too old to have another child. I hate him."

I wince. "You don't hate him. You're just very angry and disappointed right now. And if you're angry with me, I accept that. But this is your father's story to tell, not mine."

"Gahhhh. I hate it when you're so calm and rational when I just want to rant and rave. How can you be so . . . forgiving?"

"I wouldn't say I'm all that forgiving, but I've had a few days to get used to the news. You wouldn't have thought me calm and rational when he called to tell me. Interrupting my tour of the Louvre, abruptly ending my day with Geoffrey." Until he came to my room afterward, but that was my little secret.

"I'm going to have a brother or sister twenty-five years younger than me! That's so . . . *Desperate Housewives*!"

I bite back a smile. She's right. When this news gets out in San Sebastian, it will be uncomfortable for a while. People may look at me with pity, or scorn, but it won't kill me, and eventually some other local scandal will take over, and this one will be forgotten. At least Abby is far from the blast zone.

"And I can't believe he had the nerve to invite me to their wedding!"

That last bit got my attention. My breath left in a rush. But what did I expect? It shouldn't come as a surprise given Phoebe's pregnancy.

"So, they're getting married. That I didn't know," I say, as a collapse onto the bed. "When?" I'd like it to be a speedy affair —and over with before I get home.

"Next month."

So much for that plan.

"In San Sebastian?"

"No. It's a destination wedding in St. Kitts."

Thank God for small favors.

"I don't want to go. I don't want to be around that—that . . . tramp."

Tramp? There's an old-fashioned word.

"Do I have to go?"

I smile. That was a refrain when she was a teenager and didn't want to go to some school function. "You're an adult, Abby. You can decide whether you want to go or not. But, I will say this—Phoebe is now part of your father's life, and as much as I detest her for what she did, I do think you and your father need to patch up your relationship. He does love you."

Abby snorts. "If he loved me, he wouldn't have screwed around on you. Or gotten his harlot pregnant."

It's my turn to snort. "Abby, where are you coming up with these words?"

"Mom," she huffs out in frustration, "that's beside the point."

"Listen, you've always wanted a sibling. Now you'll have one." I've always felt guilt over my inability to give Abby a sibling.

"I wanted a little brother or sister who was two or three years younger. Not twenty-five!"

"I know. But I bet the moment you hold that baby in your arms, you'll fall in love. And you're going to be the best big sister ever."

"Maybe the *oldest* big *half*-sister ever," she says with a watery laugh.

Relieved that I've talked her off the ledge, I say, "Maybe that too." I glance over at the clock and realize I'm going to be late if I don't get going. "Are you okay now?"

"I suppose. But I still reserve the right to get pissed off again."

"That's fair. I've got to go and get dressed."

"Got a hot date with Geo-ff-rey?" she sing-songs.

"Dinner." I don't elaborate, because I don't want to break Geoffrey's trust.

"Mom, any chance this could turn into something real?"

The hopeful note in her voice makes my stomach flip. She needs some good news right now, but I can't give that to her. Even if he is attracted to me, nothing can come of it. We live in two different worlds on two different continents.

"Sweetheart, I know you want that, but no. This is strictly a relationship for show."

She sighs. "Well, damn. At least Dad thinks it's real. That's something."

Geoffrey

To maintain the privacy of Ava and Geoffrey's relationship, the wedding dinner is being held in a small private dining room at the Four Seasons. Immediately following the official ceremony, they posed for pictures, before heading back to the hotel.

Upon entering the room, I quickly scan it searching for Ellie. Disappointment fills me when I realize she isn't there yet. I glance at my watch. It isn't like her to be late.

"She'll be here," Iris whispers, giving me a smile.

"What?" *How did she know?*

"Ava told me your—what do I call her—your girlfriend? would be joining us for the dinner." At my frown, she continues, "I'm happy for you Geoffrey. You deserve to have someone in your life who cares for you."

"Oh, but—"

"She's here." Iris nods toward the door behind me.

I practically stumble over my own feet to turn toward the door. Ellie is standing there looking hesitant but stunning in that violet dress she wore to our first dinner. Her hair falls in soft waves around her face. I'd only seen her with straight hair. My fingers itch to plunge my fingers into that thick mass of silver hair and capture her mouth with mine. My feet refuse to move, and before I can coax them into taking a step, Ava reaches Ellie. They exchange a few words, then Ava presses a kiss to her cheek, before taking her hand to lead her to me.

My mouth is dry. My pulse is racing. What the hell is the matter with me? Am I having a heart attack?

"Papa, look who I found," Ava says as she presents Ellie's hand to me.

I reach out blindly and take it, my gaze locking with hers. The corner of Ellie's mouth lifts, and she murmurs something to Ava, who walks in the direction of her husband.

"I'm so sorry I'm late. Abby called. Barry told her about the baby."

This broke my trance. "Ah. And she didn't take it well."

"You could say that. But I think I calmed her down by the end of the call."

I like sharing this intimacy. I like that Ellie feels comfortable sharing this with me. "Do you think she'll come around to the idea of having a baby brother or sister?"

"I do. But enough about my family drama. How was the ceremony?"

"It was . . . civil," I say with a cheeky smile.

"What?"

"Let's just say tomorrow's ceremony will be the romantic one everyone expects."

Eleanor

I admit, I was dreading meeting Geoffrey's ex-wife, but the fact that she is remarried helps. Turns out she and her husband, Johannes, were both kind and charming. And I think I talked them into visiting San Sebastian.

And Ava is such a sweet young lady, and the same age as Abby. The two of them would really hit it off. Her handsome groom, Gervais, made for interesting conversation. Geoffrey had said he was in the financial industry, but what he hadn't said was that Gervais's area of expertise was the fashion industry. I took advantage and picked his brain for industry analytics.

What I thought would be an uncomfortable evening turned out to be an enjoyable one instead. Excellent food, lively conversation, toasts to the couple, and lots of laughter. It was an evening I'll never forget.

And then there's Geoffrey. When I entered the room and saw him standing close to Iris, a petite blond beauty, a flash of jealousy shot through me. Which I realize is absurd. What right do I have to be jealous? He's not mine, nor will he be. But god, he looked so debonair in his navy suit and powder blue tie, the light from the chandeliers sending shots of silver through his hair. And when he turned to gaze in my direction, those blue-gray eyes connected with mine and I'd been transfixed.

He's been by my side off and on throughout the dinner. Understandable, as he is the father of the bride. But whenever he was next to me, it was as if he found any excuse to touch me. His hand finding mine under the table or sitting possessively on my thigh. Whenever we were standing, his arm rested around my waist, or his hand settled on my lower back. The sexual tension between us feels as if it's building to a breaking point.

At one point, while the dessert course was being served, he'd leaned over and whispered in my ear, "I can't keep my eyes off of you. You're so beautiful, Ellie. So, desirable." His warm breath tickled my ear, making me shiver, and the scent of his rich cologne filled my senses, and I'd wanted him with every cell in my body. I'd thought after Barry's infidelity, and after my bout with cancer, that part of my life was behind me. But Geoffrey's charisma and warmth had brought it out of hiding.

And dammit, I'm tired of being afraid. Afraid of being hurt. Afraid of revealing the effects of age and cancer treatment. Maddie is right. I am going to grab this chance and enjoy the hell out of it—and damn the consequences.

Tonight.

Geoffrey

"Would you like to come in?" Eleanor asks as we approach the door to her suite.

My heart stutters. Come in? Like for a drink? Conversation? What? I take the direct approach. "Ellie, in the interest of open communication, I need to know what you mean."

A blush colors her cheeks, and she hesitates before saying, "I'm inviting you to bed." She stops, as if mortified, and begins to ramble. "That is, if you want. It's okay if you don't. You don't need to feel obligated." She pivots toward the door with her keycard, her head down in embarrassment.

"Obligated?" I choke out and turn her back to face me,

lifting her chin. "My god, Ellie. I've wanted you since day one." Her violet eyes widen. "How can you think otherwise?" I take the keycard from her and open her door. Table lamps cast a soft glow on the room. And through the open balcony doors, the Eiffel Tower sparkles in the night like a Christmas tree, lending its own light to the room.

I set the card on the console table by the door and reach out for Ellie, reeling her in. When we're pressed together from chest to hips, her full breasts cushioned against me, I lift her chin and graze her lips with mine. My lips brush back and forth across hers, just a whisper of a touch, until she moans and opens her mouth to me.

Her fingers play in the hair at the nape of my neck, and I shiver at the contact. Her kisses, so hot, so sweet, have me at the brink. I break the kiss, wanting to savor the desire I have for her. It's a push-pull of needing to take her hard and fast, and wanting to taste every inch of her, and make it last.

Ellie steps back and then circles the room, turning off the lamps, so that the only light is that from the Eiffel Tower. She faces me, looking a little nervous. "I'd prefer the lights off."

I read uncertainty in her gaze. A self-consciousness that saddens me. This beautiful woman has nothing to be ashamed of. I want to fight her on this. Tell her how I long to see her—and feel her. Instead, I approach her and place my hands on her shoulders. "Whatever makes you feel more comfortable."

She tosses her bag onto the sofa behind me and steps close, her hands resting on my chest, as she gazes up into my face. "Thank you." Her subtle perfume fills my senses, and my hands fist at my sides to keep from pulling her with me to the couch and tearing the clothes from her body.

One of her hands slides down my arm and, threading her fingers with mine, she leads me to the suite's bedroom. I know this is a big step for her, and my knees go weak with the trust she has in me. When we enter the bedroom, I walk to the bedside table and turn off the glowing lamp, casting the room in shadow, the twenty thousand lights of the Eiffel Tower providing enough light to see Ellie, the alluring shape of her.

I stalk her with deliberate steps, waiting for her to change her mind. When I reach her, I cup her cheek, my thumb stroking her bottom lip. "You're sure?"

She nods her head. "I—it's been a long time. And . . ." She laughs and shakes her head before returning her gaze to mine. "I know it sounds old-fashioned, but I've only ever slept with one man—my ex-husband."

An odd mix of lust and tenderness sweeps through me. That this magnificent woman would choose me as only the second man to share her body with humbles me. "I promise, Ellie, I'll make it so good for you."

Eleanor

God! I couldn't be any more nervous than I am right now! It's true. I was a virgin when I met Barry. As hard as that is to believe, he is the only man I've ever had sex with. Until now. My body has changed so much since the early days of our marriage. My body bears the scars of life. I had a difficult pregnancy. A difficult birth. And my breast! Thus, the darkness. I'd prefer to close the shutters on the tower's lights, but then we'd be groping in utter darkness. I bite my lip. Maybe it's dim enough in here . . .

"Ellie." Geoffrey encloses me in his arms. "You're shaking."

"Am I?" I mutter against his chest. His hard, muscular chest. A chest he'd exposed in *From Paris, With Love*. A chest I would very much like to see for myself. Drawing in a deep breath that fills my senses with his scent, I tilt my head back. "Kiss me."

"With pleasure."

His mouth descends on mine, tasting and nibbling, but I want more. I open to him, and he takes the invitation, his tongue stroking and teasing mine. My breasts press against his hard chest, and the contact sends heat straight to my center.

He changes the angle of the kiss, as his hot mouth plunders mine. I want to crawl inside this man. My body aches with a desire that I thought had faded long ago. He'd taken off his tie earlier in the evening and unbuttoned the top button, leaving a masculine V visible. I start working on the remaining buttons, needing to feel his skin. To taste him. Breaking our kiss, I press open-mouthed kisses to his heated skin and take comfort in his sharply indrawn breath. I must be doing something right. Maybe it *is* like riding a bicycle.

His mouth trails along my jaw, to my neck, his tongue drawing hot little circles on the tender skin there. Then he sucks my earlobe into his mouth, and I gasp. Drawing the shirt over his shoulders and down his arms, I step back to view what I just unveiled, the lights from the tower casting him in shadows and light. He is still beautifully formed. Where so many men our age have gone soft, he's all hard muscle and sharp planes. I cover his firm pecs with my hands, thrilled at the hard nipples that jut into my palm.

"Your turn," he murmurs, sending a shiver down my spine. His fingers graze the zipper at my mid-back, drawing it down at a slow agonizing pace. Suddenly, the snug bodice feels too tight, too confining. Trepidation fills me. Without a bra, I will soon be bare to him. Finally, the dress falls away. The bodice grazes my bare nipples, tightening them into little buds, and I no longer care that my breasts will be bared to him. I am too desperate to feel his big warm hands cupping me. To feel his hot mouth on my sensitive nipples.

His gaze drifts lower, and in a whiplash of feeling, I yearn to cover myself again. In the dim light, I know he can only see shadow and shape, but the modesty is there just the same.

Then his hands are on me, and nothing else matters as I arch into their warmth.

"Ellie. So beautiful. So luscious," he murmurs, as his hands knead and shape my breasts. I am mesmerized by the shadowy view of his hands on me. His thumbs rub over my nipples, and I moan at the pleasure. He lowers his head and his tongue flicks out, teasing a nipple, and I throw my head back with a cry, while his hand works over my other breast. Then he takes my aching nipple into his hot mouth, and I arch into him, as heat shoots along my spine, pooling between my legs.

He slides the zipper lower. My dress falls to the floor in a whisper, and I'm left standing in my heels and panties, completely exposed. His free hand glides along my belly, then cups my sex over my panties. I stiffen, and he pulls back. "What is it?"

Heat burns in my face. Will I be ready for him? I don't know what impact the hormone blockers have had on my sexual response.

"Ellie, please. Talk to me."

"I don't know if I am . . . wet . . . enough. I—"

"Ah." He cups my face in his hands and kisses me gently. "Let me worry about that."

His hands continue their exploration of my body. Skimming down my back, then cupping my ass and squeezing. "You have such a luscious ass." He presses my hips against him and I can feel the hard ridge of his erection against my stomach. He groans at the contact.

"The things I want to do to you, Ellie—you have no idea." His hand drifts around my hip and back to my sex, where he cups me again, his fingers grazing me, and I flinch with the pleasure of it.

"I'd say you have no worries," he murmurs against my breast, as his mouth finds my nipple again. He suckles, and my knees go weak. He releases me and whispers, "You are so wet for me Ellie."

Relief floods me as his fingers dip beneath my panties to the silky wetness I now feel. He groans against my neck. "Sweet Ellie."

I gasp, knowing it won't take long. "Geoffrey," I pant, "I'm so . . ."

"I know." He slides two fingers inside, and with only a couple of strokes, I shatter. My orgasm rocks me to my core, and my legs give out. He lowers me to the bed, his fingers still working in delicious rhythm, my body shuddering with the longest, hardest orgasm I have ever experienced.

I return to earth, to find his arms around me, his hand gently fondling my breast. "You're so beautiful. So . . . real."

I'm spent, but I find enough energy to reach out and cup his straining hard length through his trousers. He groans and pushes into my hands. "I want you. Inside me. Now."

"I thought you'd never ask," he says with a grin.

Geoffrey

I am so hard it hurts. I'd like to think that, at my age, I have acquired patience and the ability to control my body, but not tonight. I won't last long.

I strip off my remaining clothes, my gaze raking over Ellie's silhouette laid out before me like a wedding feast. My eyes stop at the little tuft of curls covering her. I want to taste her, but that will have to wait for round two.

I take a condom out of my wallet and roll it on. Thank God I had one with me.

Ellie props herself up on her elbows and says in a husky voice, "Confident, weren't you?"

"Let's just say hopeful." I lower myself to the bed beside her and skim my hand along her beautiful body. "How would you like it?"

She lifts her head and looks at me, her brow furrowed in confusion. "What?"

"What is your preferred position?"

She bites her lip a moment, then says, "I don't know that I have one."

"Well, we'll figure it out later." I cover her with my body, my erection making contact with her hot skin, and I groan. The pleasure of her naked skin pressed to mine is enough to send me over the edge. I clamp down on my resolve as she opens for me, her hips cradling mine. I enter her wet, welcoming body in one smooth motion. Her chin lifts, her neck arching as I fill her. It. Is. Devastating.

She clasps my ass, pressing me deeper, as her hips thrust upward. "Please, Geoffrey."

No need to beg. I begin to move in slow, deliberate strokes, picking up speed with each downward thrust into her tight body. "I won't last long, Ellie," I grind out through gritted teeth. I pump harder and faster, her cries urging me on until I feel her climax pulsing around me, and I fall over the edge with her in a rush of uncontrollable, shuddering pleasure.

Chapter Seven

DAY SEVEN

Geoffrey

I wake to dawn light filtering through the sheer curtains. Rolling to my side, I'm met with the beautiful bare back of the woman in my bed. I could get used to this view. I slide closer and press kisses along her spine before closing the distance between us, pressing my erection against her lush bottom.

Ellie sighs, pushing back against me, and I groan at the delicious contact.

Brushing her hair aside, I nip and kiss the elegant column of her neck and glide the tips of my fingers along her arm, loving her breathy whimpers. Wanting more of her, I roll her on her back, pleased when the bedsheet slips, baring her breasts to me. My first clear view of the luscious globes.

Something catches my eye, but with a gasp, Ellie yanks the sheet up to cover herself. "No, don't look. It's horrid." Her hands grip the bedclothes like a lifeline.

"Ellie? What is it, love?"

"It's nothing. A scar," she whispers.

A scar? I prop myself up on my elbow and gaze down at her. "It's clearly not nothing." I can't fathom what's the matter. We'd shared all manner of intimacies last night. Why this . . . shame? "Ellie, talk to me. Did I do something to hurt you?"

Her eyes fly open and she shakes her head. "No. No." She worries her lower lip with her teeth and turns her head to gaze out the window at the ever-increasing light, her hands still covering her breasts over the sheet.

A feeling of dread settles over me as I consider the possibilities. Breast cancer? Is this trip some sort of once-in-a-lifetime trip because she doesn't have a lifetime? Feeling sick, I inhale slowly and release my breath on a sigh. "Ellie, you're worrying me."

Her head snaps around to look at me, a frown between her brows. "What?"

"My mind is filled with images I don't like and I'm feeling . . . frightened."

"Why would you feel frightened?"

"I don't know. Why don't you tell me whether I should feel frightened?"

After a few stressful heartbeats, she lifts her hands from her breasts and nods.

I take that to mean that I can remove the sheet. My gaze pinned to hers, I slide the sheet lower, watching for any signs of regret in allowing me this intimacy. I let my gaze fall to her breasts. There—on her left breast, near her armpit—the thing that caught my eye—a scar about two inches long, a slight indentation in the middle. She doesn't have to tell me what it is.

"When?"

"Three years ago."

Life. Is that what she meant when I asked her why she'd

never been to Paris? "And the prognosis?" I have to ask. I have to know.

Before answering, she pulls the sheet back over her. "It's good. Very good, in fact. Best-case scenario. We caught it early. Early enough for a lumpectomy and radiation."

My breath leaves in a *whoosh*. I don't want to think of Ellie facing a long battle, rounds of chemo and radiation, only to lose to the evil disease.

"Even so, the radiation discolored my breast for a time. And the scar . . ." She huffs out a laugh. "Don't get me wrong. I'm incredibly grateful. Grateful to see Abby graduate, fall in love, marry someday. Give me grandchildren." She smiles and her warm gaze finds mine.

She is brilliant. This warrior. This woman who'd found her way into my heart.

"You're so brave."

Confusion flashes across her face. "What? No. I'm just one of many who have gone through this and, lucky for me, came out the other side. I'm not brave. I'm—"

"Beautiful. Brave. Bright. Bold."

She laughs. "Nice alliteration."

I kiss her quick and sweet, then I lift my eyes to hers and place a hand over hers still covering her breasts over the sheet. "Let me, Ellie."

Her fingers tense beneath mine, then relax.

I slide the sheet lower once more and look my fill of her. Her breasts are beautiful, round, and milky white. Her nipples the color of a dusky rose. The scar on her left breast a battle wound. A visual reminder of her bravery.

I ease down and press a kiss to that scar, unsure what her reaction will be. But I want her to know it doesn't mar her beauty. It enhances it. When I rise again to look into her eyes, they sparkle with unshed tears.

"I stopped seeing my breasts as a source of pleasure.

Instead, they became a threat to my life." She sniffs. "But you've reminded me that I *can* find pleasure in them again."

"Oh, Ellie." I settle into the pillows and pull her across my chest, wrapping my arms around her and holding her close. Tucking her head beneath my chin, I stare up at the ceiling.

This can't be happening. I can't be falling in love with this incredible woman I only just met. Or could I?

Eleanor

Geoffrey's comforting arms around me soothe the ache of memories. Of the fear. Of the uncertainty. Of the discomfort at the end of my radiation treatment. And it seems, no matter how many times the surgeon and oncologist says you've had the best outcome anyone could hope for, there is always a doubt in the back of your mind. Will it return? Will you have to face this all over again in the future?

I give myself a mental shake. I'm here now with this incredibly kind, sexy man. What I did last night is so beyond my comfort zone—having sex with a man I'd only just met. And yet I feel . . . renewed. For the first time in a long time, I feel beautiful.

I'm becoming aware of the heat of his bare skin beneath mine. The fullness of my breasts pressed against his hard chest. The feel of his mouth against my temple. A hunger, warm and liquid, blooms in my core and spreads down my legs and up my spine. I want Geoffrey. I want to feel him inside me again. I want to feel the deep connection I felt last night when our bodies were joined.

I press an open-mouthed kiss to his chest and smile at the

sharp intake of his breath. Lifting my head, I gaze into his cool blue-gray eyes, now dilated with desire. "Love me, Geoffrey," I whisper.

"With pleasure."

He rolls me to my back and captures my mouth with his in a kiss—hot enough to singe the sheets. Tongues tangling, teeth nipping, lips gliding, awakening every nerve in my body. He begins a slow descent, his tongue circling, drawing wet lines along my collarbone, then down to my chest, and finally across a taut nipple. I gasp and arch into him, offering him more, no longer caring about my scar.

He continues mapping my body with his tongue, heading south. When he circles my navel, I twist and buck against him, laughing.

"Ah, a ticklish spot," he murmurs against my skin, sending shivers along my torso. I look down the length of my naked body at his heated gaze, and it is the most erotic image I have ever seen. "Any others?" He doesn't wait for a response before dragging his tongue in a straight line from my navel to my mound. I groan at the sheer ecstasy of it.

When he settles between my legs, spreading me wide before him, my first instinct is to pull away. Then his mouth is on me and I cry out.

"You like that?"

I gasp. "What's not to like?"

His hot breath escapes with a chuckle. "It just occurred to me . . . we never had a follow-up intimacy talk. Are you comfortable with this?" The grin on his face sends a jolt of desire through me.

I groan in frustration and arch my hips.

"I'll take that to mean you're okay with my mouth on you here." He strokes me again, and my head falls back onto the pillow.

"Oh! Geoffrey! My god!"

He takes his sweet time, his tongue and mouth doing wicked things to me, until I feel the orgasm building, and then the explosion that sends shards of pleasure out to every cell in my body. He lingers there until the shudders fade and I've rejoined my body. I reach for him. "I want you, Geoffrey. Now. Please."

He crawls up my body, his hard length hot against my skin, and I ache to feel that inside me. He reaches over to the nightstand and opens the remaining foil package. "So glad I had a few with me."

After sheathing himself, he pulls me from the bed, and I wonder what he's doing.

"Bend over," he instructs, his voice gruff.

Oh. What he wants dawns on me. Before I can stop the embarrassing confession, I blurt out, "I've never done it this way."

The slow glide of his hand down my spine halts. "Really? Do you not want—"

I push my bottom back against his hardness in response. "I didn't say that." A thrill shoots through me at the thought of him covering me from behind.

"God, Ellie. I wish you could see how beautiful you are. Your smooth skin, your round ass." His hand continues its path down my spine and my desire rockets to a new level.

"Geoffrey," I grind out.

He chuckles and steps closer until I feel him poised at my entrance. He grips my hips and, in a slow deliberate motion, enters me until he's fully seated. My breath catches. I've never felt so . . . filled. "Oh my god," I groan.

"Sweet heaven, Ellie." He begins to move in an easy gliding rhythm, but it isn't long before he begins to thrust hard and fast, taking my breath away with the pleasure of it. His grip on my hips tightens, and I welcome the pressure of his fingertips digging into my flesh.

Another orgasm breaks over me and I collapse onto the mattress with the force of it. Geoffrey is right behind me, his deep-chested moans filling the spaces between my helpless whimpers of pleasure.

He folds over me, his breath hot against my skin. I don't think I've ever felt so thoroughly used. His lips graze along my back and I shiver.

"You okay?" he asks.

"More than okay. I'm . . . replete."

"I like that word." He lifts his weight from me and helps me to stand, patting me on the butt. "I'll be back."

I watch him walk toward the bathroom, admiring the broad shoulders that taper to narrow hips, and then the firm globes of his ass. "Beautiful man," I murmur as I crawl back into bed and gaze out at the gauze-filtered Eiffel Tower.

If someone had told me three years ago that I'd be in Paris right now sharing a bed with Geoffrey Harrison, I would've shaken my head at the ludicrous notion.

Completely unconcerned with his nakedness, Geoffrey retraces his steps and joins me in the bed, pulling me to him, pressing a kiss to the top of my head.

"I have a confession to make." I frown immediately after the statement leaves my mouth. My sex-fogged brain seems to have lost its filter.

"What's that?"

Well, in for a penny, in for a pound, as my mother used to say. "I watched one of your movies." I sit up so I can see his reaction.

"You did?" He draws back to look into my face. "Which one?"

"*From Paris, With Love.*"

He smiles and nods, then the smile fades, and I can see the wheels turning.

"One scene in particular seemed very familiar to me—almost a case of déjà vu." I say, recalling the scene where Alex feeds Emma.

He has the grace to look chagrinned. "Busted."

"Have you replayed any other scenes from your movies? The ice cream analysis?" I pin him with a reprimanding stare.

He holds up his hands. "No. I swear. I see now that it was wrong. I was hoping to score points with my fans familiar with the movie."

"Uh-huh." I lie back in his arms again. "If you decide to do it again, I'd appreciate a little warning."

"Done. I mean, I don't plan on doing it again, but if inspiration strikes, I'll tell you ahead of time. I promise."

There's a pause of a few heartbeats, then, "And dare I ask what you think, otherwise?" His voice held a note of reticence.

"I enjoyed it. Except for the part where you and Emma kiss, and . . . go to bed." I wince. Damn brain fog. I hadn't meant to say that.

"Jealous, were you?"

"A little," I say with a shrug.

"I like it."

I snort. Men and their egos.

"Any other confessions you'd like to make?"

I bite my lip, uncertain if I should say what I'm thinking. Oh, go for it. What more do you have to hide? "I think you're more handsome in person."

"You do?"

"I do." I play with the smattering of hair on his hard chest sprinkled with gray. "Because in person, I can feel your warmth, I can inhale your scent. And I can taste your lips."

He stretches his arms out wide. "I'm all yours, Ellie. Feel, smell, taste every last inch of me if you want."

"With pleasure," I say, echoing his earlier words to me.

Geoffrey

I glance at my watch and stride to the room set aside for Ava's use. We're bumping up against ceremony time and I've heard nothing from Ava or Iris. I knock, then enter, and stop in my tracks at the sight of my daughter in her wedding dress. She is a vision! I blink back tears thinking of all the years I missed. Years I'll never get back. But I'm here now, and I am beyond happy to share this day with my beautiful girl.

Then I notice her wringing her hands. "What is it? What's wrong?"

"Oh, Papa. I have torn the hem of my dress. What am I going to do? I'm afraid I'll trip with the front of my hem out." She drops her hands and indicates the drooping section of her hem.

"You know I can't sew a button, much less repair a wedding gown," Iris reminds me. "Perhaps one of the hotel staff?"

"No. I have the perfect person for the job. Don't worry, *mon petit rayon de soleil*. I'll be right back." I step out of the room and pull my phone from my pocket. Thank goodness I decided to keep it with me. I dial Ellie, hoping she's already dressed.

"Hello?"

"Ellie, we have a dress emergency. Can you come to the room across the hall from the wedding venue?"

"On my way."

I pace the hall for a few minutes then glance up to see Ellie walking down the hallway, looking drop-dead gorgeous in a dress the color of green grass, its nipped in waist giving way to a full skirt that falls just above slim ankles, her feet in strappy flesh-colored sandals. Sweet Jesus. I could throw that full skirt up and take her all over again like I did this morning.

Not the time or place, I remind myself. Later.

"What's wrong?"

"Ava somehow ripped the front hem of her dress. Please tell me you know how to sew."

"Of course, I do. You can't design clothes without knowing how to sew. Tell her I can repair it so she doesn't worry, and I'll go ask for a sewing kit."

I grab her by the shoulders and kiss her on the lips. "Thank you."

She shakes her head with a laugh then retraces her steps down the hall toward the lobby. "Remind me later to tell you how beautiful you look," I call to her.

Eleanor

I knock on the door of the room before entering. Geoffrey is still waiting when I arrive. He is so sexy in his pearl-gray suit, white dress shirt, and pale pink tie. And to think, I now know what he looks like beneath that suit. And what he feels like. I feel heat rise to my cheeks.

"They're bringing a sewing kit. Oh! Ava, you are stunning." She'd chosen a vintage-style bateau neck A-line gown. The satin bodice fit her delicate frame and the full-length tulle skirt enhanced her long legs. A satin bow at the waist and a band of satin at the hem of the skirt were the only embellishment. The satin band at the front of the dress hung loose from the tulle of the skirt.

"Oh, dear. I can see why you need the hem repaired. That won't do, will it?" I ask with an assuring smile.

"I'll leave you in Ellie's capable hands while I check on the groom," Geoffrey tells Ava.

"I'll join you," Iris says, as she leaves the room with him.

A member of the hotel staff arrives with the sewing kit, and I work quickly to thread a needle with ivory thread. I kneel in front of Ava.

"Oh, but your dress!" she exclaims. "It will wrinkle."

I gaze up at her. She is such a beautiful bride. "Never mind that. It's your day, not mine. Just stand still for a few minutes and I'll have this repaired in no time." I concentrate on the neat, even stitches for a few breaths.

"My father likes you very much," Ava says, and I freeze with the needle halfway in the fabric.

"Well, I like him too. You have a wonderful father, Ava." Despite his past mistakes.

"*Non*, you misunderstand. I mean he likes you as a man likes a woman."

I shake my head, not looking at her. I know Geoffrey has confided to her that our relationship is fake, not wanting to deceive her any more than I wanted to deceive Abby. "No. It's all part of his social media campaign."

"You fool yourself, Ellie." The lilt of her French accent places emphasis on the last syllable of my name. "I saw the way he looked at you last night at dinner. And that was not for the social media campaign. That was a man enthralled."

Enthralled? No. Perhaps Ava is so steeped in the romance of her wedding and new marriage that she thinks she sees romance where it doesn't exist. I don't answer, unsure what to say that won't hurt her.

"Did you know he is foregoing a meeting with a famous director because he doesn't want to leave before your holiday in Paris is over?"

"Oh no. He passed on the meeting because he didn't want to miss any of the wedding activities."

"Yes, of course. He made a promise to me, and he has kept it. But the director was willing to meet tomorrow or Monday. Papa told him no, because he had another commitment." I can feel her gaze on me, but I focus on the last stitch, not glancing up. "That commitment is you."

My mind whirls with this news. What is Geoffrey thinking? This could be his big chance. The whole purpose of this blasted social media campaign, our agreement—our fake relationship—is to break through the roadblocks he's been facing the last few years. No. Ava must be mistaken. She likely has a case of bride-brain. No point arguing over it.

I tie off the thread and snip the needle from it with a tiny pair of scissors. "There. You're all set." I rise to my feet, suppressing a groan. Seems my sexual escapades with Geoffrey have left me sore.

Ava surprises me by taking me by the shoulders and pressing a kiss to each of my cheeks. "*Merci beaucoup*, Ellie. You have saved the day for me." She gives me a broad smile, and for a moment, I can see Abby standing before me on her own wedding day.

"Go marry the man you love." And I'll try to wait until after the festivities to confront your father.

Geoffrey

Ava told me that in small French villages, the groom would collect the bride from her home and they would proceed to the church in a sort of caravan with musicians leading the way. Children would hold out white ribbons to block the bride's path, to symbolize the bride overcoming obstacles married life might bring. The bride would have to cut the ribbons to proceed into the church.

Today, however, couples cut a heart shape into a white sheet for the bride and groom to go through together following the ceremony.

There are no bridesmaids, maids or matrons of honor, groomsmen, or best men. Only two witnesses. But Gervais's niece and nephew, Chloe and Lucien, will precede Ava and me down the aisle.

For the ceremony, Ava chose the hotel's Cour de Marbre, a stunning outside courtyard. As the name implies, the space is paved with magnificent marble tiles that add to its grandeur and sophistication. The beautiful and tranquil courtyard creates an oasis in the midst of the busy city. Little decoration is needed, since the courtyard features manicured gardens and seasonal décor. A fountain in the center lends the sounds of cascading water as a backdrop to the stringed quartet playing in a corner of the courtyard.

After ensuring Ellie is taken to her seat, I return to Ava for one of the greatest roles of my life—father of the bride. She's smiling and a little teary-eyed. "Papa, thank you. Thank you for being here."

"Shhh." I cup her cheek. "There is nowhere else I would rather be. Now stop crying. The guests will think you've changed your mind."

She laughs and shakes her head. "It is too late for that, *n'est-ce pas*? I am already a married woman."

We line up behind Gervais and his mother, who will walk down the aisle first, followed by the children, Chloe scattering rose petals, Lucien carrying the ring.

The strains of *Sinfonia in G* begin—our cue. I have never felt such a mix of emotions—pride, regret, longing, and most of all love. This beautiful person is my daughter, and I missed most of her life because of my chosen profession. Was it worth it? Would pursuing this desperate campaign to rehabilitate my flagging career be worth it if it meant missing out on potential future happiness, like grandchildren? And is Ellie part of that future? I spot her among the guests, a beautiful smile on her face, and are those . . . tears in her eyes?

Before I can ponder the reason for the tears, I must present Ava to Gervais and take my seat next to Iris and Johannes. Unlike most other western wedding traditions, where the bride and groom stand for their vows, French couples are seated on red velvet chairs for the ceremony.

Ava and Gervais exchange their own heartfelt personal vows. Much more romantic than the impersonal vows exchanged during the civil ceremony. As I watch my daughter embark on her new life with a partner by her side, I feel another pang of loneliness. This feeling isn't helped when I glance over and see my ex-wife and her husband holding hands. My shoulders twitch with the need to look behind me. To find Ellie. To see her violet eyes gazing into mine.

Has what started as a fake romance developed into something real? But even if it has, the situation is untenable. She lives in the U.S. She has a life, a business there. She could never live in England, or France, or even New York, for that matter. She could never follow me from movie location to movie location, as Iris once did in the early carefree days of our marriage. And the near-constant separation would slowly erode the relationship, just as it did between Iris and me.

No, even if this isn't fake, it's just a fling. Destined to burn out as quickly as it began.

But as Ava kisses her groom, I can't shake the now-deep feeling of loneliness.

Eleanor

I feel a little like a fifth wheel, with no other friends or acquaintances attending. I would even welcome the company of Iris, but she, her husband, and Geoffrey are all occupied with the usual post-wedding photos. I wander into the hotel's Salon Auteuil for the cocktail hours—and I do mean "hours." Geoffrey warned me the *le vin d'honneur* can last two to three hours! He'd also warned me the reception will last all night. I can't remember the last time I stayed up past midnight, much less all night, but I am determined to pull it off.

I only hope Geoffrey won't be occupied the entire cocktail time. I am sorely tempted to return to my room and have him text me when he arrives.

Coward. You're a mature woman. You know how to talk to people. And it gives you more opportunity to speak French.

So, I suck it up and enter the elegant space furnished with pub tables set with ivory linens. The room itself is elegant, with lush carpeting, gold sconces, white paneled walls, and chandeliers dripping with crystals. Closed double doors at the end of the room lead to what I assume is the ballroom, where the sit-down dinner will be held.

This wedding must cost a fortune. It appears no expense was spared. Small by American standards, with wedding guests numbering only about fifty or so. I'm sure the list was limited to friends and family who will be discreet and not post on social media, outing Ava as Geoffrey's daughter. It's a miracle it's remained a secret for this long.

It's a relief not to be followed by Hélène and Stéphane. Not that they aren't lovely people, but I am happy for a respite from the cameras. The only cameras permitted here are those of the hired photographers. Guests were asked to leave their smartphones with a hotel attendant to be picked up at the end of the night. I left mine in the room after Geoffrey called me about the wardrobe issue.

A waiter carrying a tray of mini tarts approaches and says, "Madame?" I'm famished, so I take a cocktail napkin and a tart before thanking the young man. Scanning the room, I spot a table laden with wines. Selecting a crisp chardonnay, I pop the delicious flaky tart into my mouth. And of course, that is when an older man who was also selecting a glass of wine turns to me and asks in French how I know the bride or groom.

I freeze for a second, using my full mouth as an excuse. I hadn't considered this possibility. Oh, where is Geoffrey when I need him? What do I say? *Oh, I'm having a fake romance with the bride's father? Or maybe I'm just having sex with the father of the bride?* I swallow the tart, but it becomes a lump in my throat, and I respond in French, "I am a friend of the bride's father." Sweet and simple. "And you?"

He eyes me quizzically, and I wonder if he's on social media and has seen my face. But he simply says, "I am a friend of the groom's parents." We chat for a few more minutes—small talk about the ceremony, how beautiful the bride looked, whether they will be serving the traditional *bœuf bourguignon* for dinner, etc. Then he nods and takes his leave. I breathe a sigh of relief.

After a few more rounds of the reception area and more small talk with guests, I'm thinking a trip to the ladies' room would be a good way to waste a little time, when a voice whispers in my ear, "I've been thinking about you." I shiver involuntarily at the warmth of his breath on my ear and turn toward Geoffrey. He is devastating, his eyes warm with happiness. Then I wonder what people will think when they see us standing close together like this, and I step back.

He lifts a brow in question. "What is it?"

I glance around to see if we're being watched. God, I'm

getting paranoid. "I don't know how to act. Are we pretending to be a couple here? Or are we just friends?" Like I told the gentleman earlier.

He snakes an arm around my waist and pulls me to him. "We aren't pretending anything. You're my date. I'm yours. Now, let's go enjoy ourselves. Would you like a sneak peek at the ballroom?"

"Yes!" After the lavish wedding ceremony and this reception, I've been dying to see the ballroom.

"This way." He takes me out of the room and down a hallway to another set of double doors. "This is the staff entrance, but I didn't want other guests to see us entering the ballroom before the designated time." He flings open the doors, and I gasp at the luxurious décor.

Tables surrounded by Louis XIV chairs upholstered in cream brocade are set with the palest of pink linens, encircling a parquet dance floor. Towering vases of antique roses, their centers pink, their outer petals cream with hints of green, fill the room with their scent. The bright ceiling and gold-leaf architectural details of the space lend an old-world elegance to the atmosphere. "It's gorgeous!"

"It is, isn't it? This was all Ava's vision. I'm so happy I could give it to her."

I step next to him and wrap an arm around his waist, knowing how sincere he is about this.

Hotel catering staff, who are putting the final touches on the meal, give us a curious look.

He hauls me behind a potted palm and turns toward me. "I have been waiting all evening for this."

"For what?" I ask, as I gaze into his eyes.

"This." He leans down and takes my mouth with his, gently at first, tasting my lips, before parting them with his tongue. I moan into the kiss, wrapping my arms around his neck and pulling him closer. Even when his body is flush against mine, it's not enough. I need more.

He breaks the kiss with an indrawn breath, and we're both panting like we've just surfaced from the bottom of a deep pool. He touches his forehead to mine with a wry smile. "If it were up to me, I'd lift the skirt of that beautiful dress and have you against the wall, right here and now."

The words spill over me like warm honey. "But I suppose tupping a woman at your daughter's wedding dinner would be frowned upon."

"To say the least." He leans down again and nips at my ear before saying, "Later."

I shiver in anticipation, but first things first. While we have this moment of complete privacy, I ask, "Why aren't you meeting with the director?"

He stiffens. "Who? Ava."

I step back. "She said the director was willing to meet with you tomorrow or Monday."

He's already shaking his head. "I made a commitment to show you Paris. I won't break that commitment."

"Do you think I would hold you to that, given the whole purpose of this," I gesture between the two of us, "fake romance? It appears you're getting the result you hoped for."

His mouth is set in a firm line. "Bad timing. Another opportunity will come along."

"Maybe. But what if it doesn't? I don't want you to regret passing on this meeting, especially for something as trivial as this."

Geoffrey

. . .

I release Ellie and step back.

Trivial? Is that what she thinks of us?

Of course she does. What else is she supposed to think? After all, this is just a fake romance I cooked up to gain attention. I'd do well to remember that. But I'm still not meeting the director. I'm going to enjoy these last three days with Ellie. Then our "romance" will end with a fond farewell.

The thought makes me sick. Even the thought of a new film project doesn't interest me like it used to. All I can think about are long days and even longer nights without Ellie. All the more reason I won't give up the remaining time we have together.

"I won't regret it. We'd better go. They'll be opening the doors to the other guests soon." Ellie doesn't argue further and allows me to escort her from the room.

We reach Salon Auteuil just in time for the staff to open the double doors leading into the ballroom. Standing back, I wait for the flood of guests to precede us, Ellie standing next to me. As soon as the guests are seated, Ava and Gervais will arrive to great fanfare.

Traditionally, newlyweds make their entrance in the "broom car" or *la voiture balai*, which could be a horse-drawn carriage or vintage car, neither of which would work in the hotel, for obvious reasons. Ava and Gervais selected a little something different.

"We're at table three." I guide Ellie to a table set along the dance floor and pull out her chair. After seeing her settled, I take a seat myself. Leaning over, I murmur, "Ava and Gervais should be here any moment."

The low hum of voices fades away at the sound of an electric motor. To the delight of the guests, the bride and groom arrive on a white electric scooter decorated with tulle and roses. Ava sits side-saddle behind Gervais, her long skirts draped over one arm, a bouquet in her hand. Her other arm is wrapped around Gervais's waist.

I glance over at Ellie, and she's smiling from ear to ear, her eyes bright with laughter, her previous pique evaporated. "Oh, this is wonderful!"

I can't resist. I lean over to her and press a quick, ebullient kiss on her mouth, catching her off-guard, our teeth colliding. She lifts her hand to her mouth and laughs again, shaking her head. I love seeing her like this—happy. Relaxed. Free.

A horde of hotel wait staff parade into the ballroom, their arms laden with plates of food covered with gold cloches. The *repas de noces*, or wedding meal, is being served. Of course, the food will be excellent, reflecting the finest in French cuisine, with selections like *bœuf bourguignon*, potatoes *au gratin*, and *coq au vin*. French onion soup will be served around 4 a.m., before the guests leave.

And of course, the Champagne is flowing with a *fontaine de Champagne*. The fountain, arranged by a professional, consists of flutes or coupes arranged in a pyramid shape. The Champagne is poured into the topmost cups, allowing it to flow down into the cups below.

"Champagne?" I ask Ellie.

"Please."

After snaring two glasses from the fountain, I return to find her in conversation with Iris. It's odd to see my ex-wife chatting amiably with Ellie. Initially, our divorce had been acrimonious, but over the years, we've mended our relationship, mainly for Ava's sake. But I consider Iris a friend, if not a confidante, and I'm glad to see her and Johannes happy.

Tapping Ellie on the arm, I present her with her glass.

"Thank you." She takes a sip, closes her eyes, and her lips lift in a small smile. "Delicious."

The urge to take her mouth again, to taste the Champagne

there, is overwhelming. Instead, I take a sip from my own glass and direct my attention to the plate of food laid before me.

"Will there be a wedding cake?" Ellie asks, as she eyes the sumptuous feast before her.

"Not in the American sense. In France, the 'cake' is called a *croquembouche*."

Ellie frowns in confusion. "Crunch in the mouth?"

I laugh at the translation. "Roughly. It's a pyramid of cream-filled profiteroles in all different flavors. Guests take three or four of the cream puffs, rather than a slice of cake."

"Do the bride and groom feed each other?"

"Yes. After all, it's a symbol of the commitment to provide for one another, remember?" I say, reminding her of our conversation at Angelina, and the scene in *From Paris, With Love.*

She smirks and turns to her meal now that all guests at the table have been served.

"I'll get you another glass," I say, pointing to her empty Champagne glass.

"Oh no. I shouldn't."

I draw close to her. "Ellie, when was the last time you let go? Besides last night?"

Her eyes widen as her cheeks pinken, then she opens her mouth, frowns, and then closes it again.

"Right. So another glass it is."

Eleanor

"This is my cue," Geoffrey rises from his chair. He'd already told me he and Ava would be opening the dancing with a father-daughter dance. These things always play on my emotions, and as the first strains of Stevie Wonder's "You are the Sunshine of My Life" begin, I blink back tears. It's the perfect song for him to dance with his *petit rayon de soleil*.

The two are so lovely together, swaying to the music as he whispers to her, her arms wrapped around his neck. I worry that Barry and Abby's relationship will not recover. I'd hate to see that. As angry as I am at Barry, I want to watch their father-daughter dance someday, just as I'm watching Geoffrey and Ava's now.

Feeling a little morose, I reach for my glass of Champagne. I've lost count and, thanks to the efficient hotel staff, I can't even rely on the empty glasses to keep track. There had been countless toasts, and fresh glasses have been appearing as if by magic. I'm feeling a little woozy, but I kind of like the sensation and can't remember the last time I've been tipsy, so I take another deep pull of the bubbly, enjoying the tickle.

In keeping with tradition, Geoffrey gives Ava away to her groom, and they finish the dance together.

After the dance, the bride and groom make their way over to the towering confection that is the *croquembouche*. Amid yet more toasts, the couple each feed the other a cream puff and kiss to the applause of the guests. Seems feeding cake (or cream puffs) to one another is a well-recognized tradition, and I think back to our tea at Angelina, and how intimate and sensual Geoffrey's feeding me felt.

Speaking of Geoffrey, I've lost track of him, and Iris and Johannes are out on the dance floor, so I'm left alone at the table. Wishing I had another cold glass of bubbly, I turn in the direction of the fountain, only to see Geoffrey making his way back to the table, juggling a plate of what appears to be cream puffs and two glasses of Champagne.

The sheer masculine grace of Geoffrey knocks the breath from my lungs, and I want to climb him like a tree. I shake my head. "I'm drunker than I thought," I mutter.

He takes his seat and eyes me.

"What? Do I have something on my face?" I ask, brushing the side of my cheek.

"No. But you look like you'd enjoy taking a bite out of me."

I shiver at the gruff words. "Maybe I would." I prop my chin in my hand and smile. At least I hope it's a smile and not a grimace.

"Maybe I'll let you. Later. In the meantime, you're a little plastered. Eat some cream puffs."

"Your fault," I point out. I gaze longingly at the delicate cream puffs on the fine bone china plate. I lean toward him. "Aren't you going to feed me?"

He grins. "You're cute when you're toasted."

He lifts a profiterole to my lips, and I take the sinful creaminess into my mouth, sucking some of the escaped cream from his fingers. His eyes dilate, and he releases a groan deep in his throat. "You're killing me, Ellie. We're here for at least another three or four hours. You keep that up, and I might lay you out across this table and feast on you instead of dessert."

Warmth pools between my thighs. "I think I'd like that."

"Okay, time for some fresh air. I've apparently created a monster." He takes my wrist and helps me from my seat.

"Where are you taking me?" My eyes widen. "Ooh, are we going somewhere private so you can take me against a wall?"

Geoffrey curses before saying, "Tempting. But no."

We reach glass double doors that open onto a quiet terrace, and he escorts me over to the railing, his big warm hand on the small of my back. The air is cool after the stuffiness of the ballroom, and I shiver slightly. My head begins to clear, but for some reason I don't want to lose my buzz. It's loosened my tongue and given me the courage to tell Geoffrey what I want—him.

"Better?" he asks, as he pulls me into the circle of his arms.

"No."

"No? Do you want me to get some coffee for you?"

"No. I don't want to sober up. I want to stay loose and have fun."

I can hear the laughter in his voice. "Okay. We'll get more Champagne then. But first, look." He points to the sky in the direction of the Eiffel Tower.

"Oh," I breathe. A full moon hangs suspended above the Eiffel Tower, adding its soft glow to the Paris skyline. "I had no idea it was a full moon."

"Ava and Gervais selected this date for that very reason."

"Very romantic."

"Ellie." He takes me by the shoulders and gazes into my eyes. "This is not trivial to me. I *want* to spend the last three days of your visit together. Understand?"

I nod, unable to speak. The warmth in his eyes takes my breath. Finally, I stammer, "I—I'm glad. I want to spend them together too."

His head lowers to mine, and he nips at my lower lip, the bite sending a bolt of desire up my spine. "I plan to make good on my promise to feast on you. But for now, how about a dance?"

"I thought you'd never ask."

Geoffrey

"I am exhausted. I had many a long night when Abby was a baby, but I was much younger, then." Ellie drops onto the bed in her suite and then flops back on the mattress, arms akimbo. I laugh and drop to a knee to remove her shoes.

"Oh god. Yes."

Her moans send my blood racing south. As much as I want to make love to her, I also want her coherent when I do. I massage her feet, knowing full well it will elicit more breathy moans, so I brace myself.

Ellie doesn't disappoint. "Oh yes. Right there," she groans as I press my thumb into her tender arch.

I clench my teeth, trying to think of anything other than burying myself deep inside her. The final bill for my daughter's extravagant wedding should do the trick.

Ellie sits up. "Bathroom," she mutters as she rises to her feet, then presents her bare back to me. "Zipper."

Sweet Jesus, she's killing me. Just the sound of her zipper rasping as I pull the tab down is enough to make me hard enough to pound nails. As soon as the zipper is open, I pat her on the bottom, and she heads for the bathroom.

I take advantage of the suite's second bathroom and get ready for bed. I close the room-darkening drapes so that first light, which isn't too far away, won't wake us. I'm naked and in bed when the door opens. She's in the silk robe she wore the first night I visited her room, and from the way it hugs her subtle curves, I can tell she's wearing nothing underneath.

She flips off the lights, casting the room in darkness, heightening my other senses. The swooshing of the fabric as she crosses the room. The scent of lavender from her lotion. The soft sigh of relief as she crawls into bed. The feel of her warm, bare skin as she presses her back to my front.

A few hours may be too long to wait to make love to her again, but I suck it up and drape my arm over the curve of her waist and bury my face in her hair. "Good night, Ellie."

I'm met with a soft snuffle as she falls asleep in mere moments.

As exhausted as I am, I can't fall asleep. Ellie's warm, fragrant body pressed against mine has my imagination in overdrive. So many things I want to do with her, for her, to her, and only three days left. As much as I'd like to spend those three days in bed, I want to show her more of Paris before she leaves.

Before she leaves.

I don't want her to leave. I want her to stay. I want to experience her every mood. I want to wake up in the morning with her in my bed. I want to spend the evenings alone with her, watching the moon rise high in the Paris sky and watching the sun usher in the day. In short, I want more of Ellie Marshall.

Much more than I can ever have.

Chapter Eight

DAY EIGHT

Eleanor

I slowly drift up through a fog to awareness. Aware of the hard male body pressed to my back. Aware of the large, warm hand resting on my abdomen. Aware of the hot erection insistent against my *derrière*.

I can't help the smile of pleasure. Then I sigh, remembering this romance has an expiration date that is closing in fast.

I wiggle my ass against Geoffrey's erection, hoping to rouse him from his sleep. Then I open my legs and reach between them to grip his hard shaft and guide him to my opening, surprised at how ready I am. I push against him until he glides inside me, eliciting a low throaty groan from him.

The hand on my stomach skims over me until it settles on my breast, kneading and fondling, as his lips find the sensitive skin where my neck meets my shoulder. His hips move in slow thrusts, sliding in and out, in and out, in a sleepy rhythm.

"God, I could get used to this." His warm breath tickles my skin.

"Mmm. Me too." I lift my top leg, allowing him better access, and he takes it, using it to our advantage. As he pumps into me from behind, his hand glides down to where we are joined, giving me what I need as the tension builds. I reach behind me and grip his hips, squeezing as he thrusts with more insistence.

"Oh, Geoffrey," I moan, as a gentle, but by no means lackluster, orgasm breaks over me like an ocean wave, leaving me breathless and shaking.

"I've got you," he groans, before thrusting into me one last time, his own orgasm carrying him under the same breaking wave.

Only then do I realize we didn't use protection, and it was . . . glorious.

He pulls out with a sigh, apparently realizing the same thing. "I'm sorry, Ellie."

I roll over to face him and lay a hand over his cheek. "Not your fault. At least I can't get pregnant," I say with a laugh.

"There is that. Ellie, I promise I'm clean. I haven't been with a woman in over a year."

I nod. "And I haven't been with anyone since Barry."

He places a soft kiss on my cheek. "Now that that's settled . . ." He rises from the bed and pads across the floor, drawing open the drapes to let in a sliver of sunshine, then to the chair where his clothes from the night before are draped. Reaching into a pocket, he removes a small pouch and brings it back to the bed. "This is for you."

I sit up in bed and my gaze drops to the pink silk pouch in his hand, then back up to his face. "What—"

"Happy anniversary." A smile spreads across his face.

"Anni—?" Completely confused, until I recall the date, and it dawns on me. "But how did you know?"

"You told me when you finished your treatment." He shrugs, "I did the math."

Tears blur my vision at his thoughtfulness.

"Open it."

I untie the strings on the bag and shake the contents out into the palm of my hand.

"It's pink lapis," he volunteers.

Lifting the pale pink beaded necklace, I see it forms the shape of a ribbon, like the iconic pink breast cancer ribbon. I blink, and a tear rolls down my cheek. "It's . . . I don't know what to say." I grip the back of his neck and pull his mouth down to mine, pouring all my emotions into the kiss, tasting salt as another tear slides down my cheek.

He's killing me. Inch by inch, Geoffrey is killing me—with kindness and thoughtfulness and romance. How am I going to let him go in just two short days? Just when I think my heartbreak over Barry is healing, another one lies just around the corner.

We're both panting when he ends the kiss, then thumbs away my tears. "Don't cry. This is a day to celebrate, and I intend to do just that. Here, let me put it on you." He takes the necklace from me and fastens it around my neck, then glides his hand over the stones before settling it over my left breast. "Brave, beautiful Ellie."

He kneels before me and takes my left nipple into his mouth. With a breathy moan, I give myself over to him, all thoughts of my impending heartbreak dissipate like a Paris fog in the face of the sun.

Geoffrey

. . .

"Where are we going today?" Ellie asks as we exit the elevator.

"Well, since we slept till the crack of noon and missed breakfast, I thought we'd start with a late lunch, then walk around the Luxembourg Gardens. I promised we'd return when the weather was better."

"Yes, a walk sounds perfect." She sighs, slips her arm through mine, and leans her head on my shoulder, an affectionate gesture that melts my heart, yet also sends my brain into panicked overdrive. *She's leaving. In two days.*

Shut up, and enjoy what's left, I tell my panicked brain.

I glance down at Ellie's breezy pants and tank top, a pair of comfy-looking flats on her feet. Stylish but practical. A thrill of pleasure courses through me at the sight of the necklace I gave her lying against her skin.

The flowy fabric of her clothes hides the lovely curves I'd kissed and licked and touched just an hour ago, and yet I'm ready to do it all again. In our rush to get out and enjoy the day, she'd left her hair to air dry, revealing the lush waves she'd been hiding all week. The waves give off a different vibe—carefree and sensual. A hidden side of Ellie. Her bold sunglasses will block the sun, on full display this glorious mild afternoon. Yes, a walk beside this beautiful woman does sound perfect.

With Ava's wedding behind me, I can truly relax. Nothing pressing on my mind. Oddly, not even running down my next role. I'm all Ellie's.

"But first, we'll take the car to La Maison du Jardin because I'm famished." I lean down and whisper in her ear, "I worked up an appetite," then watch as a flush creeps up her neck and into her cheeks. I love that I can make her blush. So many women in my profession are jaded and no longer seem capable of blushing.

I open the car door for Ellie and greet the driver, Maurice.

Hélène and Stéphane are meeting us at the café, although, to be honest, I couldn't care less whether they meet us or not.

This is no longer about the social media campaign. It's about me and Ellie and making the most out of an experience that has been one of the best of my life, second only to Ava's birth and wedding.

"What do you know about the gardens?"

"Not much. I know they were created at the behest of King Louis XIII's mother—"

"Queen Marie de Médici," I interject.

"To complement the Luxembourg Palace she'd commissioned, and that the Orangerie Museum is in the gardens. That's about the extent of my knowledge."

As we make our way through the traffic to the café, I recite what I remember about the gardens to supplement Ellie's information. "The gardens were opened to the public sometime in the 1790s and have been ever since. Today the gardens are around—" I quickly do the conversion in my head, "—fifty-six acres, give or take—and are a popular recreation spot for locals and tourists. Of course, the most popular attraction is the monumental Fontaine Médicis—"

Ellie reaches out and places her hand on my upper thigh, and I halt mid-sentence. "What?"

"Thank you, Geoffrey," she murmurs, her face earnest.

"For what?"

"For this." She lifts her hand and waves it to indicate Paris, and then us. "You helped make a dream come true for me. You brought Paris to life for me, and I'll never forget it."

Yeah. Me neither.

Eleanor

"There's L'Orangerie," Geoffrey points out.

The Orangery. We visited the museum on our third day together. After his preposterous idea to fake a romantic relationship. I reach up and touch the necklace, the lapis warm against my skin. Now here we are, only five days later, and so much has changed. More than I ever could have imagined.

Is this real? Or is he still faking it? It doesn't feel like it. But then again, he *is* an actor. He spent his very successful career making people believe he was madly in love with his co-stars.

I want to believe our private moments together have been anything but fake. I glance over at this beautiful man as he gazes out the car window, his handsome face in profile. The straight line of his jaw, the blade of his nose, the fullness of his lips, the impossibly long eyelashes no man should have. I repeat—he is one beautiful man.

The insecurities resurface. The insecurities that are part and parcel of Barry's infidelity. What could Geoffrey possibly see in me? He could have any woman he wants—a woman years, if not decades, younger than me. A woman without the physical and emotional scars of not only cancer, but life. If Barry didn't want me, how could any other man?

Geoffrey reaches over and takes my hand, his eyes intent on mine. "You okay?"

I give him what I hope is a convincing smile. "Of course. Just thinking I leave in two days."

"Let's conveniently forget that and enjoy today."

"Yes. Let's."

The car arrives at one of the entrances to the gardens. Geoffrey steps out and, ever the gentleman, reaches in to take my hand to help me from the car. Hélène and Stéphane climb out of their own car and ready their equipment. This public display is wearying. Yesterday had been bliss without a spotlight shining on my every move.

"Do you have a particular destination in mind, or would

you just like to wander?" His hand clasps mine, and I allow myself to believe that this is real. For two more days.

"Wandering sounds perfect."

I'm relieved to see no crowd awaits us. "Where are your adoring fans?"

He grimaces. "I stopped telling Malcolm and the film crew where we're going."

"You don't trust them?"

"Let's just say I'm not taking any chances."

We follow a path through the garden. The day is warm and breezy, and I relax in the serenity of the environment. It's Sunday, so in addition to the tourists, the residents of Paris are out in full force. We pass groups of people engaged in various activities. Some are lounging on the iconic green chairs scattered across the park, basking in the sunlight and engaging in lively conversations.

Others are engaged in chess matches, their concentration evident as they strategize their next moves. Children chase each other, their laughter echoing through the air. The air is filled with the scent of flowers, and the sound of spring green leaves rustling in the breeze creates a soothing ambiance. The park's well-manicured lawns stretch out, inviting visitors to find a spot to sit and enjoy the serene atmosphere.

Flowerbeds border the tree-lined pathways, creating a kaleidoscope of color—a rich tapestry of tulips, roses, and other blooming flowers. Spring in Paris is truly breathtaking.

We continue to walk hand-in-hand in silence. Before long, I hear the trickling of water nearby. "Do I hear the famed fountain?"

"Good ear. Yes, it's just down the steps ahead."

We descend the stairs and turn right.

The Fontaine Médicis.

My first glimpse doesn't disappoint. Nestled amid greenery, its basin is surrounded by white marble urns filled with ivy and pink geraniums. The fountain cascades from smaller basins into larger ones and finally down into the main basin, where a pair of ducks bob on the surface. Chairs line the path around the fountain, inviting visitors to sit and enjoy the tranquil atmosphere.

As if reading my mind, Geoffrey asks, "Would you like to sit?" The cool shade offers a refreshing respite from the warm day.

"Sure."

Geoffrey pulls a chair alongside another, and we sit companionably, his arm draped casually over my shoulders. The camera shutter intrudes on the otherwise peaceful atmosphere, and I hold in an annoyed sigh.

"Do you have any remaining locations you'd like to visit?"

I hesitate. I had planned a solitary visit to a market for business purposes, but that was before Geoffrey and I wound up spending almost every moment together. I am somewhat reluctant to ask because I think he will balk at it since it's work-related. "I do have one request."

"What's that?"

"I would like to visit the antique flea market."

"Really? Why?"

"My boutique. I like to offer a selection of one-of-a-kind items, whether it's jewelry, small furniture pieces, books, or vintage accessories like well-preserved purses. I also like to buy vintage clothing for design inspiration."

"I think we can manage that. There are a couple of places I'd like to take you tomorrow, followed by a very special dinner at one of Paris's best restaurants—"

"Oh, you don't need to do that," I interrupt. He has already spent more money on me than the prize package provided.

"I know I don't. I want to." His voice becomes raspy. "It will be our last night together. Let me make it special."

I look into his earnest gaze, and think I see . . . regret? "Okay."

He leans toward me, and my heart stammers at the knowledge that he's going to kiss me. His warm mouth brushes mine with fleeting butterfly touches, and my pulse goes into overdrive. It's only been a few hours since our bodies have been entwined, finding pleasure in one another, and yet I want him again with a fervor that overwhelms me.

He retreats, and it's all I can do not to follow his mouth for more kisses. His eyes drop to my mouth once more, and as if giving himself a mental shake, he sits back in his chair.

"Do you have a favorite time period or designer?"

My muddled brain can't keep up. "What?"

"You were talking about your love of vintage fashion. You must have a favorite time period or designer."

"Oh. Right." I give myself my own mental shake. "I'm drawn to 1940s Dior and Chanel."

"That's it!"

"What's it?"

"The perfume you wear. It's Chanel No. 5. Am I right?"

I pull back, amazed. "Yes. How did you know that?"

He shrugs. "I didn't at first. It's been haunting me, that scent. It's timeless and sophisticated, like you."

The heat of a flush blooms in my cheeks at his words. "You think I'm timeless and sophisticated?"

He leans in close again and cups my face, his thumb brushing my hot cheek. "Ellie, I think you're the most beautiful, intriguing woman I have ever met."

I shake my head. How could that be, with all the stunning women he's co-starred with?

He mutters a curse. "Don't shake your head. Damn Barry and his stupidity."

"Barry?"

"Yes, Barry. His affair has turned you into a woman who

doubts her value, and I'm not just talking about your appearance. I'm talking about your intelligence, your strength, your courage. Don't let him do that to you. You deserve so much more."

I blink a few times, then say, "Thank you. Sincerely."

"You're welcome. Sincerely." He smiles and winks at me. "You're an interesting woman, Ellie. And your boutique sounds like one of a kind. I'd love to see it someday."

Before I can stop myself, I say. "Maybe I could show it to you sometime."

Silence follows the invitation, and heat floods my face at the absurdity of him accepting such a mundane invitation. As if Geoffrey Harrison is going to visit the island of San Sebastian to see my store. "Never mind," I say with a chagrined expression and a wave of my hand.

He takes my hand and kisses it. "Ellie, I would love to."

I think he is just being polite, but I let it pass.

"I have a request of my own," he says.

"You do? What is it?"

"When we return to the hotel, I want you to pack an overnight bag."

"What for? Where are we going?"

"It's a surprise."

Geoffrey

I open the door to my flat and allow Ellie to precede me. Although she was here only a few days ago, I am unaccountably nervous. I want her to feel at home here, which is, of course, absurd, I know. She's leaving the day after tomorrow and going back to her life, and I have a movie role to pursue. At least I hope I do.

For some reason, the excitement I usually feel when a new project is in the works eludes me. Maybe because it's been a while, and I feel out of practice. It will be better once I'm immersed in a project.

We stopped by the hotel for Ellie to pack a bag. Watching her pull together the items she wanted with efficiency and certainty felt intimate in a way that even sleeping together had not. It had been a glimpse into Ellie's private moments. There had been no hemming and hawing. She'd been decisive, selecting a few items of clothing and tossing in what appeared to be a makeup bag and a couple pairs of shoes.

"You have a blow-dryer?"

"I do." I'd let my gaze wander over the lush silver and pewter waves brushing her shoulders. "But wear your hair natural. I like it."

"We'll see," she'd replied, absentmindedly. "Should I bring something to wear to dinner, or will we return to the hotel?"

"Bring something for dinner."

I'd given Hélène and Stéphane the night off. I wanted Ellie all to myself. They'd meet up with us again tomorrow. Our last day together. The thought made me almost ill.

I set Ellie's bag at the bottom of the stairs to the lofted bedroom and walk over to the balcony doors, throwing them open to the fresh spring breeze. It had been quite warm at midday, but it would be a cool evening.

There's a knock on the door, and Ellie looks first at the door and then at me. "Hélène and Stéphane?"

I cross the room to the door. "No. Food. My favorite bakery is delivering pastries for tomorrow morning."

"Bonjour, Monsieur Harrison," young Michel says. "Here is your order." He glances behind me, presumably at Ellie, and smiles. "Have a *very* nice evening."

I smirk at him before closing the door. "Cheeky fellow, Michel." As I move to the kitchen to put the food away, I ask, "Can I get you something to drink? Wine, champagne?"

"Just sparkling water, if you have it."

I can hear her as she wanders my flat. Picking up photos, then putting them down. Stopping before the various vintage movie posters—all of them authentic—I have framed and hanging on the walls. Cary Grant and Katharine Hepburn in *Bringing Up Baby*, Cary Grant and Irene Dunne in *My Favorite Wife*, and Grant and Rosalind Russell in *His Girl Friday*, among others.

"You really love old movies, don't you?"

"I do." I hand her a glass of Perrier on ice with a twist of lime, just as she likes it. "Especially the old rom-coms."

She takes a drink and then points with the glass. "And how about Cary Grant? You seem to have a few posters of him."

I glance at her in shock, "You really don't watch movies, do you?"

"No. Sorry," she says with a chagrined smile.

"Well, Cary Grant was such a versatile actor, playing in the screwball and romantic comedies you see there," I say with a nod to the posters, "but also in thrillers like *North by Northwest*, *To Catch a Thief*, and the tragically romantic *An Affair to Remember*. And then there's the fact that Cary and I share the same hometown."

Ellie's eyes widen. "You're both from Bristol?"

"Indeed."

She turns in a full circle, then stops, facing me. "No posters from your movies?"

"Now, why would I want those hanging in my flat?"

She shrugs. "Bragging rights? Impressing the other women you bring here?"

I take the glass from her and set it on the console table behind her. I place my hands on her shoulders and pin her with my gaze. "I don't bring women to my flat. You're the first."

Her brow furrows, and then her lips part. I take full advantage and swoop down, claiming her mouth with mine, tasting the tart lime there. She sighs and wraps her arms around my neck, meeting my tongue stroke for stroke. My hands glide along her supple back to her taut ass, and I press her hips to my growing erection.

My thoughts race to where I'd like to take her first. So many possibilities. I could set her on the island counter and thrust into her heat. Or I could bend her over the sofa and take her that way. Or she could straddle me in a dining chair and ride us both into a pleasurable oblivion.

Counter. It's closest and would take the least effort. I start backing her up to the kitchen island, as her fingers plunge into my hair, grasping and holding my mouth to hers. Clutching her hips with my hands, I lift her up.

And then there's a knock on the door. "Goddammit," I mutter, raking my hands through my hair.

"Hélène and Stéphane?" she pants, her eyes now wide in surprise.

"No," I say curtly in my sexual frustration. "They're not invited. It's dinner, and their timing couldn't have been worse." Well, I guess it could have been worse—they might have interrupted us mid-coitus.

Wincing, I adjust myself and take a deep breath before flinging open the door, apparently startling the young man standing there with the fragrant bag from Les Vins de Montmartre. "Merci," I practically growl. Taking the bag, I try to smile politely. But given the expression on the pimply young man's face, it's more like a grimace.

"*Bon appétit,*" he squeaks, before beating a hasty retreat, and I close the door with a slam.

Eleanor

I place a hand to my racing heart, and despite my sexual frustration, I can't help but laugh at the situation and the expression on Geoffrey's face as he mutters a string of curses on his way back to the kitchen.

He continues to mutter as he sorts through the food in the bag, delectable scents of roast chicken redolent with thyme and rosemary. "This is what I get for trying to have a romantic dinner—a hard cock and a racing libido."

I snort in amusement. "Poor guy," I murmur, as I approach him from behind and wrap my arms around his lean waist. I slide my hand lower and grip the bulge in the front of his jeans. He groans and curses once more, before placing his hand over mine, adding more pressure. "Fuck."

"Will that keep for a few minutes?" I ask, indicating the dinner, not his erection.

"A few minutes is all it will take, I guarantee that."

I laugh. "That's not what I had in mind." I turn him to face me and unfasten his jeans before slipping my hand inside to feel the heat of him. After a few strokes, I shimmy the jeans from his hips and drop to my knees in front of him.

"God, Ellie," he groans. "You don't have to—"

His protest is cut off by a guttural moan as I take his erection into my mouth. I admit, I rarely performed this particular act on Barry, but the desire to pleasure Geoffrey is an acute need.

His hand tangles in my hair and his breathy curses of pleasure send heat to my already overheated core. In my limited experience, I'm not sure what to do, but as his hips buck at each stroke of my tongue, I know I must be doing something right. A feeling of power fills me, knowing it's my touch and my tongue that's making this man writhe with pleasure.

"Sweet Jesus," he mutters. "No. I want to be inside you. Now!"

He lifts me to my feet and onto the countertop before sliding my pants from my hips and down my legs, tossing them behind him. He parts my thighs and steps between them, raking his hot erection against my wet heat, and I'm lost. "Now, Geoffrey," I echo. "Now!"

He enters me with one hard thrust, and I shudder.

"I'm sorry," he groans. "I wasn't kidding when I said this wouldn't take long." Three more thrusts, and on the fourth he releases a guttural cry, and I know he has found his release.

Several moments pass as I stroke his back, his breathing returning to normal.

"I'm sorry, Ellie," he whispers into my hair.

"Shh."

Leaning back, he gazes into my face. "I promise I'll make it up to you tonight. And tomorrow morning, and tomorrow night."

A shiver races through me at the possibilities.

"It's your fault, you know. That mouth of yours was my undoing."

"I'll gladly accept the blame." I place another kiss on his lips, feeling another thrill of power that I drove him over the edge. Maybe I'm getting my mojo back.

"If you'd like to clean up before dinner, the primary bathroom is upstairs." I nod, and he lifts me off the counter and pats my bare ass. Color rises to my cheeks as I retrieve my discarded pants from the floor and struggle to summon the courage to walk bare-ass naked across the flat and up the stairs.

As if reading my mind, he leans down and murmurs,

"Ellie, I've seen this of you—and much more—up close and personal. Don't be embarrassed." Which only turns up the heat of my blush. I wouldn't be surprised if my face wasn't the only part of my body with red cheeks.

Geoffrey

I push my plate aside and reach for my wineglass, my hunger sated with roast chicken, *la salade parisienne*, or French potato salad, and crisp-tender *haricots verts* from my favorite Montmartre café. Two small crème brûlées await us for dessert.

We're seated at a café table on my veranda overlooking the Basilica of the Sacré-Cœur, its large central dome glowing white in the cool twilight. A French music station streams softly in the background. A very romantic setting—as planned.

"What is it about Dior and Chanel that you like?"

She toys with her wineglass and shrugs. "I love the clean lines and absence of embellishments of Chanel. She preferred to use luxurious accessories like faux pearl necklaces instead. As for Dior, I love the sophisticated, feminine shapes and luxurious fabrics."

"I can see that about you—in the clothes you wear. Simple, elegant, tasteful."

"Thank you," she murmurs, as her cheeks turn a lovely shade of pink.

"I love when you do that."

"Do what?"

"Blush at my compliments. If it were up to me, I'd make that blush appear several times a day."

A smile plays at the corners of her mouth, and she shakes her head.

I don't want to think about her leaving, but I want to know more about her and her life in Florida. "What will you do first when you get home—besides unpack?"

"I'll call Abby. Then I'll call the store."

"What do you look forward to most about being home?"

She ponders the question a moment and then says, "My bed."

"Tell me what your evenings are like."

"My evenings . . . are quiet."

"What do you do? Walk me through a typical evening."

"Well," she sighs, "I get home from the store around seven or eight. If I haven't eaten yet, after kicking off my heels for my slippers, I grab a light supper, check emails, maybe call Abby. Then I take a bath, read for a bit, then go to bed."

"Sounds very . . . tranquil."

"Translation—boring." She pauses with a frown. "Besides, I thought we weren't going to talk about my departure? I thought we were going to pretend it wasn't imminent?"

"You're right. It's just that," I hesitate a heartbeat or two, "I want to picture you at home, immersed in your daily routine, so when I think about you in the middle of the day, I can imagine what you'll be doing."

"And you'll think about me, will you?" she asks, a note of doubt in her voice.

"Yes," I say unequivocally.

"Why?"

"Because, Eleanor Marshall, you are an intriguing woman. You fascinate me with your incongruous blend of quiet confidence in your abilities and uncertainty in your remarkable beauty. I admire your love of all things French. Your laugh lights up my soul, and your smile warms my heart."

She gives me a dubious look. "That sounds like something from one of your movies."

"It's not. I promise." I make an X across my heart. "It is straight from my heart."

I rise from my chair and circle to Ellie's. Holding out my hand, I say, "Dance with me." She stares up at me, her gaze warm on mine, then places her hand in mine. I reel her in, my arm around her waist, and press her hand to my chest as we sway to the strains of Édith Piaf singing her signature song, "La Vie en rose."

Eleanor

I close my eyes and let Piaf's words wash over me. As she sings about holding you close and fast and pressing me to your heart, my throat gets tight, and it's as if the words were written for me. For us. This moment. But when she croons about giving your heart and soul, tears sting my eyes.

And then, when Geoffrey's arm tightens around me and he presses his lips to my temple, it's all I can do to hold in a sob.

How did I let this happen? How did I allow myself to fall for him? How did I allow myself to love a man I can never have? We live an ocean apart. His career takes him all over the world, while I'm tethered to Florida and my boutique.

I need to accept the facts. This will never be anything more than a fling, and I will have to live with the consequences of flying headlong into a recipe for heartache.

He tips my chin up. "Hey. Don't cry." He thumbs away the tears on my cheeks, then brushes his lips against mine in the sweetest, most heartbreaking kiss. My arms encircle his neck, and I pull him closer, begging him to take the kiss deeper. When he does, I resign myself to the pain I know I will feel. But for now, I relish the pleasure I feel in his arms in this moment.

Chapter Nine

DAY NINE

Geoffrey

Whistling "La Vie en Rose," I descend the stairs, a decided spring in my step. The image of Ellie's body slick with water and fragrant soap suds, and the echo of her throaty moans brings a grin to my face.

I left her to finish dressing while I make coffee and lay out the French pastries I had delivered. This feels so right. Waking with her in my bed, going about a morning routine I could definitely get used to, and having breakfast together.

I could hear her puttering around upstairs, probably repacking her overnight bag. At that thought, I'm filled with a sense of panic, like the clock is ticking on an explosive device and there's nothing I can do to stop it from going *boom*—destroying my life.

I'm frozen, a flaky croissant in my hand, wondering how I will be able to let her go when she descends the stairs, her hair still damp and drying in waves around her face.

"Mmm. Coffee smells delicious! And is that a chocolate croissant?"

I look blankly at the pastry in my hand, as if wondering how it got there. "Uh . . . yes." I hold it out to her, and she takes it from my fingers, her own brushing mine, sending a shiver up my arm and down my spine.

"You okay?" A frown creases her brow.

"Yes, of course. Just thinking about the day's itinerary."

She pulls apart the croissant while I pour a cup of coffee for her, remembering to add sugar with a splash of cream, just the way she likes it. "We could have a picnic in Bois de Boulogne."

She chews thoughtfully, her head tilted, considering my idea, then shakes her head. "No. Let's just skip lunch."

"Or we could pick up something in the market."

"Yes. Let's do that instead. I'm sure tonight's dinner will be sumptuous." She breaks off another bite of the pastry and holds it out to me. I can't resist taking it directly from her fingers, then placing a kiss on their tips.

Smiling, she leans across the bar and purses her lips for a kiss. I can't resist that offer either, so I press my lips to hers, tasting the chocolate there. Yes, this is a morning routine I could get used to. Too bad this will be the only morning like it.

Eleanor

In the car, Geoffrey reaches over and takes my hand as I gaze out the window, gorging on the scenery as it flies by, storing it away like a squirrel hoards acorns for the winter. I'll cherish these memories, and like the squirrel in winter, I'll rely on them once I return to my lonely single life.

This has been the experience of a lifetime, not only because of the location, but because of Geoffrey. These last few days have been some of the best days of my life.

A pang of . . . something makes me want to lay my hand over my chest and soothe the ache.

"Have you been to Central Park?" Geoffrey's question breaks through my reverie.

"Yes, many times. Why?"

"Just for reference, Bois de Boulogne is more than double the size of Central Park—some two thousand acres."

"I had no idea."

"It's one of the city's most popular green spaces, offering a variety of activities and attractions for visitors. It's a shame we don't have more time. They have boats for rent to paddle across the lakes, and then there's the Parc de Bagatelle, an elegant rose garden with a diverse collection of roses. They even offer horseback riding and tennis. Do you play tennis or ride?"

"Neither, I'm afraid. While I like to stay fit, I wouldn't call myself an athlete. But paddling the lakes sounds fun."

"When you come back." He grips my hand, and I glance up into his face. His gaze is serious and maybe a little . . . pleading? "Ellie, I want you to know you're welcome back here any time. With or without me, you can stay in my flat, though I hope you'll consider coming to see me."

I thrill at the offer, but I know it won't work. The last thing I need is a long—really long—distance relationship. "Won't you be off on location somewhere?"

He scoffs. "First, I have to have a movie role."

"But you will. I know you will. The right part will come along." I switch to my stern mom voice, "You might have had the right role if you'd just taken that meeting with the director."

"And miss this? No way."

The car pulls to a stop. After Geoffrey gives Maurice directions, Geoffrey opens the door and helps me out. "You up for a walk?"

"Always."

"We won't take long. I know how anxious you are to hit the market."

We follow a tree-lined path, hands entwined, birdsong filling the air. Trees are wearing their spring green leaves, and the air is fragrant with the scents of earth and flowers.

"It's beautiful," I whisper, reluctant to disturb the peace of the surroundings. Then I realize I'm not hearing the sounds of a camera shutter. "Where are Hélène and Stéphane?"

"I gave them the day off. Well, that's not entirely true. They completed their assignment."

"Completed? But we still have two days."

"Yes, but it's not about the social media anymore. It's about you. And me." He pulls me around to face him, his hands gliding up my bare arms. "I don't want to share the time we have left with anyone. I want you all to myself." His gaze lowers to my mouth, and my body reacts to the anticipation. Almost as if reading the signs of my body, he draws out the anticipation, his mouth hovering just above mine, until I can't wait any longer, and I stand on tiptoes and claim his mouth with mine.

His fingers thread through my hair as his mouth plunders mine. Not for the cameras. Not for social media. But for him. For me. I press my body close, and he moans, taking the heat level up a notch or ten.

This is so damn complicated. How did this happen? I never expected to fall for a man in seven short days. What started as a lark has now become a cause for heartbreak. I'd like to blame Maddie for planting the seed. But I can't. Even without her not-so-gentle nudges, I would find myself in this same situation. Entangled in a relationship that could never be.

Geoffrey

I've never been to the Les Puces de Saint-Ouen or Les Puces, even though it's one of the largest and most famous flea markets in the world. If I need something for my flat, I pick up the phone and call my interior designer, and she does the work for me. But I find I'm looking forward to experiencing it for the first time with Ellie.

"According to my research, there are fifteen hundred sellers in several different sections, each with its own specialization—furniture, vintage clothing, books, and art." Her voice carries a note of breathless excitement, and I can't help the smile that crosses my face. She's like a kid in a candy store.

"We should start at the Office de Tourisme to pick up a map and other useful information. A friend of mine who owns a boutique in Atlanta said the rue des Rosiers is the market's spine and your North Star. She urged me to visit the most notable markets including the Marché Vernaison, the first and oldest market, known for its winding allées, the Marché Paul Bert Serpette outdoor stalls, and the area around *rues* Paul Bert and Jules Vallès."

Ellie's excitement is contagious, and I'm as eager as she is to get started.

"But I'm heading straight to Chez Sarah's," Ellie continues, almost bouncing in the backseat next to me. "It's a three-hundred-foot-long corridor that's said to feature a breathtaking array of designer clothes dating from the turn of the twentieth century to the early 2000s."

Maurice drops us off, and after picking up our map, we head directly into the fray—a maze of narrow streets, alleyways, and covered passages, all bustling with activity.

"There are other vintage clothing shops like Merveilles de Babellou's two boutiques, but it's a little too rich for my blood. Especially if I want to pull the garment apart to, uh, copy it."

"In a nod to 'imitation is the sincerest form of flattery'?"

"Exactly."

We pass shops displaying vintage furniture—carved wooden pieces, ornate mirrors, and velvet settees from a bygone era.

"Here we are," Ellie says, drawing my attention back to the task at hand.

We enter a shop displaying a mind-boggling collection of clothing, and I wonder how anyone goes about sifting through it all. But Ellie clearly has an approach in mind, and she dives right in.

Lifting a simple dark blue dress from the rack, she eyes it critically, front and back. Checking seams, the zipper, and tugging on the material. Apparently, it makes the cut, because she drapes it over her arm.

She continues sorting through the clothing, then stops at a black outfit and raises it for inspection. She mumbles to herself, "Chanel, circa 1949. Excellent condition."

A moment later, it joins the blue dress.

"Look at this! A 1920s flapper dress!" She holds up an intricately beaded number. "Beautiful, but . . . I don't see my customers in the market for a flapper dress." She hangs it back on the rack and continues her search.

Before it's all said and done, and with very little wasted energy, she picks out five dresses, one beaded evening dress, several Hermès scarves, and a cashmere sweater.

At Marché Serpette, another vintage clothing stall, she

selects a Dior handbag, which she *oohs* and *ahs* over, and a few pieces of costume jewelry. "These I'll sell in the boutique along with the Hermès scarves. The cashmere is for me," she adds with a wink.

Watching Ellie haggle in French over unmarked items was a joy in itself. She has a clear idea of the value of the items, while also offering fair prices.

I follow behind her like a gosling following its mother goose. She stops abruptly, and I almost run into her. Reaching out, she pulls a sweater off a shelf in front of her, eyeing it critically. "Hermès," she murmurs. "Fine cashmere. Excellent condition."

To my surprise, she turns and holds the sweater up in front of me, as if trying it out for size. "Perfect, I think. Would you wear this color?"

It's a gray-green—what I've heard referred to as sage. I don't think I would've selected it for myself, but I think I like it. "Sure." I reach for it, intending to buy it for myself.

"No." She holds it tight to her chest. "This is my gift to you, for making my first trip to Paris memorable."

"Thank you. Although it's not necessary." I'm very touched by her gift, and then it dawns on me what she said, "First? Does that mean you'll be coming back?"

"It does. I think I could swing an annual trip to come to the flea market." She continues to examine the sweater, not looking at me. "For business reasons, of course."

Ah. Not to see me. Well, what did I expect?

"Are you up for more shopping?" Oblivious to my disappointment.

I paint a smile on, bow, and say, "Oui, Madame!"

Eleanor

. . .

"Insane. I must be insane," I mutter. I'd gone a little overboard with my purchases, but they were all too good to pass up. And now I have to ship many of them, since there's no way I can take them with me. Thankfully, the aptly named Ship Antiques on Rue des Rosiers is happy to send purchases home for shoppers.

Like the perfectly preserved Louis Vuitton trunk I bought, which will serve as a beautiful display for other items in the boutique. Then there are the art deco perfume bottles in pale blues and purples. And I can't forget the vintage typewriter. Some antique books and maps will find their way to my home office, while a vintage camera will be used as a display in the store.

After a quick lunch at Le P'tit Landais on Rue des Rosiers, I arrange for the shipping.

"You certainly clean up," Geoffrey says, interrupting my musings, as we walk to meet the car.

"I'm sorry—you were probably bored."

"On the contrary, I enjoyed the afternoon, watching a pro at work."

I raise a skeptical brow.

Geoffrey takes my hand and lifts it to his lips, a grin on his face. "Truly. You have a keen eye, discerning taste, and you know what you want. It was like watching a master artisan plying their craft. What will you do with everything? Use it in your boutique?"

"Most of it. I like to create a story with my displays. I'll use the trunk and vintage camera to display a travel collection I have arriving for summer. The typewriter and books will sit on a display shelf featuring trendy reading glasses. I'll offer the perfume bottles for sale."

"I really have to see this boutique of yours. It sounds beautiful and unique, like its owner."

My stomach flips at the compliment, and at the idea of him visiting my store. But I can't put much stock in the comment. The odds of Geoffrey Harrison, famous heartthrob, visiting Ellie's are higher than the odds of Christian Dior or Coco Chanel visiting.

Geoffrey

After visiting the Palais Royale, Ellie and I returned to my flat for a much-needed rest before dinner tonight. We'll be right back at the Palais Royale for dinner at the famed Le Grand Véfour.

That rest had turned into passionate, almost desperate lovemaking, with the knowledge that it would be one of the last such encounters.

My heart squeezes, and I wonder for a moment whether I'm having a heart attack. After a moment, the pain recedes, and I realize it's my heart breaking in agonizing increments.

Ellie kicked me out of the bedroom before she was dressed, telling me to wait downstairs for her. I'm trying my damnedest not to pace when I hear her coming down the stairs. I glance up as she steps into the living room, and my breath catches. Now, instead of suffering from a heart attack, I'm suffering from asphyxia.

Dressed in what I can only guess is a vintage satin dress the color of smoky purple that clings to her shape like it had been tailored just for her, Ellie is a stunning throwback to another era.. The snug bodice and waist give way to a full pleated skirt that stops just below her knees, displaying her shapely legs to perfection. Her luscious silver hair is pulled back in a sleek twist, revealing her graceful neck, tempting me to press kisses to the tender skin there. Around her neck is the pink lapis necklace I gave her. Black stiletto pumps—Louboutins, from their iconic red soles—complete the look. "My god," I say, when I can finally draw a breath.

"Do you like it? I found it today." She smooths a hand along the bodice, and just as I'm regaining my equilibrium, my blood rushes south.

"How?" I croak out, then clear my throat to try again. "How did you buy that without even trying it on? It fits like the designer—"

"Dior," she interjects helpfully.

"Dior made it for you."

"Geoffrey, I do this for a living. I can tell what will fit and what won't."

I shake my head. "I'll say. I'll be fighting the men off all evening."

She laughs, that throaty, brandy-soaked laugh. "I seriously doubt it, but I'll take the compliment just the same. I may be fighting the women off all night." Her gaze rakes over me, and I feel it right down to my toes. I chose a charcoal gray suit, white dress shirt, and pearl gray tie, which turns out to complement the deep purple of her dress. "You look handsome." Then she sighs. "It's so nice to see a well-dressed man."

"Happy to oblige, Madame," I say as I bow.

She steps closer and places her palms on my chest before lifting her mouth to mine. Needing no other encouragement, I lean down and brush her lips with mine. She pats my chest and says, "Thank you."

Eleanor

. . .

My breath catches the moment I walk into the restaurant. The elegant space holds all the opulence of Versailles, with red velvet upholstery, embellished carved paneling, priceless gilt-framed paintings, mirrored walls, crystal chandeliers, and tables set with snowy white linens, gold and white china, and fine crystal wineglasses.

The maître d', a stout, round-faced fellow, greets us in French and guides us through the main dining room. Geoffrey's hand found what has become its customary place on the small of my back, warm and possessive. Rather than seating us there, though, we climb an elegant stairway to the first floor, where we enter a room that serves as a foil to the extravagant décor of the main rooms. In stark contrast, the private lounge is all pearl grays and whites. The room soothes, rather than excites.

The walls are adorned with what appears to be paper sculptures. I step in for a closer examination, my fingers itching to touch, but of course, I resist the urge, not wishing to damage the ethereal sculptures.

"Madame Claudine Drai," Geoffrey offers. "I'd like to add one of her pieces to my collection, but they are difficult to obtain. As soon as she completes one, it's sold."

A waiter enters, a white cloth draped over his arm, carrying a silver ice bucket containing a bottle of champagne. "*Bonsoir*, Monsieur. Madame. Please take a seat at the table of your choice."

I lift a brow at Geoffrey. Are there no other patrons tonight?

"I reserved the entire room," he murmurs.

I shake my head. There are eight other tables in the room. What must this have cost him?

"How about here, by the window, looking out onto the Rue de Beaujolais?" Geoffrey offers.

After sitting, with Geoffrey's gentlemanly assistance, the waiter places the ice bucket by Geoffrey. "May I serve the Champagne?"

"Oui."

"The chef has selected a very special dinner for you tonight," he says as he pours the sparkling wine. "Please relax and enjoy the champagne while we prepare the first course."

He leaves, closing the door behind him. That's when I notice the classical music playing softly in the background—Claude Debussy's *Clair de lune*. Geoffrey has clearly gone all out for our last dinner together. My stomach clenches at the thought. This is it. This is the end of this little fantasy. Tomorrow, I will reenter real life, and all its stresses, legal battles, and emotional woes.

"A toast." Geoffrey's silken voice invades my morose thoughts.

I lift my glass, noticing my hand tremble a little.

"To a whirlwind romance!"

Whirlwind is right! I smile and clink my glass to his, though the smile feels fake. Like the ones I turned onto his adoring followers.

We sip, then set our glasses aside. I'm sure the champagne is excellent, but it settles like dust in my mouth. He reaches across the table and takes my cool hand in his warm one. "Stay." His blue-gray eyes implore.

I shake my head. "I can't stay. I have a life. I have responsibilities. And so do you. You have a part to pursue."

"Dammit," he mutters. "I'll come visit you then."

My heart stutters. "No, you won't. You'll be busy with your new movie. And then another. Life will get in the way. So please, don't make promises you can't keep."

His beautiful, lush mouth forms a thin line.

The waiter takes this moment to present the first course—delicate blinis with caviar and *crème fraîche*.

Before Geoffrey can resume his argument after the waiter leaves, I blurt, "Tell me about the restaurant," as I look around the room once again. I don't want to argue. Not tonight.

He releases a gusty sigh, but then nods, as if in understanding. "The restaurant has been around since before the French Revolution, making it one of the oldest gourmet restaurants in Paris. In fact, Napoleon Bonaparte and Joséphine dined here. As did Victor Hugo and Jean-Paul Sartre." He takes another sip of champagne. "It boasts three Michelin stars, and its sommeliers are some of the best in the city."

The remainder of the exquisite meal, including pan-seared salmon, roasted pork loin, roasted potatoes, and *haricots verts*, is congenial, if not romantic. I hate that the discussion put such a damper on the evening, so I reach across the table and place my hand over his. "Geoffrey, I want you to know that I had a wonderful time."

His eyes soften. "I'm glad. I did too."

I smile and shake my head. "To think I had planned to spend the past nine days in Paris alone. What a dreary thought that is now."

He rotates his hand so our palms are facing and laces his fingers with mine. "Ellie, promise me when you return home, you'll pick one activity each week that's just for fun. Whether it's dinner with friends, attending a play, spending a day at the spa, anything. Don't go home every day and shut yourself away. Life has far too much to offer, and far too little time to experience it."

"I promise." He's right. It's so easy to get into a rut. I will miss him dreadfully, but I will do my best to take his advice.

"Monsieur, Madame, may I clear the table?" the waiter asks, startling us out of our conversation.

"Yes, thank you, Guy."

"Dessert will be served shortly. Would you like coffee or tea?"

"Tea, please," I say.

"None for me," Geoffrey says.

After Guy leaves, Geoffrey rises from his chair across from me and takes the one next to me, wrapping his arms around the back of my chair. "I had the chef prepare a special dessert. One that has special meaning to me."

"Really? And why is that?"

"I'll tell you when it arrives."

"You're very mysterious, tonight."

Guy returns with a cart laden with a silver teapot, delicate china cups, creamer, and a sugar bowl. After laying out the tea items on the table, he sets two dessert plates on the table with a flourish. I glance down and then laugh, shaking my head. It's a *mille-feuille* with roasted strawberries, mascarpone, and a dark chocolate drizzle—the same dessert I had on our "first date" nine days ago. "Why?"

Geoffrey glances at Guy, who is pouring my tea, and shakes his head.

As soon as the door closes behind Guy, I give Geoffrey a pointed look.

Geoffrey

"That first night, when I watched you eat this very dessert, I wanted to whisk you up to my room and have my wicked way with you."

She giggles like an ingénue, and I feel it in every corpuscle, making my blood sing. "Have your wicked way with me, huh? And why was that?"

"First, I expected you to order black coffee for dessert, not some puff pastry decadence. You were so uptight and proper, I didn't figure you would let yourself enjoy something so rich and indulgent. Then you took that first bite, and you let out this low, sexy, throaty moan. My god! I wondered if that was what you sounded like during sex." I lean in close and whisper, "Turns out it is," enjoying the shiver in response.

A blush suffuses her face. "It is not!"

"I love that I can do that."

"Do what? Embarrass me?"

"Make you blush," I say with a grin. "Watching you savor your dessert was sexual torture." I pick up a fork, cut into the delicate pastry, and hold the fork up to her mouth. She hesitates, then opens those plum-colored lips, takes the fork into her mouth, and my breath hitches, the sight reminding me of when she went down on me in the kitchen. I shift in my seat at the visual this elicits.

When she releases a throaty moan, I am undone. "There it is!" Her eyes widen, and I can't help the laugh that escapes.

She swallows and then says, "You're incorrigible!"

"But you love it! Admit it!"

She sniffs, Miss Prim and Proper, and I love the challenge this role poses. I know how to get behind that façade with the right coaxing, and I'm up to the task. Just as soon as she finishes this blasted dessert.

Eleanor

. . .

I lean my head against Geoffrey's shoulder in the back of the car as we drive through Paris back to the Four Seasons. His cologne is driving me mad. I just want to bury my face in his neck and inhale.

With a will of its own, my mind takes this moment to remind me that this is our last night. *Oh, shut up. Can't you leave it alone and let me enjoy what's left?*

Geoffrey presses his lips to my hair, and I sigh in both contentment and resignation. I try to picture our farewell. Will we say goodbye at the hotel? Or will he go with me to the airport? Will I cry? Or will I hold it together until I'm home alone. And how will they handle the social media? Will our "relationship" just fade away? Or will there be an announcement that we have gone our separate ways, the distance making it too difficult to maintain a romance? And how long before his next flavor of the month is trending?

My stomach roils at that thought. How will I handle seeing him with another woman? How will I accept his sharing a bed with another woman? I inwardly scoff. Probably about as well as I accepted Barry sharing a bed with another woman.

But here's the thing. The pain of that knife wound has lessened. It's healing, and the scar tissue is only making my heart stronger.

At least I hope it is. Because I'm going to need all the strength I can muster to walk away from Geoffrey and never look back.

Geoffrey

. . .

I escort Ellie to her hotel room, her overnight bag in one hand, her hand in the other. I have been thinking about what I plan to do to her—with her—since dessert. This is not the time for slow and easy. This is the time for hard and fast. We can slow it down next time. And there will be a next time, because I plan to make the most of our last night together.

Ellie has been quiet and withdrawn since we left Le Grand Véfour. I can relate. That's why I need to rock both our worlds tonight. That full skirt she's wearing plays perfectly into the scenario I have in mind.

As soon as we enter her suite, I drop her overnight bag and press her back against the door, my hands going to her waist, my mouth descending on hers. She hesitates for a split second, then her hands are in my hair, stroking and grasping.

Our tongues tangle, and I taste chocolate, strawberries, and champagne. I work her skirt up to her hips and yank down her panties, while she gasps and moans into my mouth. Once I have her naked, I unfasten my trousers and release my erection, guiding it to her entrance, where she's slick and wet. "Wrap your legs around me," I groan. Thrusting up and into her is sweet bliss. She cries out as I bottom out inside her.

"My god, Geoffrey," her voice raspy with desire.

I slam into her repeatedly, not caring that anyone walking down the corridor can hear us. There is only one thing I want, and that's to pleasure us both. My focus narrows in on where we are joined, and nothing else matters.

Ellie clings to me, her arms wrapped tight around my neck, as I plunge into her. I can feel her tightening around me, and I know she's close. "Come, Ellie. Come for me!"

She explodes in my arms, her orgasm rocking us both, just as mine slams into me in a crushing wave of pleasure. I bury my face in her neck.

This woman! How will I ever let her go?

Chapter Ten

DAY TEN

Eleanor

Light filters into the room, signaling the start of my last day. Well, my last morning, really. My flight is at 1:30, so I'll need to be at the airport by 10:30.

I lay quietly, listening to Geoffrey's deep, even breathing. His arm is heavy and warm around my waist, his muscled chest pressed to my back.

My limbs feel heavy, and I'm sore in all the right places. We made love all night, taking breaks in between to catch some modicum of sleep. I'll crash on the flight home, for sure. But it was worth it. Geoffrey is an attentive, caring, passionate lover—not that I have anyone to compare him to besides Barry. But I think he's everything a woman would want in a lover.

And up against the door last night? I've never in my life! It was like something out of a steamy romance novel or movie. Look at me referring to something I never would have considered until now.

I wonder idly what plot point this is? The Deeper Attraction phase?

Despite this being it—the end of our "relationship"—I feel . . . oddly tranquil. Or maybe I'm just exhausted.

Geoffrey's hand glides up my rib cage and around to my breast, giving it a little squeeze. "You're awake," I murmur.

"No. I think I'm still dreaming, because I have a beautiful, warm woman in my arms."

"Then I must be dreaming too, because I have a hard, sexy man holding me in his arms."

"Mmm. Let's just keep dreaming then."

As much as I hate to break up this interlude, my bladder is becoming insistent.

He groans as I get to my feet, wrapping the hotel robe around me. He might not mind padding around naked, but I do.

After relieving myself and brushing my teeth, I head back to the bedroom, grabbing my phone off the nightstand to turn it on and check my flight status.

As soon as the phone connects to the hotel Wi-Fi, it blows up. Buzzing with incoming texts—dozens of them. What the —? My stomach drops as my mind is bombarded with all manner of tragedies. Abby was in an accident. My boutique burned down. My lawyers have bad news. We didn't take our phones to dinner last night, and now I'm regretting that decision.

I open the first text from Abby. At least she's safe. I immediately breathe a sigh of relief. That is, until I read the message.

> Abby: Mom! I didn't know you planned to announce that your relationship with Geoffrey was fake! What is going on?

What?

Maddie: Ellie! I thought this was supposed to be a secret?! What the hell?

Phoebe: Well, well, well. Look who's a little liar!

"What the hell is going on?" I shout.

Geoffrey sits up in bed, and I'm so disturbed by the text messages that I can't even appreciate his bare torso.

"What is it, Ellie? What's wrong?"

I don't respond, as I open an Instagram link Abby sent me.

Splashed across the post is:

IT WAS ALL FAKE!

This links to a story in a British tabloid:

Was it All an Act?

For the last nine days, Geoffrey Harrison and Eleanor Marshall have been carrying on a very public whirlwind romance, but was it all a farce? If so, Harrison played his best role ever! Making us all believe he had fallen for the woman who won the Dream Date Contest. The question on everyone's mind is whether she was part of the whole stunt or Harrison played her.

I can't finish. My eyes blur and the phrase "whirlwind romance" repeats in my head. Geoffrey used those same words in our toast last night!

"Ellie, I'm worried." I glance up to see Geoffrey standing in front of me. Thankfully, he had on a hotel robe as well. "What's going on?"

Anger and pain rockets through me. "How could you do this?"

"Do what? Ellie, talk to me!"

I thrust my phone out to him, the humiliating story still

on the screen. He takes the phone, and I walk away, unable to bear his proximity.

"Shit. Ellie, I didn't do this. You have to believe me."

"Do I? What about that phrase 'whirlwind romance'? You used those exact words last night."

"I don't know. A—a coincidence." He rakes his hand through his hair, making it stand on end, looking for all the world like he's as shocked as I am. But then he's an actor, right? He just *acted* like he cared for me. Just like he would do in any rom-com. He played the role of the smitten lover. Well, he'd played *me* for sure!

"There must have been a leak."

I jump on him. "By who? The only people who knew were the two of us, our daughters, my best friend, and Malcolm."

"My daughter knows how to keep a secret." He murmurs.

"Are you accusing *my* daughter of breaking my trust?"

He throws up his hand. "Or maybe Maddie."

I cross my arms over my chest. "No, she wouldn't do that."

"Maybe not intentionally."

"No." I jab my finger at him. "You don't get to blame my friends and family! And what about Malcolm?"

His lips thin, and he hesitates. "No. He's been my agent for over thirty years. He wouldn't do that."

"I'd point the finger at him before I would my daughter or Maddie."

He's pacing the room. Oh yes. He was good. Playing the wronged man.

"It's all been a game to you, hasn't it?" A thought occurs to me. "All those people who seemed to know where we were going to be. This *whole* thing has been a game to you. The 'Where's Geoffrey?' social media game. It was you all along, wasn't it? Or Malcolm. The whole point of this publicity stunt was to attract attention. Why would you want to keep where we were going a secret? That would defeat the whole purpose, right? And what better way to prove you've still got it as a romantic lead than to fool the whole world into thinking you were falling in love with me?"

"No! Ellie, no!" He strides over to me and grips my shoulders. "It wasn't me."

I shake his hands off, not listening. "This is all so humiliating! I don't know which is worse—that people think I was a willing party to this fake romance or that I was an unwitting dupe in it all!"

How will I face everyone at home? Barry? Phoebe? I thought of Phoebe's mean text, and my stomach drops. I'd have to go home and face the humiliation. Phoebe's smug expression. Her gleeful participation in the gossip.

And the boutique. It had been trending on social media, according to my social media manager. This little escapade had the side benefit of boosting sales by over seventy percent! Would people stop shopping there? Or would they come out of morbid curiosity to see the woman who was duped by Geoffrey Harrison?

"I guess this is what you referred to as the Black Moment," I mutter. "It's aptly named."

"Ellie, please—"

"I need you to leave." My voice is so quiet, I'm not sure if he heard me.

"Ellie."

"Please leave. Needless to say, I'll catch a taxi to the airport."

"Ellie, give me time to figure this out. Give me time to—"

"No." I cross my arms over my chest, whether to protect my heart from his quiet plea or to try to hold the broken pieces together, I don't know. "I'm done."

He finally nods in resignation and turns to retrieve the

clothes we'd thrown off in the living room last night. Last night. That seems eons ago.

I stare out at the Eiffel Tower—a view that never grows old. Now I don't care if I ever see it again. Before he walks out of the bedroom, I say, "You know the worst part in all of this? I never planned to like you so much."

Geoffrey

I slump into a chair in my flat, utterly defeated and exhausted. I'd had to exit the hotel through the kitchens to avoid the paparazzi and fans waiting out front. I wonder what Ellie will do. Would hotel security take care of her?

I'm worried sick about her, even as I'm hurt that she thought I had done this on purpose. That I had played her and humiliated her for my own gain, without remorse.

Apparently, it had all started blowing up during dinner last night, unbeknownst to us. Neither of us had brought our phones to dinner, by tacit agreement. An Instagram post about the story in the tabloids went viral, getting over two million views.

I texted Malcolm and told him to get his ass over to my flat, pronto. I'm too enraged to speak to him on the phone, and I don't need to add any more fuel to the fire by talking to him about this in the presence of my driver, Maurice.

I have to make this right. Even if Ellie never speaks to me again, I need to make this right. I need to relieve her humiliation and heartache. But how?

There's a knock on my door. Malcolm.

I jerk it open. "Come in."

He seems a little too jovial. A little too pleased with himself. I get a sinking feeling in the pit of my stomach.

"Tell me you didn't do this," I murmur, barely holding my rage in check.

He rocks back on his heels. "Of course I did this, and by God, what a boon this has been. I have received five phone calls from directors who want you in their next rom-com. And not as the father of the bride! As the romantic lead. Turns out baby boomers want to see themselves on screen—older heroes and heroines falling in love."

My rage boils over. "What the *hell* were you thinking?!"

He finally takes a step back, understanding dawning on his now sweating face. "W-why, it occurred to me last night that if everyone learned it was all fake, they'd be amazed at your acting skills. Nine days of an intense fake love affair. How can anyone but the best actor sustain that kind of emotion?"

"Did you ever stop to consider the consequences to Ellie?"

"Why, I—" A frown furrows his brow. "But it was fake! She agreed to it."

"Dammit, Malcolm! Did you ever stop to think it wasn't fake?"

Malcolm blinks.

I scrub my hands through my hair for what must be the hundredth time since this godforsaken day began. "It wasn't fake. It may have been in the beginning, but not at the end."

I'm not sure when it morphed into something real—into *love*.

I don't want to go back to being alone again. I want someone special in my life. I want—no, I *need*—Ellie. She doesn't fawn over me. She doesn't put up with my shit. She likes me for who I am. Not because I'm an actor, or because I'm wealthy. I scoff. At least I *thought* she liked me. But now she hates me.

"I'm sorry, Geoffrey," Malcolm says quietly behind me. "I

didn't realize. But look at the bright side—you're back, baby! Five scripts are coming your way. The long drought is over."

I turn and level him with a stare. "I couldn't give a flying fuck. You want to talk about a drought? I just *devastated* the one woman I've come to love after years of loneliness and believing I was destined to live the rest of my life single and alone. You could give me a thousand scripts, and I wouldn't give a damn. There is only one thing I want. Ellie."

Eleanor

As if my heartbreak isn't enough, I'm hounded on the way to the airport despite my slouchy hat and big sunglasses. Then again in the airport until I blessedly make it through security. But people stop and point at me on the concourse and in the airport club prior to my flight. The whispers are like claws scraping along my skin, tearing at me, leaving me torn and battered.

One woman even had the audacity to ask for my autograph.

A flight attendant took pity on me and moved me to the last row in first class with no one in the seat next to me.

My phone continued to buzz with text messages and phone calls until I turned it off for the flight. I texted Abby and Maddie and told them I couldn't talk, just so they wouldn't worry. I only wanted to get home, crawl into my bed, and pull the covers over my head until this all blew over. If it ever blew over.

How do people endure this kind of public excoriation? I think of famous athletes, actors, and musicians, people in the public eye, whose lives are lived under the microscope of public opinion, and wonder, how do they do it? But the difference between them and me? They *chose* to be famous. I certainly did not.

But didn't you, though? The voice inside my head asks.

First, when I agreed to accept the Dream Date contract. Then again, when I agreed to spend nine days with Geoffrey in the spotlight. And even worse, when I agreed to this godforsaken fake relationship. I have myself to blame for my current situation. But Geoffrey holds some of the blame as well.

This is what I get for allowing myself to trust another man. I swore I'd never trust another man as long as I lived, even if it meant spending the rest of my life alone. After all, I had a rich life already, didn't I? My beautiful daughter, my best friend, a supportive community, and a thriving business. Assuming the community will still support me and my business will continue to thrive after this debacle.

But in the confines of the dark, quiet airplane, I can't help but feel the loss of Geoffrey. I hadn't realized what my life *had* been missing—that special someone to share it with. And he was special. At least I *thought* he was.

Geoffrey

I hang up the phone and drop into the chair I hope is behind me. In my nervous pacing, I've lost track of where I am in the room. Solid wood greets me as my ass hits the seat. I shake my head, still trying to comprehend what just happened.

After years of attempts to revive my career, I'm offered not one rom-com but five! All in a new rom-com subgenre—seasoned romance, where the hero and heroine are mature silver-haired adults. Just eleven days ago, I would have read the scripts with relish and chosen the one that best suited me. Malcolm would have negotiated a seven-figure deal, and I would have been on top of the world.

But not now.

Now, none of the roles held any interest for me. Now, they all seemed shallow and unfulfilling. There was only one role I wanted—to be Ellie's lover, friend, partner, maybe even husband.

But the phone call I'd just ended didn't involve any of those roles. No. It involved the role of a lifetime. And what's more, the in-studio filming will be in Georgia, of all places—an easy distance to Ellie.

The director, Sean Martin, contacted me to see if I was interested in playing a man I've admired all my life. A man whose career mine had followed. A fellow Bristolian—Cary Grant. My stomach does a backflip at the idea that I will be portraying this iconic and versatile actor.

Apparently, this biopic of Grant has been in the works for the past two years, with an adaptation of the bestselling biography by theater and movie critic James Bleinhem. According to Martin, they had cast everyone but the leading man himself.

I couldn't help but laugh when Martin told me Steven Cassel had recommended me for the part, despite my refusal to meet with him when he'd wanted. I thought for sure I would be on his shitlist.

Life can take some unexpected turns. This is just one. Meeting Ellie was another. And now, I have a very real chance of making this work. If she will forgive me, that is. It will take some serious groveling, but I am more than willing to do whatever it takes, even if I never make another movie after this one. I don't care if this is my last film—I'm going to kill it.

I've allowed my career to interfere with too much of my life—the relationship with my daughter being the worst casualty. I won't let that happen with Ellie. Now that I've found her, I'm not going to let her go so easily.

With that motivation in mind, I had to come up with a plan for the most important Grand Gesture of my life.

Eleanor

I walk into my cool, quiet house and breathe an exhausted sigh of relief. I didn't get too many looks in the Atlanta or Jacksonville airports, and I made it to my car without incident. Maddie called on my way home, but I wasn't ready to talk. I told her we'd catch up tomorrow after I settle in. I touched base with Naomi about the boutique, a little worried I might be carrying spring inventory into fall if traffic fell off as a result of the story. She'd said they were busy, and many people had come in asking for me. She said she thought one was probably a reporter.

Lovely.

Unable to bear another public outing, I'd order my groceries online for delivery. And for now, I'd distract myself with unpacking, laundry, and catching up on mail and email. Tomorrow I would have no choice but to face the derision I had likely earned by faking a very public relationship with a famous actor. But I had neglected my boutique long enough. I had to get back to it.

As I unpack and sort through my recent acquisitions, my hand finds a rolled-up piece of paper, a little worse for wear after the trip overseas in my suitcase. It was the drawing Geoffrey had bought for me in Place du Tertre. I had planned to have it framed to give to Abby, but as I unroll it, I'm having second thoughts. Would she want something that would remind her of her mother's public affair? It would be better if I threw it away. Why would I keep something that reminds me not only of Geoffrey and what we might have had but also of a humiliating time in my life? Probably even more humiliating than Barry's infidelity, our divorce, and the drama that is still playing out with Phoebe and my boutique, because this latest is so very public.

I'm about to wad it up, but my hands freeze. I can't bring myself to do it. "Fine," I sigh. "You get a reprieve," talking to the drawing of myself as if it understands. "You're losing it, Ellie. Completely losing it."

Then I spot the pink silk bag containing the pink lapis breast cancer necklace Geoffrey had given me. I pull it from the bag, and a tear slides down my cheek. It was such a thoughtful gift. Why would he go to the trouble of giving me such a meaningful gift if he didn't care for me? I slip the necklace back into the bag. Maybe someday I'll be able to wear it without feeling the heartache I feel now.

My phone buzzes again with an incoming text. Irritatingly, every time my phone buzzes, I hope it's a text from Geoffrey, apologizing, offering me some proof that he didn't leak the story. That he hadn't been acting when he'd treated me like I meant something to him. When he'd made love to me. Not a single text from the man. If he really cared, wouldn't he at least send me a text? Ask if I made it home okay? "Get over yourself. He's already moved on, and you should too."

The text is from yet another reporter asking if I'd like to tell my side of the story. "Umm . . . that would be a no." Delete and report as junk.

Before I can delete the last text, my phone buzzes yet again! It has been buzzing with text messages from other friends and reporters. How the hell did these reporters get my cell number anyway?

"That's it!" I shoot a text to Abby and one to Maddie,

telling them I'm fine but that I'm turning off my phone. It seems the only way I'll get any respite—at least for today.

Geoffrey

"You're the reason she left the way she did. Now you're going to help me get her back."

After settling everything with the movie deal, I told Malcolm to come to my place for a strategizing session.

"Have you tried texting her?" Malcolm asks, as if I hadn't thought of that.

"*No*. She would just ignore me, or worse, block me. This goes far beyond texting or even a phone call, man. This needs to be big. Think the Grand Gesture from my movie, *A Sunday Kind of Love* or *To Have and To Hold*." In *A Sunday Kind of Love*, the hero, Luka, hires a billboard on the heroine's route to work asking her to marry him. In *To Have and To Hold*, the hero hires a skywriter to write a message over Manhattan saying he was the world's biggest ass—would she please forgive him?

"Ah, I see what you mean," Malcolm taps his lips, thinking. Then he breaks into a slow smile. The kind that he displays when he's conniving.

Eleanor

"It's been like this since that first Instagram post—the one where you're at the Eiffel Tower and Geoffrey is holding you,"

Naomi says as she joins me at the counter and follows my gaze to the storefront, where women are lined up like they're at a Black Friday sale. "It's gotten crazier since the, uh, well . . . since the bomb dropped."

"But are they buying or just gawking?" I ask, trying to ignore the pain in my chest at the memory of Geoffrey's arms around me. "And has this affected my loyal customers?" I can't imagine the wealthy women who shop here during the season will welcome such crowds.

"A bit of both, I'm afraid. Some women want the dresses you were wearing in Paris. Others just ask if you're here, and if not, they leave."

I sigh. Well, from my perusal of the store inventory and my review of the sales numbers in the last month, sales are definitely up. That's something, I guess.

"I have to warn you, though, a few could be reporters. There's been more than one asking for you."

My morning coffee curdles at the thought of encountering a reporter. The last thing I want is more publicity. But it can't be helped. I can't hide out forever. This is my business. My livelihood. The thing I've worked so hard for these last few years.

"All right." I glance at my watch. "Let's open the doors."

After a brisk morning of shoppers and gawkers, I'm dead on my feet. But duty calls. A tall, slender woman in breezy slacks and a silk shell holds up a linen dress in pale sage.

"That color would be great on you," I say as I approach. The color would complement her dark hair and olive complexion. "Would you like to try it on?"

She turns to me and smiles, before leaning over conspiratorially. "What I would really like is to help you tell your story."

I stiffen. "No, thank you."

She returns the dress to the rack. "The world is only

hearing and seeing the negative. There are two sides to every story. Tell yours. I'll help you," she prods.

"No. Now, if you're not interested in that or any other items in the store, I have customers to attend to." I pivot on my heel and walk away. Spotting Holland Conti, a dear friend of Maddie's and thus not a reporter in disguise, I rush over to greet her. My shoulders twitch, feeling the reporter's eyes following me.

Eleanor

The shipment of the smaller items I'd purchased in Paris arrived. Unpacking them and setting them up in the boutique would be a welcome distraction, except I'd have to do it after hours if I expected to get anything done without unwelcome interruptions from the press and the public like the ones I experienced today. Naomi texted me to tell me the trunk had arrived at the boutique.

But as I remove the items from the shipping container, each brings a reminder of Geoffrey, and I wonder if he kept the cashmere sweater I bought for him.

My doorbell rings, and my heart tries to crawl out through my throat. Is it a photographer hoping to get an ambush photo of me when I open the door? Or a reporter or journalist ready to stick a microphone in my face and interrogate me?

I tiptoe over to the peephole and let out the breath I'd been holding.

"It's me, Ellie. Open the door."

Maddie.

I unlock the door and yank it open, then grab her forearm, pulling her into the house before closing and locking the door.

"It's that bad, is it?" she asks, eyebrow raised. She takes in the closed plantation shutters on all the windows.

"You have no idea. The emails and text messages have been relentless. Friends, family, high school classmates I haven't heard from in decades. They all want a piece of the story that they can sell to the tabloids or gossip about to their friends." I tuck a stray strand of hair behind my ear. "Drink?"

Maddie nods and follows me to the kitchen, where I grab a can of her preferred diet soda I keep on hand just for her. She pops it open and takes a drink, then leans against the kitchen island, giving me one of her looks. The kind I saw frequently when news of Barry's affair first came out. It said, *Please tell me what I can do.* "I should cancel—or postpone. I can't possibly leave you at a time like this."

Maddie had an upcoming trip to L.A. to view a new artist's work for her gallery. "No. I'm a grown woman—not some lovesick teenager. This isn't my first heartbreak." But it *will* be my last. I'm not going down this road ever again. "Some other scandal or titillating story will come along, and this will be old news." *Eventually.* "Go to L.A. Have a great time with your artsy friends, and don't worry about me. I have the Boutique Retailers Association trade show in two weeks, and Abby is coming down for a week between semesters."

"I'm sorry," Maddie's voice is earnest and full of regret.

"What on earth for?"

"If I hadn't entered you in that contest, you wouldn't have met Geoffrey, and you wouldn't be in this situation. I wanted you to forget your bastard ex-husband and do something good for yourself. Instead, I made matters worse. I'm the one who encouraged you to have an affair, for God's sake! How can you ever forgive me?"

"Please don't castigate yourself. I finally got to see Paris, and in a way few people get to—guided by an expert. And a celebrity."

"An expert who broke your heart."

Trying to brush off her dramatization, I say, "I'm the one who agreed to everything—accepting the prize package, spending nine days with Geoffrey when I didn't have to, and more importantly, faking a romantic relationship with the man. This was doomed to blow up in my face."

"But—"

I can see she's not about to give up falling on her sword, so I interrupt, "On a positive note, look at all the loot I found at the Flea Market." I point to the pile I'd set out on the dining room table, and I take one of the Hermès scarves I bought and hand it to Maddie. "This is for you."

"What? No. I don't deserve it. I've made your life hell."

"Pfft. I would hardly call it *hell*. I'm hurt, but I'll get over it," I say, trying to shrug it off. No such luck.

"I'm not buying it. You didn't need this on the heels of Bastard Barry's perfidy." She hands the scarf back to me.

"Take the damn scarf, Maddie. I picked it out with you in mind." Eyeing her blouse in her customary bold colors and patterns, I observe, "Now, whether you have something solid you can pair it with, I can't recall." She frequently resembles one of the abstract geometric paintings she sells in her gallery.

She sighs theatrically. "All right. But I won't wear it in good conscience."

I take the scarf from her again and drape it around her shoulders, tying it at a jaunty angle, then turn her to face the mirror on the dining room wall.

She lifts a hand as she stares at her reflection and touches the delicate silk, a dreamy expression on her face. "Fine. I'll keep it."

Chapter Eleven

Eleanor

The next day, I startle at a knock on my door. So far no reporters have been brash enough to show up at my house, but still . . . there's always a first time. In bare feet, I tiptoe to the door and look through the peephole. Barry! What on *earth* is *he* doing here?

I peer through the peephole again, trying to see if Phoebe is with him. He wouldn't be that cruel, would he?

"Open the door, Ellie. I can see you're looking through the peephole."

Sighing, I unlock the door and swing it open. "Come to gloat?"

He makes a face, then says, "No, I come bearing gifts."

My gaze drops to the large manila envelope he's holding. "What kind of gifts?" I ask, my voice laced with suspicion. "Another bomb?"

"If you let me in, I'll tell you."

"Fine." I hold the door open for him and catch a whiff of

his cologne as he walks in—Calvin Klein's Eternity for Men. The refreshing, spicy scent used to delight me. Now, I only want the scents of bergamot and citrus.

Barry strides through the foyer and into the kitchen like he owns the place. Well, he used to anyway. Laying the envelope on the island, he opens it and pulls out a stack of documents —legal documents—making me stiffen.

"Now don't get your back up. Phoebe agreed to the settlement on the boutique. It's signed, sealed, and . . . delivered." He hands them to me.

"What did you have to give her in return? Never mind." I wave my hand. "Forget I asked." I hold the documents in front of me, skimming them. "So, the store is all mine again?"

"Yes."

A wave of relief washes over me. We're done. The divorces, both the marital and the professional, are concluded. I own this house, and I own my boutique. At least something is going right.

"Why'd you do it?" The "it" he's referring to requires no explanation.

I glance up at his still handsome face, then sigh and rub my forehead. "I don't know, really. He asked, and I just . . ." I shrug.

"Was it to get back at me? At Phoebe?"

"If I'm honest, partly. The two gut punches you delivered while I was on that trip didn't help."

"I know you don't believe me, but I am sorry about the timing. I just wanted you to hear it from me first."

"Unlike your affair." I cross my arms over my chest, suddenly feeling vulnerable. He doesn't respond. "And you and Abby?"

This time, he sighs and rubs his forehead. "She's pissed. Said she won't come to the wedding."

I feel a little sorry for him—mind you, a *very* little—but still. "She'll come around. Just give her time."

"I hope so. I can't bear the idea of my daughter hating me."

"She doesn't hate you. She's just . . . hurt." *And with good reason*, but I keep that thought to myself.

There's one question that's been circling in my head since I first happened upon Barry and Phoebe cozied up in that restaurant booth. Since we're being civil, now is my chance. "What happened to us?" I ask.

"The truth?" Barry's brows lift in question.

"Of course," I say.

He gazes at me for a long moment, then says, "You forgot how to have fun."

I almost fought him on that, then thought better of it. He was right, of course. Geoffrey taught me that. My heart aches at the thought of Geoffrey, and I wonder what he's doing at this very moment and whether he got the movie role he so desperately wanted.

"You were so focused on your business that you no longer had time for anything else. Not me. Not even yourself."

"And you, yours," I protest.

"And me, mine," he concedes. "But how many times did I ask you to dinner, only to be told you couldn't because something at the boutique needed your attention? How many times were we invited to a party only for you to beg off at the last minute?"

"Pot, meet kettle." Annoyance flares. "You never supported my dream the way I supported yours. For *years*, I worked for your dream, then when I finally pursued my own, you didn't support me."

"I supported you. I was proud of you. But then it became almost an obsession."

"You should recognize it," I fire back. "Yours was an obsession."

He sighs and scrubs a hand through his hair. "You're right." He gives me a sad smile. "We were *both* obsessed. I'm a selfish bastard, I admit it. I wanted all your attention." He opens his mouth to say something, but hesitates, then says, "I missed you. I missed our work together. I loved having you at the practice with me—part of my dream."

"But it wasn't *my* dream."

"I know. As I said, I am a selfish bastard. Always have been."

"Not always," I say. "You cared for me when I was sick. You nursed me after my surgery and after every radiation treatment." He had. I wouldn't have made it through without his care and support.

"When you were diagnosed, I knew you had the best possible prognosis. It was going to be a battle, but the early detection and the type of breast cancer were greatly in your favor. I had hoped that, once you made it through the treatments to remission, you would embrace life and take a step back from your business. But you didn't. You seemed to pursue it with even greater vengeance."

Again, I want to deny it. To blame everything on him. *He's* the one who had an affair, after all. But he isn't wrong. When my mortality was in question, instead of taking that step back and enjoying what life had to offer, I dug in and worked even harder. I started my business later in life, and when I was sick, I felt I had even less time to make it what I wanted it to be. Less time to accomplish all the things I wanted.

"Do you love him?"

It took me a moment to realize Barry had spoken. "I'm sorry?"

"Do you love him?"

"Who?"

"Don't be coy, Ellie. You haven't a coy bone in your body."

"Newsflash, Barry! It was all fake." I throw my hands up in exasperation. "Maybe you haven't heard."

"Maybe it started out that way. But I've known you for thirty-three years, Ellie. You can't lie to me."

"Lie—"

He pins me with olive green eyes that used to take my breath away. Now, the only eyes I want to look into are blue-gray ones. All right. I sigh. I do love him. But do I really want to share that with my ex-husband, when I haven't even shared it with Geoffrey? "It doesn't matter. What would he want with me when he could have any woman he wants?"

Barry shakes his head. "Did I do that to you?"

"Do what?"

"Did I make you question your own value?"

He had, but I also didn't want to discuss my insecurities with him. I just shook my head.

"Listen to me, Ellie. You are a beautiful, vibrant, intelligent woman. He'd be crazy not to want you."

"You didn't," I whisper, the hurt clear in my voice.

"God, Ellie. I'm so sorry that I made you feel that way. I *did* want you. I wanted the life we had. I thought you didn't want me."

His statement stuns me. Had he really thought that? Did I really make him feel that way? Did I deserve some of the blame here? All of it? No. Before I could voice that, Barry spoke again.

"I'm not placing blame. My affair was . . ."

"Despicable? Dishonest? Disgraceful?"

"I was going to say unacceptable," he says with a wry smile. "But you're right. It was all of those things."

It was my turn to sigh. "The fact is, I guess we both

screwed up." I hold up my index finger and point it at him. "But you screwed up worse."

"I'm willing to accept that."

"You are?" I blink at him.

"Of course. I vowed to be faithful to you, through good times and bad. I didn't keep that vow."

We were silent for a few moments, then I ask, "Why didn't we have this talk *before* your affair?"

"One, I didn't set out to have an affair. And two, we were both too focused on our lives outside our marriage. We just . . ." he shrugs.

"Drifted apart," I finish for him.

He nods. "We drifted apart." He steps up to me and cups my face. "I am sorry. I do love you . . ."

"You're just not *in* love with me anymore, either."

He drops his hand, and his eyes hold a sadness in them. "And you're not in love with me anymore."

I shake my head. "No."

"Then go after the man you *do* love."

"I'm not—"

"Ellie," he admonishes. "Don't let him slip away."

The unspoken words hung in the air—*like you did me.*

Eleanor

"Have things calmed down at all?" Maddie asks, before taking a sip of her wine.

We're lounging on one of my sofas, nibbling on a charcuterie board she'd picked up. We'd normally meet for dinner at a local restaurant, but circumstances being what they are, keeping public appearances to a minimum is essential for my sanity.

"Define 'calmed down.' If you mean getting only fifty text messages a day, rather than a hundred fifty, I guess you could say that things have calmed down."

I'd already told her about the encounter with the reporter in the boutique. "By the way, Barry came by."

She sits bolt upright. "Whatever for?"

"Well, it's good news, actually. He managed to convince Phoebe to sign the papers. I am, once again, the sole owner of Ellie's."

She lifts her glass in a toast. "Hallelujah."

I tap my glass to hers and take a sip.

"What did he offer her in return?" She lounges back onto the couch again and selects a mini wedge of brie.

"Don't know. I didn't ask. Well, I asked, then I changed my mind before he could tell me." I build a little snack with a cracker, a slice of peppered salami, and a creamy Havarti. "We also had a heart-to-heart."

"Really?" She drags out the word. "Do tell. Did he drop to his knees and beg your forgiveness?"

"No." I tell her about the conversation, and when I get to the part where he tells me to go after Geoffrey, she sits up again.

"He did? Huh." She ponders that for a moment. "And will you?"

"What? After what he did to me? No."

"Let me ask you something."

"Uh-oh."

She holds up a finger. "Hear me out. What if the fake nature of the relationship hadn't been revealed in such a public way? What if you two had simply gone your separate ways, as if the relationship had burned itself out? The internet would likely still have blown up with questions, conjectures, and accusations. Some would blame you, and others would blame him. You would be the woman Geoffrey Harrison dumped."

"Or vice versa," I interject in my defense.

Maddie lifts a shoulder. "Maybe. But more likely, people would assume he dumped you. My point is, would your life be any better right now? Isn't it possible you would still be hounded by reporters, that gawkers would still show up at the boutique hoping to get a selfie with the woman who'd had a wild romance with Geoffrey Harrison, and the tabloids would still feature articles about the torrid affair."

I thought about that a minute. "Perhaps . . . but this is so much worse than that, because I'm either the hapless dupe or the unscrupulous liar. I loathe either option."

"I get that. But you'd still be a prisoner in your house." She lifts an arm to encompass the living room.

Geoffrey's words rose unbidden in my brain: *Promise me when you return home, you'll pick one activity each week that's just for fun.*

I snort.

"What?"

I tell her about our conversation that last night we were together. "Like that's possible at this point. Like I could meet up with friends for dinner or attend a play. Even visiting a spa is out of the question. None of those things will be possible until I wake from this nightmare that is my life. Ironic, don't you think?"

Eleanor

. . .

"Have you read *The Times* today?" Maddie asks as soon as I answer the phone the next morning.

"No, I haven't had a chance. I'm packing for New York. Why?"

"Go to your email and open *The Times* newsletter. I'll wait."

"You're scaring me." But I do as she says and drop into a stool at the kitchen counter, then pull my laptop in front of me and open it up, navigating to the daily email from *The Times*.

"You there yet?" Maddie prods.

"Yes, yes. What am I looking at?"

"Scroll down to the Culture section."

"Okaaay. Still don't see—oh." My gaze lands on the headline: "The Fake Romance That Wasn't." By Guest Writer, Geoffrey Harrison. I scoff. "He's just trying to rehabilitate his image."

"Maybe. But he damns himself in the beginning by admitting the fake romance was a publicity stunt to boost his career. After the news leaked, he was offered five scripts to play the romantic lead in rom-coms."

"Well, good for him. His scheme worked then."

"Yes, but here's the thing. He didn't take any of them."

That gives me pause. Why wouldn't he take them? Wasn't that the whole reason for this farce? Then anger, hot and sudden, courses through me. "You mean to tell me I have been utterly humiliated for nothing? That son of a bitch." Tears clog my throat and sting my eyes. "I got involved in this whole charade for nothing."

"Read the article, Ellie. That's all I'm going to say." And then she's gone.

Opinion: The Fake Romance That Wasn't

By Geoffrey Harrison

Sometimes the truth is stranger than fiction, and in this case, it's more romantic too.

For nine days, social media was focused on the woman suddenly by my side—Eleanor Marshall, winner of the Dream Date Contest. Some skeptics said it must be staged. Others said it was a publicity stunt. And to be fair, they weren't entirely wrong—at least in the beginning.

None of what happened was part of the original plan. The contest winner was promised a romantic dinner with me, complete with photo ops, followed by nine days in Paris—all expenses paid—to spend however they wished. The morning after the dinner, my agent suggested we spend those nine days in Paris together.

It wasn't long before I proposed the idea of a fake relationship in hopes it would further inflate my social media presence and resuscitate my flagging movie career. And, truth be told, because I wanted to spend more time with her. I liked her. She said yes—not to love, not to a lie—but to help me revive my career. She signed on, fully aware that every smile in front of the cameras was a performance. What no one saw coming—least of all me—was that somewhere between the Instagram posts and the staged affection, the act would become real.

I fell in love with her.

And now, in the aftermath of the media circus and the disclosure of the truth, all eyes have turned—unfairly—on her. She's been called complicit, manipulative, opportunistic. But let's set the record straight: She doesn't deserve a shred of the censure being hurled her way.

This entire situation was my idea. My agent and I orchestrated it. I benefited from it. She was the one who walked into it with no motive but to help, and later, no defense when things went sideways. If anything, she was the collateral damage of my attempted career-saving maneuver.

If I had it to do over again, I never would have hurt her

like this. I never would have treated her heart like a prop. Because the truth is, the woman I asked to pretend to love me became the woman I truly can't stop loving.

So, let's stop punishing her for being part of a story she didn't write. Let's stop assuming the woman in the spotlight is always playing a game. Sometimes, she's the only one telling the truth.

And maybe—just maybe—the next time love finds its way out of fiction and into real life, I'll be wise enough to recognize it before it's too late.

Because this wasn't just a PR stunt gone wrong.

It was a love story that no one expected . . . least of all me.

The words blur on the page, as my eyes fill with tears. Did he mean it? Or was this part of the act? Was he trying to rehabilitate her image, or just his?

His version isn't exactly the truth. He had presented the idea for me to get back at Barry. But maybe he is trying to protect me.

I stand abruptly, slamming my computer shut. I don't know what to believe. I want to trust him, but I can't. Nor can I trust myself.

For all his words of love, he hadn't called or even texted me since I left Paris. If he feels the way he says he does, why hasn't he reached out to me? Why hasn't he apologized to *me*?

No. I said I was done in Paris. I'm still done.

Chapter Twelve

Geoffrey

I pull up out front and park the car, my gaze landing on the sign in casual script that reads *Ellie's*, and beneath it, the tagline "refined and sophisticated vacation wear." From the looks of it, the boutique is busy, with women coming and going. Maybe the publicity has been good for her business. Hey, nothing wrong with putting a positive spin on an otherwise negative situation.

Drawing in a deep breath, I grab the enormous bouquet of flowers I bought, and I step out into the hot, humid Florida air. "Here goes nothing."

A pleasant *ting* announces my arrival when I open the door. Thankfully, no one is paying me much attention. I quickly scan the store for Ellie's beautiful face, but no such luck. Maybe she's in the back.

Then I consider the store itself, my curiosity getting the better of me. Large windows flood the space with natural light, creating an airy environment. The soft pastel hues, natural elements like seashells and driftwood, and the light-colored wood floors add to the airy feeling. Carefully curated resort wear reflecting Ellie's style is displayed in clever vignettes, along with straw hats, sandals, and accessories. Everything effortlessly chic.

A small lounge area with plush seating in sea glass colors sits in one corner of the boutique. In another corner, I see the Louis Vuitton trunk, cleverly filled with a display of resort wear, sunglasses, hats, sandals, and the camera she'd picked up in Paris.

Women peruse the racks and shelves, chatting among themselves. Two glance up, then stare gape-mouthed, while another woman stammers, "That's, that's, omigod, that's . . ."

I only give them a brief nod and a smile before I scan the store once more, hoping to see Ellie.

"You!" A statuesque brunette wearing a dress in abstract geometric shapes of bright primary colors, like an Oli-B painting, steps in front of me and crosses her arms over her buxom chest, glaring at me.

She is Jane Russell to Ellie's Ginger Rogers. No, Ellie's Doris Day. Hey—don't judge. Despite her good-girl roles, Doris Day had a hot body.

I know immediately who she is, based on Ellie's description. "You must be Maddie," I say, turning on my sexiest grin.

"Don't even try it." She eyes me like I'm a piece of gum on the bottom of her designer stilettos. "And if you think a bouquet of flowers is going to win her over, you are sadly mistaken."

The silence in the boutique is deafening. All the women are frozen in place, watching the exchange like it's an episode of *Real Housewives of New Jersey*.

I want to step around her and search for Ellie, but I know

I will need her support. Or at the very least, her understanding.

"Is Ellie here?"

"No, but if she was, I wouldn't let you near her."

Damn. "When will she be here?" I ask, ignoring her last comment.

"Never you mind. Just be on your way."

"She'll be back on Thursday," a voice pipes up.

Maddie gives the woman the gimlet eye.

"Where is she?" I ask my new friend.

"She's in New York at the Boutique Retailers Association annual trade show," she offers in defiance of Maddie's stare. "She didn't plan on going, but she needed to get away from the brutal gossip, even for just a few days."

I wince. Point taken.

"Look, uh, what is your name?"

"Naomi."

"Naomi. I just want to talk to her. Apologize. Well, grovel, really. Whatever it takes."

I scan the faces of the other women in the store to see if I have any allies. A few nod their heads, then look at Maddie.

"Come on, Maddie. Can't you see he's trying to win her back?" one of them prods.

"Yeah, like in one of his movies," another adds.

"It's so romantic," a third woman exclaims, her eyes dreamy.

I turn back to Maddie. "I have an idea." A new Grand Gesture. One that is perhaps more meaningful. "And I'll need your help."

All the women in the store start talking at once, encouraging Maddie to relent and help me.

She eyes me dubiously, then sticks her finger in front of my face. "You hurt her again, you're dead meat."

Point taken.

Eleanor

A few mornings later, I'm in my hotel room getting ready for the day when my phone rings. It's Maddie.

As soon as I pick up, she says, "Put *The Today Show* on. Now," then hangs up.

What the hell? I grab the remote and turn the TV on. There's Geoffrey on *The Today Show*, and he's live on the set. I gasp. He's here? In New York? My heart races at the thought that he's here. In New York. At the same time as me.

I drop onto the foot of the bed. He looks tired—as if he's just flown in on a red-eye.

"Have you communicated with Eleanor?" The female host asks, her face a mask of sympathy.

"No, he hasn't." I cross my arms over my chest. Don't sympathize with him. He doesn't deserve your sympathy.

A sad smile crosses his face. "No, I haven't."

"Why not? If you say you love her, why haven't you reached out to her?"

"Yeah, why haven't you reached out to me?" I mutter aloud.

"Mere words aren't enough. A phone call, a text message, a bouquet of flowers won't cut it."

I scoff and jump to my feet. "How would you know? You haven't even tried."

"Then what will?"

"Yeah, Geoffrey, what will?" I prod, as if he can hear me.

"I'm working on it." He turns his devastating grin on the camera, and my knees nearly buckle. What the hell is he up to?

Geoffrey

I'm standing across the street from the Javits Center, where I've been waiting for the better part of the afternoon, afraid I might miss her. The taxi driver I hired to wait is costing me a fortune, but I don't care. She finally steps out, and I drink her in. Her luscious silver hair is up with a few strands loose around her face. The dress she's wearing hugs her subtle curves. And her legs—my god, her legs—look a mile long in those heels. Giving myself a mental shake, I signal to the taxi driver, who pulls around and over to the curb while I run across the street, dodging traffic.

If this were a movie set, this is where the director would shout, "Action!"

Eleanor

It has been a long but productive day, despite being distracted by Geoffrey's interview. I found my mind wandering in the midst of conversations with vendor reps. *Why is he here? Is it just coincidence? Surely he wouldn't have flown all the way to New York just for the interview. It could just as easily have been filmed remotely. He isn't here for me, is he?*

Of course not, Ellie, I chide myself. I'm a smart, mature, practical woman. Not some fanciful teenager. This isn't one of his movies where the hero chases after the heroine. This is real life, and things like that don't happen in real life.

Relieved this is the last day of the trade show, I look

forward to getting back to my hotel room, ordering room service, and taking a long hot bath. Attitudes in New York being what they are with regard to public figures, only a few people at the trade show accosted me for a photo or autograph. For the most part, people were professional and focused on the business of retail—not me.

I exit the Javits Center into the humid New York City afternoon, where I'm assailed by the wail of sirens, the blast of car horns, and the general bustle of the city.

Hailing a taxi at rush hour in New York can be downright demoralizing, but my feet ache, and I can't bring myself to walk the three miles back to The Pierre. I lift my hand signaling to an approaching taxi, not expecting success. To my surprise, it pulls up at the curb, and I place my hand on the handle.

"*Excusez-moi—c'est mon taxi*, a male voice says, as a familiar broad hand covers mine on the door handle. "But I'd be willing to share the ride."

I turn my head so fast, I feel a knot in my neck. "Geoffrey!" I glance around searching for Hélène and Stéphane—or any photographer or videographer.

"You're a difficult woman to pin down. After a long flight across the pond, I had to catch another flight to New York."

"But—" is all I can stammer out.

Geoffrey opens the door to the driver berating us about whether we are getting in or not.

Geoffrey

"Well, are we?" I ask, my arm extended toward the backseat. I hold my breath waiting, wondering what I will do if she refuses.

Thankfully, she climbs in and I slide in beside her, relief making my knees weak.

"Where to?" the annoyed cab driver asks.

I look at Ellie, brows raised in question.

"The Pierre," she replies.

"Fancy," I murmur as the driver pulls out into rush-hour traffic and we buckle our seatbelts. Safety first. The drive to her hotel could take a while, which is unfortunate, because all I want to do right now is gather her into my arms and kiss her senseless.

"Why are you here?" she asks, her voice shaky and hesitant, as she wrings her hands in her lap.

I turn to face her, as much as the seatbelt will allow. "Did you read my article in *The Times*?"

"Yes, but—"

"Did you see *The Today Show* this morning?"

"Yes."

"Then you must know why I'm here."

She licks her lips, and I hold back a groan. I want to taste those lips again. "I don't know what to believe," she whispers, and her eyes fill with tears.

Oh god. "Ellie, please don't cry." I yearn to take her into my arms—damn seatbelts—but I take her hands instead. "I meant every word I said. It wasn't me," I continue. "It was Malcolm. He leaked the truth. He didn't know that by that point it wasn't fake. Not anymore. At least not to me."

She draws in a shuddering breath and withdraws her hands. "Why didn't you take any of the roles offered to you? Why did I humiliate myself for nothing?"

"Oh, Ellie. Without you, those roles no longer interested me. I think the luster faded with each passing day I spent with you. I only wanted you. I've sacrificed too much in my life for a star on the Hollywood Walk of Fame. I couldn't sacrifice you."

"But your career . . ."

"Will be fine. In fact, it will be more than fine. I passed up the roles only to get the role of a lifetime." I told her about the Cary Grant biopic and about the studio filming in Georgia.

"I'm happy for you. You're right. It is the role of a lifetime, playing the man you've always admired. But what does this have to do with me? Why are you here? With me?"

I cup her face. "You still don't understand? I'm here because I love you, and I will gladly spend every day of the rest of my life proving that to you."

"I want to believe you, I do, but . . ."

"Will this help?" I reach into my pocket and take out the Tiffany blue box tied with a white satin ribbon.

She sucks in a breath and gazes up at me, eyes wide.

"I know you've been hurt, not only by Barry, but also by me. But I promise you, I will never hurt you like that again." As I'm speaking, I untie the bow and open the box to reveal the oval-cut amethyst set in platinum, surrounded by diamonds.

"Oh, Geoffrey," she murmurs.

"It reminds me of those gorgeous eyes of yours. Eyes I want to wake up to every morning for the rest of my life. I'd get down on one knee if it weren't for this damn seatbelt."

"On the floor of a filthy New York City taxi?"

"Hey!" the taxi driver interjects. "My taxi is not filthy."

"Marry me, Ellie. Say you'll be my leading lady."

She smirks. "That's a bit cheesy, don't you think?"

I shrug. "I thought it was cute."

"Come on, man, it was cheesy," the driver says.

I ignore him. "What do you say, Ellie?" I hold my breath, waiting in agony for her answer.

"But I haven't even said 'I love you,'" Ellie protests, and

my heart sinks. "So let me rectify that now. I love you, Geoffrey." She holds out her left hand. "And yes. I'll marry you."

My breath leaves in a rush as I slide the ring onto her finger.

She lifts her left hand to my face and kisses me, her lips warm and soft beneath mine. Then she asks, her violet eyes sparkling with joy, "And what plot point is this?"

"The Grand Gesture, of course."

Epilogue

NINE MONTHS LATER

Eleanor

It's almost midnight, and the wedding reception is still in full swing, despite the small guest list. I'd long since removed my heels and padded around the ballroom barefoot.

Much to Malcolm's chagrin, Geoffrey and I had insisted on a small *private* ceremony at his Cotswold estate. No press. No photographers—other than Hélène and Stéphane, our official wedding photographers.

There was quite the social media frenzy when it was announced that Geoffrey and I were engaged, but the furor died down after a few weeks, and we've been able to live in relative peace.

Abby served as my bridesmaid, and Geoffrey's son-in-law served as his best man. Maddie and her latest beau, Mitch, flew over for the ceremony. They would depart for a two-week trip to Scotland tomorrow.

Geoffrey, devastatingly handsome in a dove gray suit, white shirt, and violet tie, is chatting with Maddie. It took some time, but he finally won her over with his charm. As for me, I wore a dress of my own design in palest silver taffeta, with a fitted bodice and full tea-length skirt. Perfect for the amethyst necklace and earrings Geoffrey had given me as a wedding gift.

With filming complete on the Cary Grant biopic and my busy season behind me, we would spend a couple of weeks here in England before returning to Florida. He'd begun exploring other career options but hadn't landed on anything yet. For now, he seems content to relax and work on his memoir.

He smiles, and his gaze captures mine. Who would have guessed that a contest I never entered—for a Dream Date I never wanted with an actor I didn't even know—would end in a wedding ceremony? But that's what happens when you fall in love under the Paris moon. You get your very own HEA. That's 'happily ever after' for those who don't know.

About the Author

Rebecca Heflin is a best-selling, award-winning author who has dreamed of writing romantic fiction since she was fifteen and her older sister sneaked a copy of Kathleen Woodiwiss' Shanna to her and told her to read it. Rebecca writes women's fiction and contemporary romance.

Never quite sure what she wanted to be when she grew up, Rebecca didn't attend college until age 30, and earned her bachelor's in literature from the University of North Florida, before going on to complete her law degree from the University of Florida Levin College of Law. Ever the late bloomer, Rebecca finally turned her attention to fulfilling her dream of writing and published her first novel at age 48.

Rebecca's pen name is an abbreviated version of her great-great grandmother's name: Sarah Anne Rebecca Heflin Apple Smith. Whew! And you wonder why she shortened it.

She is a member of Romance Writers of America (RWA), Aged to Perfection Seasoned Romance Writers, RWA Contemporary Romance, Romance Writers of Virginia, and Florida Writers Association. Rebecca and her mountain-climbing husband recently relocated to central Virginia.

facebook.com/RebeccaHeflinBooks

bookbub.com/authors/rebecca-heflin

pinterest.com/rheflinbooks

Also by Rebecca Heflin

THE PROMISE OF CHANGE

RESCUING LACEY

DREAMS COME TRUE SERIES

DREAMS OF PERFECTION, BOOK 1

SHIP OF DREAMS, BOOK 2

DREAMS OF HER OWN, BOOK 3

STERLING UNIVERSITY SERIES

ROMANCING DR. LOVE, BOOK 1

WINNING DR. WENTWORTH, BOOK 2

EDUCATING DR. MAYFIELD, BOOK 3

SEASONS OF NORTHRIDGE SERIES

A SEASON TO DANCE, BOOK 1

A SEASON TO LOVE, BOOK 2

A SEASON TO REMEMBER, BOOK 3

A SEASON TO GIVE, BOOK 4

www.ingramcontent.com/pod-product-compliance
Lightning Source LLC
Chambersburg PA
CBHW071137180726
48291CB00007B/2218

* 9 7 8 1 7 3 6 6 6 0 0 2 7 *